Worth the Wait

Also by Jamie Beck

In the Cards

Worth the Wait

Jamie Beck

This is a work of fiction. Names, characters, organizations, places, events, and incidents are either products of the author's imagination or are used fictitiously.

Published by Montlake Romance, Seattle

www.apub.com

ISBN-13: 9781477820445
ISBN-10: 1477820442

Cover design by Mumtaz Mustafa

Library of Congress Control Number: 2014913356

Printed in the United States of America

For my parents and late stepfather.
Thanks for always seeing the best in me.

Prologue

Wilton, Connecticut
Thirteen Years Ago

By the time Vivi turned thirteen, she'd learned not to expect much from life. Tragic accidents could wipe out half your family and then drive your dad to live in the bottom of a bottle. Bullies could ruin a perfectly good day by picking on your cheap clothes or the awkward things you occasionally blurted out. Loneliness could sometimes wrap itself around you so tightly you could barely breathe.

But accepting the plain truth of it—that life is hard—also helps you enjoy the little things more. To appreciate the small moments, like eating raw cookie dough right from the yellow package, or waking up with your old dog curled up on your bed, or making a new friend when you simply dreaded the first day of eighth grade in a new town.

That last fluke was how she came to be sitting at Cat's kitchen table, at her first-ever sleepover, concentrating on the final strokes of a sketch she'd been asked to draw. Cat had been bragging to her mother about Vivi's artistic ability, and Vivi didn't want to disappoint her new friend.

She took one last look at the image of the ceramic rooster she'd copied before holding up her work for inspection. Mrs. St. James's eyes widened as her hand flattened against her breastbone. "Oh, Vivi, this is wonderful. May I keep it?"

"Sure." Vivi nodded, delighted by the praise.

Cat passed the bag of Oreos back across the table. Vivi snatched three more and sat back in her chair. Contentment washed through her, prompting a happy sigh.

But her peace of mind fell apart as soon as Cat's two older brothers burst through the kitchen door, both sweaty from lacrosse practice. Although Vivi hadn't yet met them, she knew David was the brainy high school senior, Jackson the rowdy sophomore.

Like Cat, they'd inherited their mother's Spanish beauty. All three siblings boasted glossy dark hair, soulful brown eyes, and an olive complexion. The total opposite of Vivi's wide-set blue eyes and fair hair.

Vivi noticed David kissed his mom hello on the cheek before he went to the stove, lifted the lid off a pot, and sniffed its contents.

Jackson flashed a friendly smile when introduced to Vivi, but then immediately turned his attention to Cat. "I need to steal you for a sec, sis." He jerked his thumb toward the living room.

Cat rolled her eyes and leaned toward Vivi. "What do you want to bet he'll ask to *borrow* my allowance tonight because he already spent his?"

Vivi shrugged, completely out of her depth. Since her mother's and brother's deaths seven years ago, she had no siblings or semblance of normal family life to go by. She must've been frowning at her thoughts when she dunked another cookie in her milk, because David asked, "Something wrong with those Oreos?"

"N-no." She swallowed—hard. He was more handsome than any boy should be. Honestly, it really wasn't fair to all the other boys. Or the girls.

"David, look at this drawing Vivi just made. Isn't she gifted?" Mrs. St. James stood up, offered her seat to David, and began fixing him a bowl of paella.

David studied the sketch and then scanned Vivi from head to foot—which didn't take long—apparently cataloging the pink streaks in her hair, her Hello Kitty pajamas, and her scrawny limbs.

A grin curled the corners of his mouth. "This is really good. You must take art lessons."

His intense eyes seemed genuinely curious, which left her terribly flustered and overheated. Still, she couldn't look away.

"Not really." His gaze riveted her to her chair. Did he really want to talk to her? "I mostly teach myself by reading books or renting videos from the library. Sometimes I stay late after school with the art teacher."

"Impressive." He looked at her with respect. "Do you paint, too?"

Vivi sat up straighter, eager to discuss her favorite subject with him. "Yes, and I do collage. Sometimes I work with clay, but I'm not very good yet. I take photographs, too."

"You just moved to town, right? You should check out Silvermine Arts Center, a top spot around here for any kind of art class. It's just over the border, in New Canaan."

"Sounds awesome." Vivi pasted a smile on her face even though she knew she'd never set foot inside that studio. It sounded expensive. More importantly, it would require her dad to get involved, and that just wouldn't happen. She had taken care of him since the accident, not the other way around. It was probably just as well because, on the rare occasions he made an effort, he usually embarrassed her with his drinking.

David tilted his head, narrowing his eyes slightly, as if he could see her thoughts. Then his expression lightened. "Do you do portraits?"

"Not very well." Vivi grimaced and then popped another soggy Oreo in her mouth, growing increasingly disoriented by his attention.

"I'll be the judge of that." He pushed the pad of paper toward her and then leaned forward, elbows on the table. "Draw me."

"Now?" Half of her cookie plunked back into the milk.

"Why not?" He twisted in his chair and tipped his chin up. "Profile?"

Consumed by an exhilarating mix of panic and fascination, she ignored the mess in her glass and picked up the pencil. "No profiles."

David turned back toward her and sat motionless. His eyes glanced at the paper.

"Eyes up," she instructed, and when he looked at her, he smiled.

Her fingers tensed at first, her initial marks too heavy, but within a minute or so, she became absorbed by the project—for the most part, anyway. Granted, she couldn't ignore the way her heart kicked an extra beat every time they made eye contact, which, under the circumstances, happened pretty often.

Mrs. St. James placed the bowl of paella in front of him and then quietly left the kitchen. David set the food aside and continued watching. Several minutes later, Cat returned and plopped down in the chair beside Vivi. "Why are you drawing David?"

"Because I asked her to," he replied before Vivi could answer. "Shhh. Don't distract her."

"Seriously?" Cat heaved a melodramatic sigh while looking at Vivi. "You don't have to draw him, you know."

"I don't mind." In fact, Vivi rather liked the good excuse to memorize every detail of his perfect face.

He winked at her just then. Had he read her mind again?

Heat raced to her cheeks.

"I'll go find something for us to watch on TV." Cat stood, peering over Vivi's shoulder. "Come find me when you're done."

After she left, David asked, "How do you like Wilton so far?"

"It's nice . . . prettier than Buffalo." Darn it, she'd messed up his jawline. She erased a bit and concentrated on the page in front of her.

"Does sticking the tip of your tongue out of the corner of your mouth help you draw better?" David teased in a good-natured way.

Wincing, she sucked her tongue back inside her mouth and glanced at him. "Apparently."

He crossed his arms, chuckling, and continued to watch her work. Within another few minutes, she was finished. She examined the image, wearing a scowl. Portraits were a *lot* harder than ceramic roosters.

David reached across the table and tugged at the pad. "Let me see."

Reluctantly, Vivi released it and watched for his reaction.

"It's amazingly good for such quick work." A slow grin spread across his face as he intently studied her drawing. "You made me much better looking than I really am."

"I did not!" She hadn't, had she? Oh God, how embarrassing.

"You did, I think." He tore the drawing from the pad and set it to his left before sliding the previously discarded bowl closer. "Thanks."

Vivi reached out for the picture, but he swatted her hand. The contact sent tingles up her arm.

"That's mine." He then spooned saffron rice into his mouth. "In fact, sign it so someday I can prove I knew you when."

Although Vivi knew he was kidding around to be nice to his baby sister's friend, she loved every minute of his undivided attention. Unfortunately, it lasted only seconds longer, thanks to Jackson.

"Hey, bro. Hurry up, or we're going to be really late."

David glanced at the clock with surprise. "Sorry," he said to Jackson. "I'll be quick."

He set his bowl in the sink and then took the drawing from the table. "Nice meeting you, Vivi. Thanks for this."

"I think Cat is in the family room waiting for you," Jackson told Vivi as he followed David out of the kitchen.

"Oh, thanks." Vivi meandered out of the kitchen, feeling a bit light-headed.

She sank onto the sofa cushion beside Cat, who had chosen the movie *Sabrina,* starring Harrison Ford. Vivi couldn't remain interested in the story, because her mind kept fantasizing about seeing David again at breakfast.

"What's with the goofy grin?" Cat asked.

Oops. Vivi covered her private thoughts with some version of the truth. "I'm happy you invited me over."

Chapter One

Block Island
Present Day, Late July

The choppy water of Long Island Sound pitched the ferry, but Vivi knew that wasn't why she was in danger of losing her lunch. Her fingers gripped the edge of the bench seat while her knee jiggled at the pace of a hummingbird's wings. It had been eighteen months since her heart experienced this particular kind of workout.

"You look green," Cat said. "Are you feeling okay?"

Snapping from her daze, she turned toward Cat, who had extended Vivi the last-minute invitation to vacation with her and her brothers at their family's Block Island summer home.

"I'm fine." Vivi quelled her nerves and sat upright. "Just *really* ready for this ferry to dock."

And even more ready to see David, who'd been the object of her affection for more than a decade. The accumulation of years of correspondence, movies and museum outings, afternoons in Central Park, and private jokes had convinced her of their destiny. Until recently, the fact that her sentiments had been unrequited had never deflated her hopes. No surprise, considering life with her dad had taught her not to demand much of love.

Cat leaned toward her. "I'm sure you're eager to see David, but he's different now. He's distant."

Vivi stared at the floor. When he'd moved to Hong Kong after his mom's death eighteen months ago, she'd noticed a change. A sudden, mysterious withdrawal from everyone.

"He's never explained his radio silence, not even to your father?" Vivi asked.

"Especially not to Dad. Ever since Mom died, they barely speak to each other, although neither will tell us why. Maybe things will improve now that he's home." Cat grimaced. "Who would've guessed I would've missed him so much?"

Vivi would have. While others might describe both Cat and David as somewhat aloof, she knew them to be fiercely committed to and protective of their close friends and family.

She glanced out the window, over the ocean. The last time she'd visited Block Island had been several months before Mrs. St. James's cancer diagnosis. A lifetime ago, now. "Thanks for inviting me this week, Cat."

"I'm glad you could come on such short notice." Cat smiled.

"The big perk of being a teacher—a wide-open summer schedule."

"What about your singing gigs?" Cat asked.

Vivi shrugged. "Seeing that I'm maybe one step above an anonymous coffee-shop performer, I doubt I'll be missed this week. There are a handful of singers who rotate through the schedule at the bar, so I'm covered."

"You're at least two steps above a coffee-shop guy," Cat teased. "But I'm glad you made it work. I'll have much more fun with you than I would've with Justin." Cat's expression turned grim at the mention of her tumultuous relationship, which had apparently just gone south yet again.

"For sure!" Vivi winced as the words left her mouth, realizing they weren't the most compassionate.

"My life is so screwed up lately, it's driving me crazy. I really need this time away from work and Justin. I don't want to think of either for the next several days." Cat clamped her hand on Vivi's thigh. "Promise you'll help keep me sane."

"God, Cat, if you're counting on *me* for sanity, you really are screwed up!" Vivi laughed.

"Good point," Cat joked. Then her phone rang. She frowned at the screen and then pouted. "Justin."

"Don't answer."

Cat frowned, then mouthed "sorry" as she answered his call. She immediately stood and walked away, which left Vivi free to anticipate seeing David again.

He'd barely kept in touch with anyone after his move. She recalled the final letter she'd sent him on the first anniversary of his mother's passing. His cryptic reply had politely warned her to leave him be, so she'd given up and started pushing him from her mind, determined to finally get over him.

She'd nearly succeeded, too, by throwing herself into the many other things in life she loved—her elementary school art teaching job, her photography hobby, her weekend singing gigs. Then, three weeks, three days, and seven hours ago, Cat had casually mentioned David's unexpected move back to New York. Vivi had feigned nonchalance until she'd been alone. Then she'd been unable to concentrate on anything else.

The next day, he'd sent her a brief e-mail promising to get together as soon as he'd settled into work and his new home. Somehow she'd since refrained from calling to welcome him home, or worse, from wandering around his Manhattan neighborhood hoping to "accidentally" bump into him. But nothing had prevented her from fantasizing about seeing him again.

Cat reappeared, looking irritable, and shoved her phone into her purse.

"Forget about Justin." Vivi patted Cat's thigh twice. "Move on."

Cat's chocolate-brown eyes fixed on Vivi. "Easier said than done. Surely you know that as well as anyone."

Vivi's eyes dropped to her hands, clasped together and resting in her lap. *Yes, I sure do*. Today's anticipation of the long-awaited reunion unleashed a million thoughts and emotions. Might he finally see her as more than his friend, his *muñequita*, a little doll? Or had the prolonged absence from each other's lives diminished the closeness that had once existed?

Experiencing the feelings was challenging. Concealing them from Cat—clearly impossible.

The ferry horn's blast pierced the air, ripping Vivi from her thoughts.

"Grab your bag. We're docking." Cat hopped off the bench and proceeded to the deck. The breeze whipped her waist-length hair around her face. She traipsed off the ferry with her Louis Vuitton suitcase in tow.

Other passengers appeared to be admiring Cat's long legs, luminous hair and eyes, and finely chiseled features. Even when not working the runway, Cat looked every inch the high-profile fashion model.

Vivi sniffed the air and wrinkled her nose in response to the pungent stench of fish and engine fumes in the harbor. But nothing destroyed the romantic notion of a bygone era evoked by the National Hotel, a white-clapboard Victorian-era structure that dominated the landscape.

Following behind Cat, Vivi heaved her no-name duffel over her shoulder and ambled down the gangway. She tugged at the bottom of her cutoff denim shorts while discreetly searching the crowded parking lot for David.

As a teen, Vivi had been prepared to wait forever for him. Of course, forever had proved too ambitious. Now, on the cusp of letting those dreams die, she'd see him again, here on a crowded dock.

"Hey, Cat!" David waved his arms above his head. "Over here!"

His eyes widened upon catching sight of Vivi, which made the fine hairs on the back of her neck stand at attention. "Vivi? I didn't know you were coming." He then glanced at Cat with a confused expression. "Where's Justin?"

"Don't ask," Cat barked. "Don't say a word, in fact."

David raised his hands in surrender before kissing Cat's cheek. "Sorry." Then he turned to Vivi and grinned, reaching for her hand.

Only thirty-one, not a single gray strand marred his beautiful head of hair. Dark stubble covered his jaw, framing his sumptuous mouth. Although no longer captain of any lacrosse team, he'd retained an athletic build—broad shouldered and narrow in the waist and hips—and stood a full foot taller than her five foot one.

"Vivi," he murmured in her ear while curling her against his chest and kissing the top of her head. The contact of their standard hello hug filled her with longing, as always. "It's so good to see you."

When he squeezed her more tightly, her entire body resonated. *Home.* "Welcome back," she said while easing away.

"Thanks." David favored her with his shy smile.

"So, are you happy to be home, or missing Hong Kong?" she asked.

Following a pronounced pause, he replied, "I spend most waking hours at the office, so it doesn't make much difference where I sleep."

The image of him tumbled in bedsheets smacked her in the face, but she maintained her cool. His flip remark hadn't fooled her. After more than a decade of friendship, how could he not remember she could see his soul?

"I doubt that's true." Noting a faint hitch in his breath, she wanly smiled.

Although curious to discover the reason behind his hesitancy, she knew he'd never disclose it in front of an audience. *Patience, Vivi.*

"Where's Jackson?" Cat threw her luggage into the back of Jackson's beat-up green Jeep Grand Cherokee.

"At the house with Hank."

Vivi noticed Cat blanch, but David spoke again before Vivi could pry. "And Laney."

"Laney . . . from Hong Kong?" Cat croaked before shooting Vivi a worried glance. *Laney from Hong Kong?* Although the words struck like a blow to the head, Vivi plastered a smile on her face. Thankfully, neither Cat nor David noticed her clenched teeth.

"Yes," he replied.

Cat donned her giant black sunglasses before opening the passenger door. "She sure traveled a long way for a short vacation."

"Actually, she moved to New York, too." David's quiet response rocked Vivi to her core. *No, no, no, no.* Oh, God, she couldn't breathe.

Cat slid her glasses along the bridge of her nose and pinned David with an astonished stare. "Moved to New York, or moved in with *you*?"

"She's presently living in temporary housing provided by our law firm." He opened the door for Vivi, waving her into the backseat without quite meeting her eyes. His vague answer weakened her knees, making her grateful to finally be seated.

"Wow." Cat paused, fumbling for words. "Looks like this week will be filled with surprises."

Laney must be why Vivi hadn't heard from David after his initial e-mail. Before she could wallow in her misery, the car's engine roared to life and they set off toward the bluffs of Mohegan Trail.

Vivi needed to get over David, and she needed to do it *now*. It took her a minute to find her voice. "Who's Hank?"

Once again, she noticed Cat bristle at his name.

"A finish carpenter who works for Jackson. He seems like a decent guy." David glanced at Vivi in his rearview mirror. "You've never met him?"

"No. Jackson had been fairly tied up with Alison these past two years. Hank wasn't with him on the few occasions I saw him."

David's brows lowered. "Don't mention Alison unless you want to set Jackson off. Whatever happened between them must've been extremely unpleasant." He glanced at Cat. "You know anything?"

She shook her head.

Vivi sat back, unsettled. While David and Cat chatted in the front seat, she contemplated her new reality. David had brought a woman halfway around the world to be with him. He *had* fallen in love, just not with Vivi.

Nausea returned and climbed up her throat. She swallowed her bile, hoping no one detected her disappointment.

Stifling a laugh, she considered the folly of envisioning a special reunion with David. Apparently, even at twenty-six, she'd still wanted to believe in fairy tales.

An hour ago she couldn't wait to arrive, but now she was the island's captive. Nowhere to run. Carrying out a charade seemed her only viable option. Too bad her open-book face diminished her chances of success.

She squeezed her eyes shut in a childlike attempt to disappear. When she opened them, she shifted her attention to the rolling green hills. They ascended the island road, whizzing past gray and brown cedar shingle houses, which were partly obscured by tall, dry grasses and overgrown shrubbery. Sadly, the abundant sunshine and long-range views—normally a welcome change from New York—failed to lift her spirits.

However, the breathtaking vista surrounding the St. James family's house forced a grin. Perched atop the two-hundred-foot-high cliffs, it enjoyed 180-degree ocean views.

Vivi turned her back on the bluffs and looked at the three-story house, which was surrounded by mammoth blue hydrangea. The main living area was located on the middle level, with guest bedrooms on the ground level and a master suite on the top level.

She squinted in the sunlight at the picnic table parked on the flagstone patio at the side of the house. Fleeting images of Frisbee games, candlelight conversations, and body-surfing contests passed through her mind.

A light prickling sensation swept over her scalp and down her shoulders. Those trips had provided temporary escape from her unhappy life with her father. She'd had high hopes for this trip, too, but they'd all died at the harbor.

The sounds of the seagulls and ocean brought her back to the present. Vivi inhaled the briny sea air and waved off David's assistance as she lugged her bag out of the backseat. Her momentum sent her stumbling backward into the cute blue convertible parked in the driveway.

"Whose Mini Cooper?" she asked.

"Laney's."

Cat scrunched her nose. Vivi thought it was a great car, especially compared to the rental car she and Cat had driven to the island.

At that moment, Jackson scrambled down the front steps and jogged toward them. He snatched both girls up into a bear hug. Although two inches shy of six feet tall, his solid frame towered over Vivi. In his arms, her toes lifted off the ground.

He'd always been the devil-may-care St. James sibling. She'd thought of him as a big brother forever. Fortunately, Cat didn't mind sharing. Vivi squeezed him with all one hundred pounds of her might until he set her down.

"V, what a great surprise!" He ruffled her hair. "Now I know we'll have some fun this week."

"It's great to be back here, and I can't wait to meet Hank."

Jackson's gaze flitted between David and Vivi. He tilted his head and grinned. "Are you on the market?"

"Yep." She didn't dare look at David. "How about you?"

"No time for a commitment." Jackson's glib tone failed to conceal the ache that flickered across his cognac-colored eyes. "But a fling would be nice."

"I'll be sure to warn the natives." Vivi winked. Jackson laughed, revealing his deep dimples. His presence provided a much-needed comfort from her distress over David and Laney.

"So, rocks or sand today?" she asked while they strolled toward the house, with David and Cat trailing along somewhere behind them.

Jackson rubbed his hands together and flashed another grin.

"Sand. Of course, if a big storm passes through, the beach could get rocky again."

"Then let's take advantage of the good conditions now." She lightly brushed a Persian blue hydrangea bloom with her open palm. Her artist's eye noted the blossom's variegated shades of blue and purple—the colors of her bruised heart.

Once inside, she followed Cat downstairs while David and Jackson trotted up the half flight to the main living area. David's temporary departure came as a relief. A new experience for her.

After hoisting her luggage onto one of the twin beds in Cat's room, she tossed her clothes randomly across the pastel-pink coverlet. An indigo-colored tankini swimsuit, comprised of snug boy shorts and an underwire halter, landed on top of the pile. She grabbed it and changed her clothes.

She tugged the wheat-colored, windblown rat's nest some might call hair through the back opening of her worn Yankees baseball cap, shoved her feet into orange drugstore flip-flops, and grabbed her yellow beach towel. The outfit was inelegant, but she loved wearing bright colors, especially when her mood needed a boost.

Grinning, she spun toward Cat. "All set."

Only then did she notice Cat sitting on her bed, fully dressed and cross-legged, reading her phone with her brows tightly drawn together.

"Justin?" Vivi sighed aloud. Cat's preoccupation with her roller-coaster romance seriously interfered with their friendship these days. Worse, the unstable relationship made Cat edgier and more impatient. One way or another, Vivi planned to uncover the reason behind all the melodrama during this trip.

"Go ahead." Without looking up, Cat mumbled, "I'll catch up in a bit."

"Don't sit around waiting for his calls. Being too available for a man never served me well." Vivi snickered at herself. "One of us should learn from my mistakes."

"Ha, ha." Cat rolled her eyes and waved off her friend.

Fudge. Now she'd have to face David and Laney on her own. Of course, she'd had lots of practice confronting awkward occasions throughout her life. She'd survived them all, sometimes even with her dignity intact. Resiliency was the silver lining afforded by her many disappointments. Drawing a deep breath, she crossed the ground-floor hallway.

Voices descended from the kitchen. An unfamiliar velvety baritone rang out, which she presumed was Hank's.

"So who's Vivi?" he asked.

"David's shadow." Vivi actually heard the impish smile in Jackson's intonation, even as her stomach knotted. *His shadow?* "Actually, she's been Cat's best friend since middle school. But she's had a massive crush on David since we were all kids."

Oh, God. David hadn't been surprised by that horrid nickname. Had they often *joked* about her behind her back? She stood, frozen and breathless, on the fourth step.

Hank's voice interrupted her thoughts. "Is she hot?"

"How would we know? She's like a sister to us," Jackson said. "I guess she's pretty cute, in an unconventional way. A little sprite. Blond, blue-eyed, big smile."

David remained mute on the subject. A hot mixture of agony and self-disgust washed through Vivi while she acknowledged the time she'd wasted on a man who apparently only ever considered her a member of his family.

Of course, in the very beginning she'd understood their differences had been insurmountable. David had been eighteen, the captain of the lacrosse and debate teams, and perpetually besieged by perky, uninhibited cheerleaders. On the other hand, she'd been a thirteen-year-old stick figure with a camera hanging from her neck and fingers stained with brightly colored oil paints.

Regardless, she'd been undaunted. Wearing her heart on her sleeve, she'd been certain her love would eventually win him over. Now she had to face facts instead of cling to delusions. Refusing to hide in the stairwell like a mouse, she resumed her ascent, but then the men continued talking.

"What's she like?" Hank asked.

Simultaneously, Jackson answered, "Quirky," while David stated, "Exceptional."

"Cute, quirky, and exceptional. Well, if you're not interested, David, can I have her?" Hank teased.

His shadow. Seized by the need to wrest control of her situation, she charged up the last few steps, two at a time, and abruptly entered their conversation.

"I think that's a question better directed to me. After all, David's not my pimp." She smiled cheerily, as if this were a normal discussion, and prayed her flushed cheeks wouldn't betray her.

All three men stared. Reddening necks broadcast their embarrassment at having been caught gossiping. Jackson covered his laughter by coughing.

She stole a glimpse of David, who stood in silence, staring at her with his typical intensity mingled with something she couldn't quite identify.

His stiff demeanor proved he still suppressed his deep well of emotion, which made her insides melt. Her heart thudded in response to his quiet, powerful energy. *Look away.*

In order to convince everyone she'd finally outgrown her *crush* on David, she began flirting with Hank.

"Hi. You must be Hank. I'm Vivienne, but my friends call me Vivi." She shook Hank's hand and flashed a coquettish smile. "So, to answer your earlier question, I'd say you have an uphill battle since I've typically preferred brunettes." She winked at Jackson and then resumed smiling at Hank. "Of course, I dated Alex in college—a hot blond, like you—so you never know."

On that note, all three men's jaws dropped. Wrapping her makeshift ponytail around her hand and then setting it free, she laughed and crossed to the refrigerator to find a soda. She hid behind the open door, letting the chilled air cool the heat in her cheeks. Having gained a toehold on her pride, she shut the door and turned to face them.

"Cat's texting Justin, so she could be a while. Is anyone heading to the beach yet, or am I on my own?" She popped the tab of the Diet Pepsi can and took a swig. Her nose wrinkled at the tickle from the released carbonation.

"I'm ready," Jackson said. For the first time, Vivi noticed how shaggy he'd let his wavy hair become.

"Me too." Hank wiggled his brows, causing her to laugh.

His tanned, square jaw and celadon eyes made him look like the quintessential lifeguard. An old, soft T-shirt hugged his muscular chest and emphasized his swimmer's build. Most women would go crazy for this guy, but Vivi's knees weren't weakening. Nope. Despite his good looks and evident testosterone, Hank barely registered a blip on her radar. Clearly she'd procrastinated visiting a shrink for far too long.

At least the tension had eased. She tipped her chin and raised her brows at David, silently questioning whether he'd be joining them.

"Laney's changing upstairs." He studied her as if to gauge her reaction to the idea of meeting Laney. "We'll be down later."

"Super. Looking forward to meeting her." Vivi smiled sweetly, lying through her teeth. Threading her arm through Jackson's, she thrust her can of soda toward the back door. "Let's go!"

Hank picked up the cooler and followed them outside.

They crossed the yard and came to the first of the 163 rickety steps leading from the top of the cliff to the beachfront below. Vivi paused to survey the sandy beach, which stretched along the base of the cliffs several hundred yards to her left. The few homes scattered across the top of the bluff shared this spectacular view.

She fixed her attention on the sun-bleached staircase, which twisted its way down the face of the bluff. The worn wooden structure resembled the framework of old-fashioned roller coasters, and equally terrified her, too. Concentrating on avoiding splinters, she firmly gripped the railing and followed Jackson and Hank down to the beach.

While helping the guys set up umbrellas and beach chairs, she managed to conjure up distinct images of David in the kitchen. His high cheekbones, thinly sculpted nose, and square jaw made him striking beyond compare—just masculine enough to avoid being labeled a "pretty boy."

Countless daydreams had peppered so many days since they'd first met. His analytical nature and calm demeanor had been a fixed point around which she'd bobbed and whirled while battling her chaotic life and emotions throughout the years. She'd entrusted him with her secrets and fears. In every circumstance, he'd made her feel understood—known and accepted.

She'd thought they'd shared an unbreakable bond. But whatever did or didn't exist had ended when he went to Hong Kong. Laney's move proved, once and for all, David would never belong to Vivi.

Blinking back tears, she resented the inability to mourn the loss of her dream. Here she'd be forced to bury her disappointment under false laughter while interacting with him and his lover. No ice cream overload, no chick flicks, no tissues. Could there be a worse nightmare?

Paging Tim Burton.

The burn of the sun's scorching glare was nothing compared to the shattering pain inside. Watching the waves collide against the rocky outcroppings in the sea, she conceded the scenery in her personal hell was magnificent.

Chapter Two

David released the breath he'd pent up since he'd first laid eyes on Vivi. He hadn't wanted her to learn about Laney that way. But, except for a flash of surprise, her periwinkle eyes had sparkled like always.

Her diminutive appearance wasn't as elfin as he'd remembered, despite her pleasantly upturned little nose and gap-toothed smile. She'd matured and grown into her huge eyes and expressive mouth. Though not voluptuous, she filled out her swimsuit and wasn't shy about putting her lithe body on display for Hank. Not that she'd ever been very shy.

Generous Vivi had arrived brimming with energy, as always. Her presence never failed to infuse a room, or its occupants, with warm vitality—in his opinion, anyway. Proximity roused the familiar pull of their seasoned friendship, though the ties were now as fragile as the threads of a spiderweb.

He hadn't seen her since his mother's funeral. Her tearstained cheeks had mirrored his own grief that day, although he'd tried to conceal his shattered state. It was the only time she'd ever behaved with uncertainty around him, as if she'd known he'd been utterly broken.

What she hadn't known—what *no one* knew—was how he'd effectively lost his mother *and* father at that funeral. David's discovery of the torrid affair his once-beloved dad had been carrying on while his mom had battled cancer had demolished his illusions of his father, his family, and love.

The hole his mother left behind had been magnified by the deathbed promise she'd extracted from him for the sake of keeping her family united after she passed. Honoring her plea to keep the affair a secret had conflicted with David's yearning to expose his father, so he'd secured a transfer to his firm's Hong Kong office to escape temptation.

Unfortunately, time away hadn't diminished his anguish, thanks, in part, to his father's unrepentant attitude. Worse, David's retreat and secrecy had screwed up his relationship with Cat and Jackson, and probably Vivi, too. If he couldn't somehow mend fences with his father, he feared permanent estrangement from all of them.

If only they knew the truth.

"Lighten up, David. We're on vacation. Leave the office behind for one week."

Laney's voice interrupted the bleak direction of his thoughts. She sauntered into the kitchen looking like a trophy girlfriend, wearing a wide-brimmed sun hat, a beach cover-up with a gold-sequined border, and a designer gold-lamé bathing suit. Holding Armani sunglasses in her hand, she tipped her head and stared at him.

He knew she hadn't the slightest idea what he'd been contemplating. He'd never confided in her. Laney was sexy and whip-smart, but theirs was not a love affair. United by common interests and careers, they'd fallen into a comfortable relationship of compatibility and mutual respect, which he now valued over unreliable emotions like love. In this regard, they were well matched.

"Nice bathing suit." He flashed a brief smile. "Looks good."

He had no doubt she'd dropped a few hundred dollars on the racy bikini peeking out from under her glittering wrap.

She grinned and kissed him. "Well, that's better." Glancing around the empty kitchen, she asked, "Where is everyone?"

"Cat's downstairs talking on the phone. Jackson, Hank, and Vivi went to the beach."

"Who's Vivi?"

"Cat's best friend since middle school." He hid the grin that formed upon recalling the first time he'd met her, pink hair and all. "You'll like her. She's fun, creative." *And a whole lot more.*

Vivi had turned into a flirt, but not with him—not any longer. Her infatuation had never embarrassed him, despite Jackson's goading. If anything, David had admired her courage. Unlike him, she freely exposed her vulnerabilities. It provoked his protective instincts, although she'd probably never needed him as her champion. Vivi had always been brave.

He'd greedily absorbed her fawning. Looking back, perhaps he'd unintentionally treated her like a beloved family pet, doling out playful attention while assuming she'd always wait for his return with open arms. Apparently her arms got tired.

"Oh, so we've got even numbers now." She cocked her head. "Have Vivi and Jackson ever dated? He's fun and creative, too, in his design-build kind of way."

"No." Frowning, David waved his hand dismissively. "She's like a sister to him."

He'd never considered his brother's compatibility with Vivi, although he'd known they were close. Despite acknowledging their history and shared traits, the idea of pairing his brother with Vivi agitated David.

Straightening his shoulders, he twisted his neck to dispel his disquieting reaction.

"Let's go." He reached for Laney's hand before striding toward the back door.

When they arrived at the beach, they found Jackson seated near the cooler drinking a cold beer. Hank and Vivi strolled along the rocky edge of the water fifty yards away, then stopped and leaned in toward each other to inspect whatever she was holding in her hands. The dramatic effect of the cliffs rising up from the sand created a disturbingly romantic picture.

"Where are they going?" David squinted while peering down the beach.

"Vivi wanted to explore." Jackson closed his eyes and rested his head against his reclined beach chair. "Hank volunteered to wade through the surf with her."

"They look cute together despite the height difference." Laney studied them. "Their hair is even an identical color. Maybe they'll hit it off. He seems like a nice guy."

"What's hair color got to do with anything? You've got red hair and mine is black. Is there some special meaning in that?" David snapped, surprising himself with his terse tone before he tore his gaze away from Hank and Vivi.

Laney and Jackson viewed him through narrowed eyes. Ignoring their stares, he inhaled slowly and snagged a bottle of water from the cooler.

"What would you like to drink, Laney?" David asked, noting the visible waves of heat rising from the sand.

"Diet soda, please."

He handed her an icy can and sat beside her. Beads of perspiration gathered at his hairline within minutes. He guzzled half of the contents of his water bottle without stopping.

David sat back in his chair and tried not to notice Vivi gleefully stooping to discover ocean treasures. He also tried not to wonder how much more interesting it would be right now at that end of the beach with her. Hank would soon learn Vivi was never dull.

Unwittingly, a smile tugged at the corners of his mouth. Seeing her evoked so many memories.

When he'd left for college, she'd stowed a secret love note in his computer case. To this day, her brazen declaration of affection remained the sweetest gift he'd ever received from any girl. He'd kept it tucked away in his wallet for years as a sort of talisman.

Throughout his college and law school years, she'd routinely mailed him care packages. His roommates had devoured the snacks. He'd enjoyed her colorful letters most—rife with indignant opinions of high school gossip and gamesmanship, which she'd navigated poorly. Sometimes she'd included a sketch she'd drawn, or a photo she'd taken, to remind him of home and what, or who, eagerly awaited his return. He'd cherished her reminders more than he'd ever admitted to anyone.

Of course, now their attenuated relationship was yet another victim of his damned promise. But Vivi's presence offered an unexpected opportunity to reconnect. An opportunity he'd gladly embrace. For once, Justin's bullshit might yield a positive outcome.

Cat arrived on the beach and tossed her mammoth silver tote bag next to David's chair, kicking sand up against his leg.

"Nice." He peeked at her from over the top of his sunglasses and grinned. "Thanks."

"So what's with the beard, by the way?" She rested her hands on her hips. "I barely recognize you."

"It's hardly a beard." David rubbed his hand along the day-old stubble on his jaw before introducing his sister to Laney.

"Hi, Laney. I'm the pain-in-the-ass sibling, or so I'm told." Cat winked at David. He watched his sister size up Laney's attire, physical attributes, and disposition. "How long have you two been dating now? Five months?"

"About seven, actually," Laney replied.

"Oh. Well, it's nice to finally meet you. What's your accent? Midwestern?"

His sister's direct approach made him smile until Laney shot him a miffed glance. Was she angry he hadn't told his family much about her?

"Yes," Laney replied. "I'm from Chicago."

"Nice city," Cat said. "Now you've moved to New York, right? Are you on the Upper East Side?"

Cat's transparent fishing expedition drove a prickle of annoyance down David's spine.

"I'm undecided," Laney replied. "Acclimating to the new office, partners, and clients has been exhausting, so I haven't spent much time looking."

"Huh. That must be why I haven't seen much of David, either." Cat turned toward David and shoved his shin with her toes.

Before he could respond, Laney intervened. "Yes. It's quite a coup to make partner at a top firm by his age. The expectations are pretty daunting. Maybe you should cut him a little slack until he settles in at the office." She smiled pointedly at Cat.

David watched his sister's mental retreat from Laney's admonishment. Shielding her eyes with her hand, Cat turned to scan the beach and spotted Vivi and Hank. Her bothered expression echoed his discomfort with their apparent attraction.

"Is Hank hitting on Vivi?" She leaned over and lightly batted the top of Jackson's head. "You'd better have him back off. We don't need any sexual complications this week."

"Settle down. Hank's not her type," David chimed in without thinking.

He shuddered at an image of Vivi and Hank engaging in any kind of intimate behavior, a first for him. Suddenly the weight of his sister's amused glare landed on his shoulders.

"Why isn't he her type?" Cat scoffed with smug satisfaction. "Just because he's not *you*?"

Jackson laughed, David groaned, and Laney became exponentially more interested in Vivi.

"What's that mean, David?" Laney drew her glasses down her nose and locked eyes with him. "Did you date her?"

"No," he said. "I never dated Vivi." He cast Cat a warning glance.

Jackson settled back in his chair with a smirk. Cat paused, appearing pleased to lord power over her oldest brother. The creases in David's forehead deepened as she opened her mouth.

"Vivi's not David's type. But since he believes he's God's gift, he thinks no woman could ever be interested in anyone other than him."

Laney's suspicious expression remained firm despite Cat's lopsided grin.

"Yes, I'm God's gift, Laney. Lucky me, or I'd never have had a shot with you." David smiled tightly in spite of Cat's teasing, or the fact that Hank and Vivi continued their journey farther down the beach.

"Yes, lucky you. And don't you forget it." Laney tipped her chin up and resumed her reading.

Cat plunked herself down under the umbrella beside David. After slathering SPF 90 sunscreen on her body, she hugged her knees to her chest and stared across the ocean. The distant aspect of his sister's gaze tugged at his heart.

Leaning forward, he whispered, "I know I haven't been the best brother lately, but if you need to talk, or vent, about whatever happened with Justin, I'll walk with you."

She studied him and then let her gaze drift back to the horizon. "Not now, thanks." Her posture stiffened. "Maybe later."

Even if her rebuff was a defense mechanism resulting from his apparent indifference during the past year, it still smarted.

He tugged on her ear. "Whenever you need me."

He watched her, resolving to regain her trust, knowing it would take months of effort, not days. He could live with her and Jackson's displeasure more easily if it weren't for the fact that his father's relationship with them was as close as ever. *Utterly unjust.*

He stretched his neck once more to rid himself of mounting tension. Unable to recall the last time he'd relaxed, he'd desperately hoped returning to his favorite place would help him unwind this week. But now Cat seemed preoccupied with her Justin, Laney's antennae were training on Vivi, and Hank was sniffing around Vivi like a dog in heat. Only Jackson appeared to be enjoying the sun and surf.

David wished he could be like his brother, who accepted things more easily. Unfortunately, he viewed the world in black-and-white terms, having never quite learned how to deal with the gray. That trait was probably one reason he couldn't forgive his father.

He inhaled deeply and then consumed the rest of his water. Closing his eyes, he daydreamed about prior weeks spent on this beach.

Like his mother, he'd always treasured this island and the long summer days spent here with family and friends. Well, most of his family, anyway. His father had never stayed for more than two or three nights before rushing back to Connecticut. Now David doubted work was the reason he'd left them so often.

His father's duplicity proved a loveless but pleasant relationship was the smartest choice. Shared goals and interests mixed with attraction left no risk of a broken heart on either side of the equation. David's idea of the so-called match made in heaven.

He absentmindedly crushed the empty plastic bottle in his hand; the crackling sound wrenched him from his thoughts. Feeling exposed, he glanced around. No one else seemed to notice. *Huh.* He'd become invisible.

A little while later, Vivi and Hank returned to the group. Clutching a cup containing small sea creatures, Vivi kneeled beside Cat.

"Look what we found." She inched closer to Cat, eyes gleaming in anticipation of the torment she seemed to be planning, and brandished a small crab in her right hand and a starfish in her left. "Aren't they beautiful?"

"Ew, Viv." Cat shielded herself with a magazine. "Put those back in the water!"

David had often wondered how two near-polar opposites maintained their friendship for so long. Then again, he and Vivi also shared a bond despite her personality being the antithesis of his—because of it, in fact. *Yin and yang.*

The thought reminded him of the jade bangle bracelet he'd brought back from Hong Kong for her, which was engraved with carvings of a dragon and a phoenix—symbolizing the union of yin and yang. He'd placed it in his desk drawer weeks ago, waiting for the right time to surprise her.

When Vivi spotted Laney, her childish behavior subsided. After returning the crab and starfish to the cup, she wiped her sandy hands against her slim thighs and stood to introduce herself to Laney.

"Hi, you must be David's girlfriend. Laney, right? I'm Vivienne, a friend of the family." She extended her hand. "But everyone calls me Vivi."

Her dirty fingers starkly contrasted with Laney's manicured ones. David noted tremendous differences between his girlfriend's cultured refinement and Vivi's unpretentious manner. He watched Laney assess Vivi's inexpensive swimwear, old baseball cap, and unkempt ponytail, and then dismiss whatever competition she might have feared earlier.

Like most people, she'd underestimated Vivi's charm. He'd often wondered how so many could miss it.

Remarkably, Vivi appeared unaffected by Laney's presence. Her evident lack of interest or envy rattled David. He'd grown accustomed to her doting manner. More than accustomed, actually—he'd liked it and now lamented its absence.

When she walked to the edge of the water to wash her hands, he followed her into the surf, eager to reestablish their rapport.

"I'm glad you're here, Vivi," he said, yanking on her ponytail. "Now we can make up for lost time."

"That's an odd saying, right?" She kept her eyes on her hands and legs as she cupped water to rinse them. The water beaded and rolled off her skin, washing away most of the sand. "Like you can actually get back the wasted time."

"I guess you have a point." He frowned. He bent over to push a fallen section of hair behind her ear. "But we've always had a great time here. It's the perfect place to catch up. I've missed our conversations."

She stood fully and raised her eyebrows. Did he see doubt behind her eyes?

"Are you living in that same apartment in Astoria?" he asked, grasping for neutral territory.

"Yep. New York must seem humdrum to you after your stint in Hong Kong." The corners of her lips quirked upward and she planted her hands on her hips. "I guess congratulations are in order, although I'm not surprised. I always knew you'd be successful. Is partnership everything you want it to be?"

"Time will tell," he replied, unable to reach through the emotional distance between them.

"Yes, time changes everything." She tilted her head sideways. "Does Laney like New York?"

He'd never been comfortable speaking about any of his girlfriends with Vivi, preferring to spare her feelings by compartmentalizing his private life as much as possible. Today Laney's presence forced the issue. "She's not yet settled. Work takes up most of her time, and she hasn't any friends there."

"Well, she has you, anyway."

Over the years he'd learned to read Vivi's various expressions, including several different smiles. But he couldn't read this one, which made him feel untethered.

"On another note, I bought you a gift in China. If I'd known you would be here, I would've brought it with me."

"Really?" She looked surprised. "What is it?"

He smiled, envisioning her reaction to the simple jewelry he'd selected especially for her. "I think I'd rather surprise you with it in person. If you want, I'll give you a hint. It's made from something believed to bring luck and protection."

"Well, thank you for whatever you bought me. I guess I'll have to wait until you can find time in your schedule to squeeze me in." Her somber tone nipped at his conscience. He froze, grappling for the right response.

"Sorry, Vivi. I wanted to see you sooner but didn't want our first visit to be rushed. It sounds lame, but I had severe jet lag my first two days back. Then I got tagged to take over a significant client transaction that's required fourteen-hour workdays because the closing date got bumped forward. Great for my career, not so great for my personal life—not that the firm gives a fig about anyone's personal life. Fortunately we just closed the deal this past Friday, so I'd love to make plans whenever you're available."

"Okay. We'll see." She paused, as if waiting for him to offer more, then nodded and glanced over her shoulder.

He watched her survey everyone sprawled out on beach chairs. She twisted her full lips into a pout as she turned from him and approached the group. *What else might she do with those pursed lips?* he wondered. He shook his head to banish the inappropriate thought.

"I think I'm done with the sun today," she announced to everyone. "Why don't I go pick up something to cook for dinner? I got inspired by my beachcombing. So I have a surprise in mind."

She stood behind Jackson's chair, leaning down close to his ear. "May I please take your car?"

"Sure." He remained reclined with his eyes closed. "Keys are on the kitchen counter."

"Thanks, Jacks."

The chaste kiss she planted on his forehead elicited a playful grin and tug on her hair from him. A spark of envy roiled through David's veins.

"Do you remember how to find the grocery store?" David interjected.

"I think so. And if I'm wrong, I can't get too lost on Block Island." She waved. "See you all later!"

In the past, she'd leaped at any opportunity to drag him off on an errand. Not today.

As she meandered toward the steps, David noticed Hank staring at her hips. A tiny knot formed in his gut.

"She's charming." Hank exhaled as he took a seat beside Jackson.

Cat's expression grew cool. She leaned forward to fasten her warning gaze on Hank. "She's important to our family, so you'd better treat her with respect."

Hank started at Cat's words and then looked at her as if amused.

"Catalina." His inflection seemed to impart a private message to her, which David couldn't decipher. "Nice to see you again, too." Grinning to himself, Hank slouched back in his chair.

David glanced at the top of the steps and watched Vivi disappear behind the shrubs. Unspoken but well-known boundaries would always limit his relationship with her. He'd be the worst kind of hypocrite to begrudge her the attentions of another man, especially when he had Laney here.

Vivi's change of heart was for the best, even if it hurt a little.

Chapter Three

Two hours later, everyone climbed the stairs to the house to escape the sun. Inside, they encountered Vivi, standing in the middle of the cheerful blue kitchen, surrounded by bags of groceries. David noted her wet hair piled loosely on top of her head. She looked fresh and clean . . . and unexpectedly appealing.

"Oh! Scoot and go shower or relax for a while." She waved her arms over the bags to prevent anyone from snooping around the counters. "This is supposed to be a surprise."

"No problem-o," Jackson promised. Everyone obeyed her command and hustled off to other parts of the house, eager to shed the salt and sweat from their bodies.

When David descended the steps ninety minutes later, he discovered Vivi humming amid a kitchen full of seafood, chicken, and chorizo. Blissfully absorbed in her task, she scurried around the small space while throwing saffron, chicken broth, and rice in a large pot.

Like his own mother, Vivi jumped headlong into every project, relationship, and activity. Her enthusiasm always charmed him. Watching the scene in the kitchen transported him back to the days when their comfortable friendship felt as natural as breathing. It wasn't until the first fragrant whiff of the simmering ingredients reached his nose that he recoiled inside.

The aroma of his mother's paella recipe penetrated his deeply buried anguish. He steadied himself against the counter.

"What are you doing?" he asked sharply.

"I-I'm making your mom's paella." Stilled and wide-eyed, she continued, "I thought of it when I caught the crabs in the ocean."

Being here with everyone for the first time since his mother's death unearthed repressed memories of laughter, love, and all the happiness he'd buried with his mother. The conflict between those memories and his current circumstances tore at him. His throat constricted as the spicy scents drew forth an image of his mother smiling at him from that very stove. *Never again.*

The crippling reality swept through him, hot and white, scoring him.

"Why? Why did you choose my mom's favorite meal? You can't take her place. You're not even part of our family!"

"Hey, David. Shut it!" Jackson yanked him from the kitchen. "She's been more a part of this family than you have recently."

David whirled around, flustered. Jackson stepped between Vivi and him, standing cross-armed.

"What's wrong?" Laney entered the room. David noticed her eyes dart from him to Jackson to Vivi.

Regaining his composure, he snatched Laney's keys from the counter and took her by the hand, desperate to escape the visions of his mother and his memories of the "perfect family" he'd once believed in.

"We're going out tonight."

Without glancing back, he hauled her from the house and, seconds later, peeled out of the driveway.

~

Still brooding at the outdoor restaurant of the National Hotel, David poured himself another glass of Pinot Grigio from the second bottle he'd ordered. A cool breeze swept across the hotel porch, causing him to shiver.

"David," Laney began, "what upset you at the house?"

"Let's not discuss it." He swigged more of his wine.

"Well, I'd like to know what we're confronting when we return."

God, he dreaded facing everyone. He slid his fingers through the condensation on the side of his glass, staring at the rivulets formed by the motion.

"Vivi cooked my mother's favorite dish tonight. It reminded me of sitting at the counter and talking with my mom while she'd work in the kitchen. The idea of enjoying it without her felt like a betrayal, especially here," he said, gesturing toward the island harbor. "I guess I'm still mourning her death. Nothing in Hong Kong reminded me of her, so it was easy to distract myself with the novelty of the region and demands of work. But her absence here, in our family's home, is forcing me to face the loss. It's suffocating. I miss her . . ." His throat tightened, choking his words. "I miss her so much."

He avoided Laney's penetrating gaze by staring at his wine glass. He'd spoken the truth, just not all of it. More had provoked him this evening. Vivi. He hadn't been prepared to see her again or feel her indifference.

It threw him off balance—way off.

After a pause, Laney pressed him. "Why do I sense more to Vivi's relationship with you and your family?"

Discomforted by her observation, David glanced off into the distance. How could he adequately condense almost thirteen years of knowing Vivi?

"Cat befriended her when she moved to our town. She'd lost her mother and brother to a fatal car accident when she was very young.

She'd lived alone with her alcoholic father until after college. Needless to say, her home life wasn't nurturing. My mother saw the toll it was taking on Vivi and stepped in as an unofficial surrogate. It's not an overstatement to say she's practically an adopted member of our family."

While this version of Vivi's history was accurate, it excluded any mention of her precise relationship with him. When he thought about that, he wasn't sure how to define what they shared. He only knew he cherished it.

"Well, she's lucky she had all of you." Laney stabbed at her salmon and pushed it around her plate.

"Lucky" seemed like a perverted view of Vivi's situation. David had met her father only a handful of times, none of which had been pleasant. Stories Vivi told him, and ones he'd heard when eavesdropping on conversations between his sister and mother, had filled in the rest of the equally bad details.

He'd often heard pity in Cat's voice when she spoke of Vivi's life. In contrast, he'd revered Vivi's ability to maintain a sunny outlook and find joy in others' good fortune. Despite the dearth of love in her own home, she maintained utter faith in the promise of love.

If only he could be more like her.

"You might want to consider apologizing." Laney's voice drifted through his thoughts. "She must've thought she was doing something nice."

By the time David finished off the second bottle of wine, contrition weighed on him like a wet wool blanket. He'd totally overreacted. Worse, he'd struck out at someone dear to him. Someone he never wanted to hurt.

While Laney drove them home, he imagined his sister's reaction to his earlier outburst. In fewer than twelve hours, he'd lost more control over his emotions than he had since the day of his fight with his father. It didn't bode well for the remainder of his vacation.

Laney shut off the ignition and opened her door. He gulped a steadying breath before following her into the house.

"I'm going straight upstairs. Hopefully this will all blow over by breakfast." She planted a cool kiss on his cheek and fled to their room, leaving him alone in the silent house.

Through the windows of the main living area, David saw Jackson and Hank lounging outside on the deck, encircled by cigar smoke. Vivi and Cat were conspicuously absent. *Here we go.*

Wrenching open the sliding door he stepped into the night air and shivered.

Jackson cast a cold glance at David just before blowing smoke toward him. "How was your dinner?"

"Not great." David waited for the punch line.

"Ours was excellent." Jackson produced an arrogant smile.

"Where's Vivi?" He scanned the lawn below. "I need to apologize."

"You think?" Jackson's sneer emphasized his sarcastic delivery. "Find her in the morning."

"Should I expect an eye gouging from Cat?" David crossed his arms in front of his chest to fend off Jackson's next verbal assault.

"No. Vivi blamed her mood on a 'call from her dad.'"

David winced. He hated the fact that Vivi falsely implicated her father to spare him Cat's tongue-lashing.

"How's she feeling now?" he asked.

"Probably a lot like a helpless kitten who's been drop-kicked by an asshole." Jackson shook his head and flicked the ash from his cigar. "Bro, I don't know what bug crawled up inside you since Mom died, but get rid of it soon."

Hank's eyes widened while he puffed his own cigar.

David stared out over the ocean, its turbulent black water churning just like the acid in his stomach. "I'll make it right," he said without looking at Jackson, wondering exactly how he'd go about keeping that promise.

"That'll be a neat trick."

He glanced over to see Jackson glaring at him. He didn't defend himself. He'd earned Jackson's scorn. David mumbled his good nights and lumbered up the steps to his room.

By midnight, a wine-induced, guilt-riddled headache prompted him to go downstairs for a glass of water. He wandered outside onto the deck, to stand beneath the starless sky streaked with wide swaths of gray clouds.

In the expansive darkness, he recalled Vivi's final letter, which he'd received around the first anniversary of his mom's death. He couldn't remember the scented note in its entirety, having memorized only an excerpt.

I miss you. No one hears from you these days. You've disappeared from all of our lives. I know your loss is tremendous, but I sense something more going on. Share it with me, please. Withdrawing from everyone who loves you will only make it worse. Your mother wouldn't want that for you, or for the rest of us. Honor her by living, loving, and finding joy in your life. It's all she ever wanted for you.

She'd included a small charcoal portrait she'd drawn of his mother. The imperfect image had perfectly captured his mother's spirit and smile. In a weak moment that same day, he'd considered calling and confiding in her.

He'd refrained to spare her from ending up in a terrible position with his siblings. Her piss-poor poker face would make it impossible for her to keep the secret from them, too.

David gripped the railing. Despite yearning for vindication, he'd never betray his mother's wish or be the one to crush his siblings' beliefs about their father and family, even if it meant he'd continue to suffer alone.

But if his mother watched over him, she was disappointed tonight. His stomach pinched each time he pictured Vivi's devastated expression from earlier this evening. He also owed her an apology for taking her friendship for granted while he'd been away.

He wondered if it mattered now. Hell, she didn't seem to care about him anymore.

When his chin fell to his chest in defeat, he noticed something in the grass. Vivi lay in the yard with her hands behind her head, listening to her iPod with her eyes closed.

Without forethought, he descended the steps to apologize in private. Even in the crisp night air, being near her felt like standing under the sun. Warmth seeped from her body and flowed along the ground, like a river of heat seeking to penetrate the frozen places inside his chest.

Her abundant, wavy locks fanned out around her head and cascaded over her shoulders. The seductively tangled mess differed from the shorter, asymmetrical styles she'd always favored. Silvery moonlight slipped through the clouds, illuminating her paper-thin, sheer white tank top.

Abruptly, an erotic vision of climbing on top of her and cupping the heavy weight of her breast as it strained against her shirt aroused him. Startled by his desire, he backed up to steady his racing pulse.

What the hell?

They could never be more than friends.

Not ever.

As a friend he could manage the highs and lows of her volatile emotions and turbulent lifestyle. As a lover it might be overwhelming.

Much more importantly, even if an inevitable breakup didn't hurt Vivi, it could jeopardize her relationship with others in his family, and that would kill her. He'd never forgive himself if that happened, and besides, *he'd* miss their friendship if it ended.

And now he had Laney in his life. Although he'd voiced apprehension over her decision to move to New York, he hadn't strongly discouraged her, either. He'd made no promises or commitments, but she *was* sharing his bed.

Why was he even thinking about this? A romance with Vivi required too much risk. Yet, in this instant, he selfishly wished to share a passionate encounter with the girl who'd long ago claimed an essential place in his life.

Shaking his head, he returned to reality and leaned over to touch her shoulder.

Her eyelids flew open. She crawled backward on her hands and feet, like a crab.

Avoiding eye contact, she stood and removed her earbuds.

"I'm going to bed. Good night, David." She dashed toward the door.

"Vivi, wait. Let me apologize. I'm just . . . struggling with memories. I'm so sorry." David held his breath.

"Fine." She slowed without facing him. "Good night."

Unwilling to let her escape, he lunged to grasp her elbow. Her tension jettisoned along his arm.

"Look at me, please." His fingers clung to her while he fought against encircling his arms around her. "I also want to thank you for lying to protect me from Cat."

"I lied to protect Cat, not you," she said. "She doesn't need anyone else upsetting her this week."

He grimaced in the face of her pronouncement. "Vivi, I shouldn't have taken my grief out on you. I'm sorry. Do you forgive me?"

She refused to answer.

"Come on. The old Vivi would forgive me for anything," he teased.

His joke seemed to enrage her. She met his eyes with her own steely gaze. "The old David was never cruel and thoughtless."

Her rebuke sliced through him. When he clasped her hand, she jerked it away.

"Vivi, please. You know I didn't mean what I said. I'd never hurt you." He produced a weak smile. Instead of offering absolution, she stared straight through him.

"As a lawyer, you choose words carefully for a living. You couldn't have said that if you hadn't thought it first."

Seeing tears pool in her eyes twisted his gut.

She blinked them back before speaking in strained tones. "I'm fine now. And you don't have to worry about upsetting me again. I came here to have fun, and that's exactly what I plan to do. So I'll be sure to keep out of your way as much as possible this week."

Before he could plead his case further, she turned on her heel and strode inside.

Silently, he stared at the door she'd closed in his face.

Dammit. Being kept at arm's length all day had been unpleasant. Now he faced a complete shutout. How'd he get here?

And how in the hell could he get back to the way things used to be?

Chapter Four

The sound of the ocean had blown through the open window all night, lulling Vivi to sleep. Too bad the luxury carried a steep price, namely the predawn screech of seagulls' cries. As Cat's gentle snore filled the room, Vivi marveled at her friend's ability to sleep through the noise.

She bit back a whimper as she nearly peeled away her corneas trying to open her dry eyes. After several painful blinks, she tiptoed to the window and slid it shut before collapsing back into bed. Although exhausted, she couldn't fall back asleep.

Instead, she reanalyzed David's uncharacteristic meltdown and subsequent apology. Unfortunately, his remorse didn't erase the pain etched in her heart.

As his final letter from Hong Kong had predicted, he had changed, and not for the better. His words drifted through her memory.

I can't share the reasons behind my withdrawal other than to say the lens through which I view the world has been shattered. I need to be alone to pick up those pieces and fit them together again.

Lately I worry my former outlook might never be fully restored. If I return home one day a different man, I hope you'll still be my friend, as I will always be yours.

Yesterday she'd seen only traces of the sensitive man he'd always been. Of course, that should make it easier to let go of what his homecoming might have meant for them. Either way, it sucked.

Still, Vivi would muddle through the week without doing anything to widen the rift between the alienated siblings. Besides, she'd be better off using this time to extricate Cat from Justin's clutches once and for all. That relationship had only made Cat more distant and defensive with each passing month.

Heaving a loud sigh, she stared across the room at her friend. As if having sensed Vivi's scrutiny, Cat popped one eye open.

"Go back to sleep, freak." Cat flaunted a sleepy grin and rolled onto her side. "I hate how you always wake up so early."

"Ah, insomnia." Vivi propped herself up on her elbow, grinning. "One of my many flaws."

Cat groaned, then reached for her phone. After scrolling through her messages, she typed a short text, huffing aloud. Vivi noticed a satisfied gleam in her eyes.

"I take it you heard from Justin again?"

"He's not happy I came here without him." Cat's brows lowered for a second. "I half expect him to show up this week, but he may not want to risk a confrontation with David and Jackson."

Vivi's curiosity got the best of her. "Okay, time to tell me what's going on with you. I hardly ever see you lately, unless you split from Justin—which is becoming a pattern."

"Have I been a bad friend, V?"

"Not a bad friend, but you've been different. Normally you share every little detail of your relationships. Overshare, actually!" Vivi smiled, then turned serious again. "With Justin, you've been tight-lipped. Whenever I ask about it, you shut down and become defensive. It worries me, that's all."

Cat drew a deep breath and covered her face with her hands. "I . . . it's hard to talk about . . . embarrassing, actually."

"Please talk to me. You know you can tell me anything. I hate seeing you all torn up."

"Promise not to judge," she warned, her voice tinged with resignation. Once Vivi crossed her heart, Cat continued. "Justin's got serious jealousy issues. He's suspicious of every guy I talk to, at work or elsewhere. Sometimes he checks my phone history or e-mails. He makes crazy accusations and we end up *screaming* at each other—saying awful, awful things. He got so pissed once, he threw the remote across the room and accidentally cracked his TV screen."

Cat's fingers gathered the comforter to pull it up against her chest.

Vivi rarely witnessed Cat's vulnerability, let alone shame. A hot flash of resentment toward Justin streaked through her body. She bit her lip before asking the obvious question. "Why do you keep going back?"

Distress suffused the room while Vivi held her breath.

Cat choked out, "Because I love him and he loves me."

Vivi turned her face away, collecting the thoughts whirling through her mind like a tornado. Thanks to her dad, she knew a little something about codependency and guilt-induced commitment. Apparently Cat thought she could fix Justin's insecurities. She'd have to learn the hard way that no one can emotionally save another.

Vivi simplified her opinions. "Sometimes love isn't enough."

Her own heart skidded to a halt, because her love for David had never mattered.

As if reading her thoughts, Cat replied, "This isn't one-sided like you and David. Justin and I are both invested."

"I wasn't comparing our situations. I'm just saying mutual love doesn't automatically make a relationship work."

Cat rolled her eyes, so Vivi conceded with a shrug. "Fine. But when his jealousy spirals out of control, tragedy can strike in an instant."

"He'd never hurt me!" Cat's eyes flared with indignity. "He just yells a lot. He'll stop when he learns to trust me."

Vivi shuddered, convinced many battered women uttered those very words prior to receiving a first punch.

"Okay. Just know I'm here for you, whatever you need. I miss you, Cat." She shifted her body to nestle down under the quilt. Sensing the need to change the subject, Vivi teased, "I've been on my own a lot these days, so you know I'm on the verge of some kind of disaster."

Cat nodded thoughtfully and picked at her comforter. After a protracted silence, she arched one brow. "I've got to give you credit. You handled David and Laney well yesterday. I didn't honestly believe you were over him until now."

Vivi knew it was unfair to resent Cat for protecting David's privacy by never telling her about Laney. It had stung to be caught off guard. But now another white lie served everyone's interests.

"Part of me will always love David, but we've all grown and changed. I want him to be happy, with Laney or whomever."

"You're a good person. If I were in your shoes, I doubt I'd be so generous." Cat smiled. "His loss, anyway. She's no fun at all."

"Well, I'm probably not the best judge. Plus we barely know her." Vivi tilted her head sideways and shrugged a shoulder. "Maybe she's just shy, like him."

"Shy? David?" Cat drew her thumb and forefinger to her chin. "I've never thought of David as shy. He's always stolen the spotlight."

Vivi's brows shot up in surprise. "He's a total introvert. He only steals the spotlight because he excels at everything to win your dad's approval."

"Maybe you're right. I've never studied him like you have!" Cat laughed and caught the pillow Vivi tossed across the room, dispelling the final remnants of tension from their earlier discussion. "Perhaps now I'll win more of my dad's attention since David no longer cares about his opinion anymore."

Vivi had always envied the way David admired his father's dignified behavior, probably because of the marked difference from her relationship with her own father. Given what she knew, she didn't believe David had now truly forsaken his father's opinion. As for Cat, Vivi wondered how being a model wasn't enough of a spotlight.

Vivi shook her head. Vacations weren't to be wasted on sorrow or problems. "Let's go make coffee and breakfast."

Glancing in the mirror, she contemplated her scruffy appearance before going upstairs. Screw it. David was taken. Everyone could simply endure her crazy hair, boxer pajamas, and sleepy face.

"I'm desperate for a shot of caffeine." Cat moved in slow motion. "Don't ever wake me this early again!"

Moments later, taking a seat at the kitchen counter, Cat rested her head on her hands. When Vivi flung open the sliding doors to let in the breeze, her stomach grumbled loud enough to draw Cat's attention. Not an uncommon event.

Vivi whipped up an egg batter with vanilla and a touch of cinnamon, and then cooked a batch of French toast. The sizzling pan heightened her anticipation. She smothered her stack with so much butter, yellow pools formed on top and dribbled over its sides.

Following Cat to the reclaimed-wood dining table, which sat bathed in sunlight streaming through the bay windows, she settled in front of her plate and let the sun warm her back.

She'd barely sunk her teeth into her breakfast when Jackson and Hank emerged.

"Smelled the coffee." Jackson leaned over Vivi's shoulder to survey her dish. "Any more where those came from?"

"I'll make you some as soon as I finish," she offered.

"You're the best, V." Jackson patted her shoulder before taking a seat beside her. Hank nodded at her and sat opposite them. Vivi watched Cat and Hank politely avoid eye contact. *So weird.*

Ten minutes later, she loaded a heaping serving of freshly made French toast onto Jackson's plate. He dipped his finger into the excess syrup spilling over his plate before sucking it into his mouth.

Vivi was helping herself to seconds when David and Laney strolled into the kitchen. She examined Laney's pressed outfit, glossy lips, made-up eyes, and her pin-straight, silky red hair neatly tucked behind a navy headband. With some surprise, Vivi noted the severe hairstyle made the sharp angles of her face look graceful rather than harsh.

Had David waited for her to primp? Did he enjoy watching her perform her feminine rituals?

Glancing at her own wrinkled, mismatched pajamas, Vivi laughed to herself. No wonder she'd never captured his interest. Elegance and poise weren't words anyone associated with her. Swallowing a sigh, she forced her gaze up to greet them.

David's hopeful expression practically begged her for some sign she'd forgiven him, so she took pity and offered a slight smile. He winked, but then Laney cleared her throat and stared at him until he proceeded to make her a cup of coffee.

He opened the cabinet to retrieve a cup and then wandered away in search of a spoon. His bad habit of leaving cabinet doors hanging open had always annoyed his mother. On the other hand, Vivi loved his little imperfections. *Pathetic.*

After stirring cream and sugar into the coffee cup, David handed it to Laney. Vivi couldn't decide if seeing him act like a trained seal made her jealous or utterly disgusted. Maybe it just made her mad. She'd always treated him like a king, unaware he apparently preferred the role of servant.

Jackson's eyes slid back and forth between David and Vivi. *Crap.* Jackson was monitoring the situation after last night's fiasco. He didn't know about the midnight rendezvous in the backyard. Sucking it up, and dedicated to moving forward with her own life *without David*, Vivi forced herself to be cheerful.

"Would either of you like French toast?"

"No, thanks." Laney patted her washboard stomach while she flashed a polite smile. "I'll stick with coffee."

"Suit yourself." Vivi shoveled a giant bite into her mouth. "David?" Her tongue darted out to lick a dollop of syrup from her bottom lip.

She watched David's eyes widen before he grinned. "Given your appetite, I'd be shocked if you left any food behind." He shook his head in jest and joined everyone at the table. "I'll grab something in a bit, thanks."

Laney wandered over and sat on his knee. Although he spoke with Hank, David's arm automatically wrapped around her waist, and she rested her hand on his forearm. The casual intimacy of the scene threw darts at Vivi's heart.

She yanked her gaze away and fought off a fresh wave of revulsion. Obviously it would take some time for her heart to catch up to her brain when it came to getting over him. Vaulting from her seat, she rinsed her dish and announced, "I'm going hiking with my camera while the morning light is still soft. Anyone care to join me?"

Hank's head shot up. "Give me five minutes and I'll go."

"Okay." Vivi smiled at him. "Cat, join us."

"Nah, I'm on vacation from work *and* exercise. In fact, I may slink back to bed now that you won't be chirping at me." She slid off the barstool and followed Vivi down to their room.

While Vivi changed her clothes, Cat nestled back under her blanket and eyed her.

"So, what's the deal with Hank?" Cat asked. "Are you interested in him?"

Vivi wouldn't confess to enlisting his help during their walk on the beach yesterday. Thankfully, he hadn't been insulted by her plan to involve him in a conspiracy to convince everyone she was over David. After getting to know Hank, however, she thought he'd be a great catch for Cat. Cat wasn't ready to give up on Justin yet, but Vivi hoped to pique her curiosity.

"He's cute, isn't he?" Vivi tied her sneakers, trying for subtlety.

"Blondes aren't usually your thing." Cat didn't meet her eyes.

"Well, I'm not blind." While braiding her hair, Vivi hid her face to conceal her intentions. "His eyes look like sea glass, which you know is a favorite of mine. And that body! And best of all, he's super kind."

"He's too nice." Cat studied her fingernails as if she were bored. "No zip."

"Nice trumps zip in my book. Did you know he's the oldest of five siblings? He's helping to pay for his youngest sister's education. And aside from all that goodness, he's got a tool belt. Come on—a tool belt is hot!"

Cat snorted, so Vivi turned toward her. "What?"

"Nothing." Cat sat forward. "Ignore me."

"Come with us." Vivi walked across the room and sat on the edge of Cat's bed. "It'll be nice."

Cat hesitated, but then her phone trilled. In the blink of an eye, Vivi lost her to Justin. She wanted to stomp on Cat's phone so they could enjoy the week together without that maniac's constant interruptions.

"Justin, I told you to stop calling." Cat sat upright in bed, back pressed to the headboard. After a short pause, she asked, "What Facebook tag?"

Vivi's stomach dropped upon hearing Justin's irate voice emanating from Cat's phone. *Please don't let this be about the picture I posted from last night's dinner.*

"Oh, for God's sake. 'The blond dude' is Hank. He works for Jackson. He is *not* here with me. I brought Vivi," Cat said, shooting Vivi a questioning look, "who must've posted one of the pictures she took at dinner last night."

Vivi mouthed "sorry." Cat waved her away, already focused on defending herself to Justin.

Defeated and feeling guilty, Vivi left Cat behind. When she returned to the living room, she found David waiting for her. His obsidian eyes held her gaze. *Just what I need now.*

"That camera is as big as you." His shy grin distracted her. "Can you hike with it?"

"Hank can carry it for me."

"Of course." David's ghost of a smile vanished. "Does your invitation extend to Laney and me?"

"Oh." Vivi blinked. *No!* "Laney hikes? Er, I mean, it doesn't seem like her kind of thing."

"You're right. It's not." He shrugged. "You know, I only invited Laney because Cat said she was bringing Justin. If I'd known you were coming, I would've come alone so we could've spent time together like normal." He shook his head and placed his hands on his hips. "I'm trying, *Muñequita*. I'm truly sorry about my behavior last night. Please tell me you don't hate me."

He'd have come without Laney? She kept the unspoken sentiment bubbling inside her, bottled up. Those types of remarks and that pet name were exactly the kinds of things that had kept her pining for him her whole life.

"I don't hate you." She lowered her voice. "But sometimes I wish I could."

David's eyes blinked in surprise. Before he could respond, Hank raced up the stairs. Another snug, well-worn T-shirt molded to his muscular chest and shoulders. Man, he was easy on the eyes. Why couldn't she be attracted to him? Seemed her head and heart never inhabited the same space. Maybe that was Cat's problem, too, she speculated.

"At your service, Vivienne." Hank lifted the heavy pouch from her shoulder. "Shall we go?"

"Thanks." Vivi glanced back over her shoulder at David. "See you in a while. Have fun."

David tilted his head, looking as if he'd completely forgotten how to have fun. Ignoring the pinch in her heart and instinct to shake him, she turned away and followed Hank out the front door.

They sauntered along the long gravel driveway leading to Mohegan Trail.

"Thanks for rescuing me again." Vivi squeezed Hank's forearm, then released it. "You've been a savior."

"No thanks needed. I enjoy your company." Lowered brows replaced his adorable smile. "Although, I've got to ask, why David? He doesn't seem like your type."

"Why not? Because he's so sophisticated and I'm so, well . . . me?" She grinned. Deep down she knew it was true. Vivi liked herself well enough. She didn't want to change. Yet her folksy personality made her different from most women David knew.

"No." Hank's confused scowl made Vivi grimace. "You're open and enthusiastic." He paused. "But he strikes me as stiff and cold. I can't imagine you two together."

"Well, apparently neither can he!" She chuckled with a shrug. "David's not cold. He's just reserved. Although he's been more closed off since his mother died, he has a tender side. That's what I love most."

"Tender?"

"You should've seen how he adored his mother. And it couldn't have been fun having his sister's friend follow him around like a puppy when we were kids, but he always made time for me. He'd compliment my art, and he never teased me about my clothes and hairstyles. And let me tell you, I was a walking, talking *Glamour* 'Don't' back then." Vivi snorted at her own memories. "I lived alone with my dad, a belligerent drunk who never stopped grieving what he lost long enough to pay attention to me. Cat's friendship gave me a sister. David's gave me more confidence and hope."

"And he doesn't bore you?" Hank's frank tone surprised her, and for some inexplicable reason, she sensed a hidden agenda.

"Never." She frowned. Boring?

David's photographic memory enabled him to talk endlessly

about any topic. He'd even been able to make history exciting for her. No small feat!

"If anything, his reserve is comforting." She kicked some pebbles on the side of the road. "Until his mother died, he'd been my rock."

Hank stared at her. "I'm surprised your feelings haven't affected your relationship with Catalina. It must be awkward for her."

"I've never put her in the middle. Our friendships are separate."

"That's a lot of juggling. Must be hard this week, with Laney here." His eyes met hers. "You're hiding your feelings well."

"Watching him with her physically hurts, but I'm determined to push past it." Vivi paused. "That said, I can't believe he loves her. Not that he loves me, of course." She peered at Hank from beneath her lashes. "You think I'm crazy."

"Not crazy. Maybe disillusioned." He grinned at her before shoving his hands into his pockets. "Why do you doubt his feelings for Laney?"

"Laney seems nice enough, but I *know* him. He couldn't love someone so . . . dry." Vivi noted Hank's dubious expression and knew he disagreed. "Lust after her body, yes. Admire her ambition and intelligence, sure. Love? I don't think so."

The sound of hurried footsteps scattering the gravel behind them interrupted their conversation. Within an instant, David caught up to them. Heat rushed to Vivi's face. She hoped he hadn't heard.

"Laney took a conference call, so I can come after all." His hands rested on his hips and he nodded at Hank. Shifting his gaze to Vivi, he smiled. "Let's go to Rodman's Hollow, for old time's sake."

"Sure," she answered. She smiled in spite of the uneasiness wrestling her body. Had David or Hank detected the catch in her voice? "Let's go."

Together the threesome continued alongside the paved road. David's words and actions confirmed he wanted to reconnect with her, if only as a friend. Why didn't she feel happier?

Hank broke the uncomfortable silence settling over them. "So, how long have you been coming here, David?"

"Fifteen years." His stride matched Hank's, while Vivi trailed two steps behind them. "It's your first time, right? How do you like the island?"

"It's a more rustic version of Nantucket."

"Yes, there are similarities. I like the quiet here." David rubbed his neck. "It's named for the Dutch explorer Adriaen Block, but the Native Americans called it *Manisses*, meaning 'God's little island.' Whatever its name, I'm glad my mother won this battle."

"Battle?" Hank asked.

"Initially, my dad refused to buy property here because it didn't make financial sense. My mom had argued that value couldn't always be measured on a balance sheet, and time spent together here would be priceless." David clasped his hands behind his back. "Anyway, she wore him down, although he's never really taken to the place."

"Why hasn't he put it up for sale?" Vivi piped in.

David's shocked expression revealed he'd never before considered the possibility. "He'd probably love to sell it and reinvest the money elsewhere." A joyless chuckle punctuated his remark. "But Cat would kill him. He'd never risk it."

Vivi giggled. "No one wants to suffer her wrath, do they?"

"No." David shuddered with exaggeration. "No, they don't."

Hank's odd expression aroused Vivi's curiosity about the prickly vibe between Cat and him. Maybe she should scuttle her matchmaking plans.

They meandered down Cherry Hill Road, avoiding the occasional car or bike that passed by. Vivi concentrated on the rhythmic scuffing of their feet against the pavement to keep her thoughts off David. Awkward minutes stretched like hours until Vivi spied the hollow's entrance near Cooneymus Road.

"So, what is this place, anyway?" Hank asked as they descended into the wooded reserve.

"About twenty thousand years ago, glacial meltwater eroded the southern end of the island, leaving three large kettle holes." David's hands gestured as he spoke, and Vivi noted the gleam in his eye. "Most of the hundreds of depressions on the island have clay bottoms and hold water, but here the bottom is porous. Those who think parts of the hollow sit below sea level are wrong. The actual bottom of the deepest kettle hole is about twenty feet above sea level. It's also—"

"Geek!" interjected Vivi, waving her hands in the air. "Hank, we're roaming along dirt paths in the wilderness where everything is nice and quiet. Ignore him or he'll try to scare you with a story of some weird rodent—"

"The small mouth Block Island meadow vole, found only here—" David began.

"Whatever." She grinned after cutting him off a second time. David playfully nudged her, but she persisted. "To listen to him, you'd think the place were infested."

"I recall a certain someone running away squealing after we found a nest." David flashed a triumphant smile.

"Yeah, and I've got the scar to prove it." She pointed to a noticeable, half-inch-long white stripe on her shin.

"Don't whine." He placed his hand around the nape of her neck and stroked it with his thumb, sending a frisson of energy along her nerves. "I'm the one who got a hernia carrying you all the way back to the house."

His warm gaze made her forget everything except how much he'd always meant to her. Old feelings stretched her heart open. She knew her radiant smile projected the feelings she'd been trying to conceal, and she didn't care.

"So, when do you need to get back to Laney?" Hank's ice-water reminder doused her momentary happiness.

"Forty-five minutes or so." David removed his hand from Vivi's neck, leaving a chill in its wake.

She frowned. Oh *God,* how she turned into a puddle over any attention from him. Pathetic. Rallying her willpower, she stopped suddenly on a wide area of the path surrounded by lush greenery.

"This looks like a nice spot for photos."

"You've got a good eye, Vivi." Hank stood under the canopy of a shadbush tree and admired the scenery. Dappled sunlight glinted off his golden hair.

"Thanks." She inhaled the wooded scent of the reserve. "Don't move." She snapped several quick shots of him and the tree. Its multi-stemmed trunk reached up behind him like fingers extending from a palm.

"Enough!" Hank's hand blocked her from taking additional photos.

"Come on, don't play coy, Hank. You love showing off your hot body in those formfitting T-shirts."

He tossed his head with a short laugh. *Gorgeous.* Vivi snapped two more shots of him and his twinkling eyes before he moved away from the tree.

"Hey, I came to keep you company." He wagged his finger in mock anger. "Not to be the subject of your pictures."

"If you want to spend time with Vivi," David interjected, "you'll learn to tolerate the photos." He dug his toe into the dirt. Was he angry with her for taking pictures of Hank?

"Tolerate?" She pivoted toward him. "Interesting. Here I'd always thought you were a willing participant in my photo journals." Then she twisted her wrist dismissively. "Guess it's good for both of us I've found a new subject."

David glanced away before he softly uttered, "Perhaps you're right."

Vivi resisted the urge to stick out her tongue, but it was darn hard. She settled for shooting close-ups of the Northern Arrowwood shrubs. Several minutes later, she replaced the lens cap. "We should head back. Cat's probably awake and getting bored."

"Lead the way." Hank carried the camera bag for her.

David trailed behind them, his head bowed. Vivi tried not to speculate about his mood swing. She'd already frittered away years of misreading his intentions.

Twigs snapping under the crush of footsteps pierced the silence. Her stomach knotted; she hated conflict and tension.

"Let's play a game. Something easy, like the ABC game." Vivi's eyes scoured the path. "Aha! Ants. I got the *A*. David, find us a *B*."

"Bark." He pointed to a nearby tree.

"Cloud," Hank offered, looking up at the cottony splotch in the otherwise blue sky.

Behind her, Vivi heard David mumble, "ABC game." Her quick glance caught him grinning despite his downcast eyes.

Once they arrived at the house, Hank excused himself to search for Jackson. David stopped on the front steps and gazed at the side yard, apparently lost in thought. He turned to Vivi, cocking his head. "There is no going back, is there? No matter how badly I want to." His shoulders slumped as he turned to go inside without waiting for an answer.

Alone on the steps, Vivi congratulated herself for surviving another round with David, and tried to ignore the heaviness settling in her chest. With Hank's help, she just might make it through the week.

Chapter Five

Georgetown University
Twelve Years Ago

Alone in his cramped dorm room, David pushed back from his desk to hunt for his red pen. He thought he'd left it in the pencil cup. Apparently not. After turning his backpack inside out, he slouched onto his bed with his computer case and began methodically digging through each pocket. He didn't find the missing pen, but his fingers discovered a folded note wedged between two interior partitions.

Curiosity pricked him upon finding the unfamiliar letter. A faint vanilla aroma reached his nose when he unfolded the missive. He then smiled, immediately recognizing the girlish cursive handwriting, scrawled in purple ink.

Dear David,

Cat is so excited to start high school next week, but all I can think about is how you'll be off at Georgetown. I hope you don't find this note for a couple of weeks so I can have fun wondering about when it will happen, and if it will make you smile. I only wish I'd have had the guts to tell you all of this in person.

I guess a good friend would be proud to see you go off to such an amazing college. All I can think about is how much I'll miss hanging out with you in your kitchen or yard.

I'll also miss the way you talk to me like I'm mature even though I'm a lot younger than you. Most guys your age (and mine) find me weird, but you're not most guys—thank God.

A third thing I'll miss is watching you and your mom together when no one is paying attention. That's when you ditch your overachieving, perfectionist habits and relax. I like seeing that side of you.

Basically, I'll miss almost everything about you. Cat's friendship and your family mean everything to me. I love her, Jackson, and your mom (your dad still scares me), but mostly I love you.

I know I'm too young now, but when I'm grown up, I'll find a way to own your heart just the way you'll always own mine.

XOXO,
Vivi

P.S. Write to me if you ever get bored: viviennelebrun@aol.com.

David reread her letter twice, smiling. *Jesus, she's brave.* He'd been aware of her crush from the beginning, but this bold declaration surprised him. He leaned against his headboard and glanced at his watch. Three thirty.

Closing his eyes, he imagined the scene in his mother's kitchen at that moment. Jackson and Cat would be arriving home from school, probably with Vivi tagging along. He could almost smell the *patatas* and *salsa brava* his mom might have put out as a snack. Thinking of them gathered around the table, laughing about their day, made him homesick.

So far college had proven to be both challenging and exciting. Although he'd already made a few new friends, he missed the comfort of his family and old friends.

Funny that a love letter from a fourteen-year-old girl could lift his spirits. He suspected most guys would be annoyed or embarrassed by her affection. No doubt his roommates would ridicule him if they found the note.

Sometimes Vivi's attention made him uncomfortable. Mostly he marveled at her courage. She seemed to accept the futility of her crush but persist in spite of it, as if it were too big to bother hiding.

Sadly, her guileless nature also made her a target, which always made him want to punch something or someone. But high school should give her the chance to meet more people like her, especially in the fine arts department.

In any case, she deserved a response. He opened his laptop and added her e-mail address to his contacts.

To: viviennelebrun@aol.com
From: drsjjr@yahoo.com
Subject: I Found It

Vivi,

I just finished reading the letter you stowed in my computer case. I wonder when you were able to sneak into my room to hide it . . . and what else you did while you were in there. Will I be finding more surprises in the future?

Thank you for the kind thoughts, which did make me smile. I miss everyone as well. I'll always be here for you to talk to, but high school is an opportunity to make new friends, so don't waste your time thinking of me. Be yourself and others will like you just as I do. In fact, I bet by the time I return, you'll have forgotten all about me.

Until then, I'll be busy honing my perfectionist, overachieving habits. I expect you'll be spending lots of time in the art department. Maybe you could send me something new since all I have of yours is that portrait of me you drew last year.

Fondly,
David

He hit Send, closed the computer, and tried to envision a grown-up Vivi. He could picture only her tiny, skinny little body and face; with her oddly cut, wavy blond hair streaked with pink, blue, or whatever other color was her temporary favorite; and her clothes stained with all manner of art supplies. He hoped, when she did grow up, she retained her endearing optimism and energy. Would he still know her? Only time would tell.

Chapter Six

Present Day

Vivi put her camera away and searched for Cat, who she found lounging on the blue striped sofa, flipping through a gossip rag. When Vivi cleared her throat, Cat slammed the magazine on the coffee table and bolted upright.

"Hey, V, let's ride the bikes to town and have lunch." Cat radiated energy and an overly bright smile.

"So you're not mad at me about the Facebook post?"

"No. You didn't do anything wrong. Once again, Justin jumped to conclusions and reacted like a maniac." Cat glowered. "Then he wonders why I don't tell him the time and location of local photo shoots. Can you imagine what damage he could do to my career with one of those outbursts on set?"

"Good decision." Vivi decided to drop the subject rather than get Cat worked up again. "So, are the cruisers in the shed?"

Cat's scowl faded. "Yes. I think I may indulge in some wine at lunch."

"Are there laws against biking drunk?" Vivi teased as they walked outside to retrieve the bikes.

Within minutes, they were pedaling toward town.

The nearly cloudless sky beckoned vacationers to explore the island. Weaving through pedestrian traffic, Vivi noticed young families everywhere. Unbidden envy nipped at her heart for the family she'd lost on that snowy January day twenty years ago. Despite the sunshine, a chill zipped through her veins.

Murky recollections leaped to Vivi's mind: hearing her father's muffled crying behind closed doors, finding him asleep on the floor clutching a photograph of her mother, sobbing while he later packed up and banished all photographs of her mother and brother.

As time passed, he'd simply drowned his grief in Jack Daniel's one day at a time. He'd slowly withdrawn from the world and from her. By the time she'd turned eighteen, she'd become much too familiar with the sights and sounds of a drunk.

As a young girl, she'd sympathized with him, and had even romanticized his despair. Whenever self-pity had surfaced, she'd belittled her feelings as self-indulgent. After all, she'd survived when her mother and brother hadn't. Bad as it was, life with her father was better than death.

In her teens, she'd often escaped by keeping busy with her art and her job at a local kennel, where she absorbed all the love she could from the dogs. The St. James family had helped by welcoming her into their lives, for which she'd be forever grateful. Mrs. St. James, in particular, had provided a motherly affection she'd long forgotten existed.

Now Vivi wanted a home of her own to fill with love and laughter. Too bad she always derailed that goal by comparing all men to David, nitpicking for flaws to justify pushing them away. Perhaps meeting Laney, a woman who literally moved around the world with David, was the kick in the pants she needed to finally let go.

"Let's eat here." Cat swerved into the Belgian block driveway area of Beachhead Tavern. A wraparound covered porch spanned the front of the two-story clapboard building.

Opting to eat outside, they picked a two-top table along the far railing of the porch. A gentle breeze provided some relief from the hot afternoon. Vivi sipped her iced tea. Perky chatter and the tinkling sound of silverware brightened her mood. She listened inattentively to Cat's recitation of celebrity gossip, and soaked up the alfresco dining experience.

An animated group of five men seated at a large table beside them caught her attention. Colorful, overlapping ink designs of swords, vines, and unfamiliar symbols covered the biceps and forearms of two. A third wore a short ponytail and reeked of patchouli. The other two men were clean-cut. Vivi's eyes lingered on the smile of the striking, dark-haired man dressed in khaki shorts and a collarless black shirt.

Cat followed Vivi's gaze, then a knowing smile crept across her face as she lifted a single, perfect brow.

"Tall, dark, and handsome. You do have a type, my friend." Cat chuckled. "Oh, excepting Alex and Hank, of course."

"Well, it *is* a vacation." Vivi blushed. "I deserve a little beach romance."

Cat's veiled expression interested Vivi. "I guess poor Hank will be left behind for Mr. TDH?"

"Well, maybe poor Hank will need some cheering up." Vivi rested her chin in her hands. "Although, I sense some kind of tension between you two. Care to share why?"

Cat sharply withdrew, turned her face, and waved off the question. The waitress foiled Vivi's prying by delivering lunch, and Vivi never allowed much to stand between her and her food.

She eyed her giant lobster roll, then scowled at Cat's boring, undressed salad. *Ick*. Compulsive dieting had to be one of the biggest downsides to modeling, in Vivi's opinion, anyway. Lifting her gigantic sandwich off her plate, she forced the crusty end into her mouth. An appreciative moan rumbled in her throat while she chewed. "Better than sex, I swear!" She smacked her lips together after swiping off a stray clump of mayonnaise.

Cat snickered. *Good*, thought Vivi. She could always make Cat laugh.

Mr. TDH bumped into Vivi's chair when he stood to take a photograph of his friends. Her eyes were drawn to him as he adjusted the lens of his camera—an amazing Nikon D3X.

Oh my. She lusted after his professional-grade equipment. Impulsively, she jumped up.

"Excuse me. Hi." Her gaze fixated on his Nikon. "Would you like me to take the picture so you can join your friends?"

He turned to her, smiling like a fox.

"*Grazie mille*. That would be very nice."

His Italian accent sent a shiver through her body, but she willed her clammy hands to grip his six-thousand-dollar camera. Handling the apparatus gingerly, she couldn't imagine ever affording something so extravagant.

The improbable gang of friends huddled together while she fired off several shots.

"This is a great camera. The resolution must be phenomenal." When she returned it to him, his fingers grazed the length of hers. Tingles shot up her arm. "I'm Vivi, by the way."

He raised her hand to his lips. "Vivi?" His eyes twinkled when he repeated her name aloud. Despite the flush of warmth traveling to her toes, she managed to speak.

"Short for Vivienne."

"Ah." He nodded. "I'm Franco Moretti." When he released her hand, the impression of his fingers remained on her own. "Do you know cameras?"

"Yes. I'm sort of an amateur photographer. And you?"

"I freelance for various travel magazines."

"Oh, wow." Franco's appeal grew tenfold. Vivi envied his dream job. What could be better than being paid to travel the world shooting pictures of its most beautiful and interesting locations?

Cat cleared her throat.

"Oh, this is my friend Cat." Vivi stepped aside, assuming Franco and his friends would prefer to focus their attention on her gorgeous friend. "Cat, meet Franco."

Cat issued a two-finger salute from her seat. Franco nodded before placing his hand on the small of Vivi's back and snapping his fingers to gain his friends' attention. His touch sent another jolt of awareness along her spine. She couldn't believe he hadn't shifted his interest to Cat.

"Vivi, Cat, these are my friends Billy, Joe, Mike, and Ross."

Vivi observed the other men eagerly greet Cat before eventually retaking their seats and resuming their own conversation. The ragtag group intrigued Vivi.

"What brings you all to Block Island?" she asked Franco. "Are you working?"

"No, not working. We're all here celebrating a mutual friend's thirty-fifth birthday."

"Oh." Vivi considered whether she could overlook the nine-year age difference in favor of his sexy accent and handsome face. "A guys' weekend?"

"A big party."

"Sounds fun."

"A reunion of sorts. We all went to college together." He glanced at his friends. "In fact, some of these guys played in a rock band back then and are planning to perform to really stir up old memories."

"Very cool!" Vivi glanced at them and tried to picture them fifteen years younger, rocking it out on stage.

"Yes, although they're not as excited now that Sarah, the singer, had a last-minute family emergency. These guys aren't singers so much as musicians."

"Vivi can sing!" Cat interjected.

"Oh, no." Vivi's cheeks ignited. "I'm not a rock singer."

"She's being modest. She takes voice lessons and sings at a local bar in Astoria on the weekends." Cat's victorious smile shocked Vivi.

That remark caught the band's attention and thrust Vivi into the spotlight.

"Really?" Franco asked. "*Il destino!*"

His deep brown eyes coaxed Vivi to admit the truth. Darn her soft heart.

Joe skeptically asked, "What kind of stuff do you sing?"

Franco's intense gaze interfered with Vivi's ability to concentrate, causing her to stammer a response. "Um, songs by Sheryl Crow, Sara Bareilles, Ingrid Michaelson, Patty Griffin. Sometimes I'll arrange acoustic versions of random pop songs."

"What about Avril Lavigne, or Pink, or anything like that?" Joe asked. He looked her over with an appraising eye. *Oh, crap.* She doubted she had the chops to pull off those throaty rock vocals.

Anxiety crept up Vivi's neck. She had two options: get in over her head, or disappoint others. She hated disappointing anyone. "Well, I know some of their songs, but I've never performed them."

Everyone ignored the timidity in her voice.

"Wanna try? We can muddle through on our own, but if you could jump in on vocals, it would be way better." Joe's friendly eyes conveyed his sincerity. "You could bring your friend, or friends, to the party. The DJ starts at nine, so we're just planning a short set."

"I don't know." Vivi glanced at the men, silently questioning herself for considering this folly. "I've never sung with a full band. I usually perform alone."

"Let's go back to the house and test a song or two. Worst-case scenario, it's a no-go, in which case we just break out the beer."

Franco stroked her arm with the back of his fingers, sending goose bumps scattering across her skin. "Why don't you look at the songs and try." He flashed an encouraging smile. "No obligation."

"Fun! Let's go, Vivi." Cat clapped her hands. "Come on. Please! This will be so much more interesting than anything else we might do today."

Vivi regarded her friend's enthusiasm and the band's laid-back attitude. Spending a little more time with Franco also held more appeal than watching Laney with David.

The adventure might be fun. In fact, it was beginning to feel like an irresistible challenge, which was how she often ended up knee-deep in trouble. Shrugging, she heard herself saying, "Okay. I'll give it a whirl."

~

Thirty minutes later, she and Cat parked their bikes in the circular driveway of a stunning blue home off Beacon Hill. The table-top property offered gorgeous views of the island and the ocean. Pounding hammers shattered the otherwise peaceful setting as workers swarmed the yard, constructing temporary outdoor flooring and flowing white tents in the rear of the home. "Big party" was a serious understatement, Vivi thought just as a German shepherd came bounding around the side of the house.

Cat froze. "Oh, God!"

Vivi looked at the dog's high, wagging tail. "It's okay, Cat."

She put her bike's kickstand in place and made a soft clucking sound with her tongue, then stopped about ten feet in front of the dog and crouched a bit. She held out the back of her hand as the dog approached her and sniffed. Glancing over her shoulder, Vivi noticed Cat hadn't moved, her eyes wide with caution. "Really, he's fine." Then she turned back to the dog. "You are a handsome devil, aren't you?"

Franco came through the front door. "I see you've met John's dog, Panzer. He likes you."

"Vivi's great with dogs." Cat said, finally finding the courage to get off her bike.

If only people were as easy to manage as dogs, Vivi's life would be much easier, she thought.

"Everyone's inside." Franco waved his hand toward the door and followed them into the entry.

Plate glass windows brought the outdoors inside. The airy, bright home smelled of lemons and sunshine. An absence of drapes and carpeting sharpened the sound of each footstep, cough, or chair scraping along the floor. Vivi admired the juxtaposition of contemporary artwork with the otherwise traditional beach house decor.

After a brief introduction to the resident birthday boy, John, she sat at the glass dining table to scan the set list. Someone set a cold beer in front of her. Although she typically didn't drink much, a little liquid courage couldn't hurt, so she chugged a third of the bottle while reading.

Joe leaned over her shoulder, flicking his thumb and fingernail together repeatedly. Her hand grasped her stomach while she tried to ignore his hovering and refocus. She knew three-quarters of the songs pretty well because they were very popular.

"Do you modify the arrangements, or do you play songs as originally recorded?" she asked.

"We keep our covers pretty true to the originals."

Vivi nodded with a sigh. "I'm pretty familiar with many of these, which isn't the same as knowing them cold."

"Let's give one a try and see how it goes. It's not like we're Coldplay or anything."

Joe strummed the melody of Michelle Branch's "Goodbye to You" while Vivi sang the first verse and chorus. Satisfied with her vocal ability, he launched into a serious discussion of the original set list. After eliminating several songs, they whittled it down to a single sixty-minute set. When the discussion concluded, Vivi sat back in dismay at what she'd just agreed to do.

"If you have time now, we should start rehearsing so we can make it as good as possible," Joe suggested. "Afterward, we'll hang out and have a few drinks."

Dazed, Vivi responded, "Okay." She glanced at Cat, who sat chatting comfortably with Franco and John. "We don't have other plans anyway."

Cat must've felt Vivi's apprehension reach across the room. She turned and then approached Vivi, whispering, "You look uncomfortable. I thought you wanted a shot at a beach fling with Franco. Are you angry with me for putting you on the spot?"

Yes! But thanks to this commitment, Vivi wouldn't have time to think about David and Laney during the next few days. It was a step in the right direction. She should kiss Cat's feet.

"No. I could've refused. I only hope I don't screw up."

"You won't! You always underestimate yourself. Have faith!" Cat hugged her friend. "I just know this will be so much fun."

Vivi smirked. Sure it would be fun for Cat, the one without responsibility or risk of failure. On the other hand, this performance would make the vacation memorable—for something other than meeting David's girlfriend. When else might she ever have an opportunity to sing with a full band?

Vivi had always believed the fun of life lay in the thrill of the unknown. Smiling, she lifted herself off the chair and looked for a microphone.

The group rushed to set up for the rehearsal, which got off to a rocky start when Vivi flubbed the lyrics. Wincing, she felt perspiration collecting along her hairline. She bit her lower lip but then caught sight of Franco's warm gaze. Heat rushed through her, replacing her fears and doubts with determination. She noticed Cat grinning and giving her two thumbs up, so she stepped back to the microphone.

What's the worst that could happen?

Chapter Seven

Laney's perfectly trimmed fingernails tapped against the side of her wine glass, drawing David's attention away from the harbor and to her taupe nail polish—a dull, non-color shade. Most days her wardrobe and appearance reflected her personality.

Severe. Monochromatic. Professional.

The fact that he hadn't previously noticed this surprised him. Then again, in Hong Kong he'd dedicated the bulk of his focus and energy toward working on the Kessler merger.

"Thank you for bringing me here this week." Laney sat forward in her chair. "It's been nice to meet some of your family, although I'm picking up on tension."

"I've been away a long time." David straightened his posture.

"Will your dad be coming up over the weekend? I'm curious to meet him, too."

He drew a deep breath. "He and I aren't on good terms, as you've probably also picked up on."

"I've noticed." She reached across the table to touch his hand. "Would you like to talk about it?"

"Not really. All you need to know is that my mom made me promise to keep a secret about something my dad did, and I'm bitter about it."

"I'm sorry, David." She squeezed his hand. "But if this is a secret, why is it affecting your relationship with Cat and Jackson?"

"They know he and I aren't speaking, and they're blaming me. Plus, I've been keeping them at arm's length to avoid spilling everything."

"Maybe you should just tell them. Why should you suffer alone?"

"Better I suffer than saddle them with the disgust I feel toward my dad." David wouldn't hurt them by destroying their family memories solely to satisfy his thirst for justice. "Besides, my mother trusted me to keep my word. I'll never betray her."

"She'd never know. If your dad deserves to be exposed, Cat and Jackson are grown-ups." She shrugged with exasperated nonchalance. "Eventually you would all recover."

"It doesn't matter if my mother would never know. *I* would know." Laney's blasé attitude toward integrity offended him. "As for recovering, obviously it's easier said than done in my family."

Clearly Laney couldn't understand his belief that his word was his bond. It was a point of honor—one of his most prized traits. Vivi would understand, but this was perhaps the only thing in his life he would never confide in her.

"Let's not spoil the afternoon by dwelling on this, okay?" He withdrew his hand from hers.

"That's your polite way of shutting me out."

She slumped back into her chair and sipped her wine just as the harried waitress arrived to remove their plates.

"It's about time," Laney muttered. "I've been dying for a refill of my water."

The waitress winced. "Sorry, I'll be right back with that."

"It's busy today. You must be exhausted," David said to the waitress, trying to compensate for Laney's rude remark. He collected his things and handed them to her, wishing Laney didn't sulk whenever she felt frustrated. "Thanks."

Shaking her head, Laney exhaled in exasperation. Once the waitress left them, she resumed their conversation.

"Let's change the subject." Her arch glance pinned David. "My free housing ends in two weeks. Should I lease my own apartment, or am I moving in with you?"

The very idea made his skin itch. Clearing his throat, he repressed the urge to scratch his arms.

Seizing upon his hesitation, she demanded, "What's the issue? In Hong Kong I spent most nights with you anyway. Are infrequent nights of freedom so critical?"

Panic and resentment overshadowed any pleasant anticipation. Not a good sign. They'd never discussed living together. Hell, they'd never uttered the word *love*. Why was she suddenly pushing this relationship toward permanence?

If he ever married, Laney possessed many qualities compatible with his life. But he wasn't thinking of a long-term commitment with her yet. Probably not ever.

"When you suggested coming to New York, you convinced me you had your own reasons for returning to the States, namely furthering your career. I never made any promises about our future. Now it feels like I'm being rushed toward the altar." Burning indigestion spread in his chest from hurting her. God, had he totally misread her feelings all this time?

"I'm not expecting a proposal." Her impassive expression gave nothing away. "It's just more economical to share the expense of one home. Why waste money on a second place that sits empty most days?"

He couldn't deny her point. Of course, her logical arguments were exactly what landed him in this awkward position in the first place. Had she been deftly manipulating him all along?

"I'm sorry, Laney. I don't think living together is the right thing for us."

Her gaze dropped to her lap. Although he questioned her motives, guilt prompted him to lean forward and cover her hand with his own.

"It's not you." That much was true. Many men would kill to be in his shoes. "I don't want to hurt you. You know you're beautiful and intelligent, and I enjoy the time we spend together. I'm simply not looking for more from dating than what we have now. Have I misled you somehow? I honestly thought we were on the same page."

"Relax. I only suggested it because it seemed convenient." She produced a weak smile. "It's fine, David."

He hoped she wasn't lying, but he couldn't shake the feeling she was putting on an Oscar-worthy performance.

After lunch, they strolled through the quaint Victorian beach town, browsing the goods for sale in the various small, independently owned retail shops aligning Water Street and the surrounding neighborhoods. Laney insisted on investigating each store, from Water Gallery and Gift, to Mad Hatter, and Full Moon Tide.

Now and then, David caught himself scanning the crowds for signs of his sister and Vivi as he ducked in and out of each shop. While Laney picked through endless shelves and racks, analyzing all of her options, boredom provided the framework for David's mind to drift to Vivi's distant behavior.

Everything about her unnerved him now. The pain his ugly outburst wrought, her detached manner, his surprising and wholly improper feelings of attraction—all of it drove him slightly mad. For the first time since they'd met, he had no idea how to behave or what, exactly, he wanted. He wished things would return to when they could read each other's thoughts. When her eyes would meet his and fill with trust and affection.

"David, isn't this divine?" Laney held up a severely cut yellow sundress.

He didn't consider its mustard tone flattering to her coloring, but after their tense lunch conversation, he merely nodded in agreement.

Two hours later, they returned to the car carrying packages containing ceramics, shoes, sunglasses, and clothing.

When they arrived at the house, David popped the trunk open and helped unload the myriad of shopping bags. Together, they hauled her loot up to their room. Heaving the final package onto the bed, he stood awaiting further instructions. Laney began picking through the bags without looking at him. Sighing, he left her there to admire her new belongings and went to find his brother.

Jackson and Hank stood at the kitchen counter threading cubed chicken and steak onto barbeque skewers. David glanced at the clock. Five thirty.

"Where are the girls?" He opened a beer and joined Jackson and Hank at the counter.

"No idea." Jackson skewered another chunk of beef and closed the utensil drawer David had left open. "They've been gone all afternoon."

As if on cue, the front door slammed open. Cat and Vivi spilled into the entry, laughing hysterically.

"Sounds like the ladies already got this party started!" hollered Jackson.

They shouted something unintelligible back and Hank chuckled. David braced himself for more of Vivi's cool behavior, but when the girls stumbled into the living room, she smiled broadly. In fact, she glowed. Seeing her lit up made him hot all over, which completely unnerved him.

"Looks like we missed something fun." Jackson whistled. "Where'd you spend the day?"

"Franco's friend's house, with the band . . . to practice for the birthday party." Vivi hiccupped and dissolved into more giggles.

Jackson, Hank, and David paused, confused by her nonsensical explanation. Thankfully, Cat filled in the gaps.

"We met Franco and a rock band called Disordered at lunch. They're here for a friend's birthday party in two nights. The band's female lead singer is a no-show. So I convinced Vivi to step up and sing a short set with them before the DJ starts. We're all invited, by the way. From the looks of things, it's going to be a major party!"

"Awesome. V, I haven't heard you sing in months," Jackson said as he finished the final shish kebab. He held up the tray. "Voilà!"

Vivi sang? Was her singing something new, or something she'd never shared with David before he left for Hong Kong? She didn't keep secrets from him. At least, he didn't think so. Disturbed by the realization he'd missed out on some part of her life, he then scowled at the thought of his sister and Vivi spending the day with complete strangers.

"Did you two actually go to a remote location with a bunch of strange men?" Concern supplanted his dismay and sparked the beginning of a headache. "Who's Franco?"

"Oh, chill out, David. We're fine." Cat waved him off. "Franco is a beautiful Italian man with the hots for Vivi. They bonded over his fancy camera." She shot Vivi a sultry look before both women burst into laughter again.

Vivi's cheeks and ears turned pink, broadcasting her pleasure at flirting with some random Italian. David wondered what happened to her interest in Hank, but he held his tongue. He turned his attention to the vegetable skewers while Hank joked with Vivi. Unlike David, Hank didn't appear the least bit resentful of Vivi's newfound crush. *Have I entered the Twilight Zone?*

"Go shower." Jackson opened the sliding door to go fire up the grill. "Dinner in thirty minutes."

"Aye aye, Captain," Vivi teased. She and Cat spun around and marched out of the living room on wobbly legs.

Feeling off balance, too, David handed Hank his skewers before trotting upstairs to check on Laney.

~

When he and Laney came down later, Café Paris Lounge music emanated from the speakers. Vivi and Cat were setting the table and lighting candles. The combined effect of the music and lighting transformed the beach house into a chic martini bar.

Thankfully, the shower had had a sobering effect on Vivi and Cat. Perhaps he wouldn't be forced to suffer through more tittering over Franco and his merry band of friends. Hearing more details would only intensify the unwelcome images of Vivi flirting with some other man.

His sister was dressed in smart linen shorts and a crisp white top. Laney wore her new Grey Poupon–colored sundress with a turquoise necklace and earrings. Vivi, on the other hand, looked like a clean but disheveled ragamuffin in low-slung drawstring shorts and a snug, lime-green tank top.

Each time she bent over the table to light another candle, the hem of her shirt lifted, revealing a hint of her waist. Her wavy, damp hair fell in front of her face in a teasing, sensual way. David ached to touch it, as he'd done so often, but now his impulse seemed dangerous. He shifted his gaze to Cat, who was filling each glass with large pours of wine.

"Do you two need more alcohol?" David asked as he pulled out a chair for Laney.

His sister rolled her eyes. He sounded like a square, even to himself. Despite being in one of his favorite places on the planet with those closest to him, so far he'd found no comfort here.

"Yes, we do." Vivi mimicked his stance and inflection. "In fact, it seems like you could use some alcohol." She chuckled and fled to the deck, escaping his response.

Cat snickered while unfolding her napkin onto her lap, appearing to take great pleasure in Vivi's new attitude. Through the window, he noticed Vivi rest her hand on Jackson's shoulder when she leaned in to talk with him. Those two were apparently thick as thieves now. David returned his attention to Cat, suspecting she felt a measure of relief that her best friend no longer pined away for him.

He felt no relief.

He felt adrift.

Vivi and Jackson carried in platters of hot food from the grill. The smoky aroma of the charred steak and chicken kicked David's appetite into gear. Vivi plucked three skewers off one platter and filled every remaining inch of her plate with a mound of brown rice and a salad. Laney's eyes widened at seeing Vivi's heaping pile of food, then she leaned forward.

"So, David tells me we're attending a party this week where you'll be performing with a band. I didn't know you were a singer."

"I'm not a singer. I mean, I occasionally sing at small venues in my neighborhood for fun and extra money, but it's not my profession." Vivi licked her fingers and took another bite of chicken. The greasy marinade glistened on her lips, like thick gloss. "Oh, Jackson. So good!"

"I'm confused." Laney lowered her fork while staring at Vivi. "Are you joking?"

"No," Vivi replied. "It tastes amazing!"

"No, about the singing. Why'd you agree to perform if you aren't a singer?"

"Cat suggested it and everyone else involved liked the idea, so I figured, why not?" Vivi shrugged and then speared a mushroom.

"Vivi's never shied away from a challenge." David winked. His praise earned him a glimpse of Vivi's bright smile. One step closer to normal.

"How can you learn all the songs in three days?" Laney frowned before taking a bite of her steak. "Won't it be embarrassing if you mess up?"

"Yes! Hopefully it won't happen." She wrinkled her nose. "If it does, I don't think the band or the birthday boy will care. At least, that's the impression they gave me today. Besides, I'll probably never see any of them again after the party."

"Oh, you'll see Franco again," Cat interrupted. "I'm sure of that!"

Vivi leaned forward to look at Cat. "Let's hope so."

David's eyes squeezed shut to block out the excitement reflected in her expression. He pinched the bridge of his nose in a failed attempt to stave off another budding headache.

"Franco?" Laney asked, having missed the previous explanation of the infamous Italian.

"He's a photographer. Meeting him is how this all came about," Cat offered. "He was having lunch with the band."

Laney sat forward with interest. "Details!"

David didn't relish hearing more details and noted Vivi's apparent discomfort as well. At least he wasn't the only one at the table feeling awkward. He braced himself for Vivi's reply, telling himself to be happy for her. She deserved to find someone who recognized her special gifts.

"Well, he's a photographer. He was born in Italy, then moved to Canada in his teens before coming to New York for college. He's older, handsome, and sexy." Vivi smiled to herself with her final comment, a remark that didn't escape David's notice. In fact, it made him feel . . . something unpleasant.

"Pass the wine," Jackson instructed before smiling at her. "I think it's great. Just like old times. Always an adventure when you're in the mix, Vivi."

"Well, I like to go all out on vacations since I can't take many." A wistful look passed over her eyes.

"Oh, why not?" Laney asked. "Don't get much time off work?"

"Time off isn't the problem." Vivi giggled. "I'm an elementary school art teacher. Lots of free time—not much disposable income."

"Oh, sorry." Laney shifted uncomfortably. "I didn't realize."

"No need to apologize. I love my job. I wouldn't trade the affection from my students for a bigger paycheck, plus I get plenty of time to pursue all my hobbies."

"That's nice. I don't get any love at my job, *and* I have to starve myself." Cat produced a mocking frown and then she and Vivi laughed together.

"No love, but a nice paycheck," Vivi said. "The real trick would be finding both in one job!"

"David and I have that, don't we?" Laney's hand ran along David's back and she kissed his shoulder.

He choked on his drink as ten eyeballs bore down on him. Hadn't she heard what he'd said at lunch? Vivi shifted her focus back to her plate, but not before a shadow flickered across her eyes. Her reaction indicated she still cared for him, at least a little bit. For the first time all day, David's emotions settled. Then he looked at Laney and tried to sidestep the firecracker she'd lit.

"I think Vivi's talking about loving the work, not a workplace relationship," he said. Laney raised one brow and looked away. When did his life become an endless minefield for which he had no map? Forks and knives scraping against the plates were the only sounds in the room now, save for the lounge music playing like a lame movie soundtrack.

He didn't want to hurt Laney in front of everyone, yet he couldn't let her pretend they were in love. Now he felt like a shithead. The kind of insensitive guy he'd never respected.

His fucking father.

Fortunately, Hank broke the silence.

"I love my work." He pushed his empty plate forward to rest his elbows on the table. "But I do envy all your free time, Vivi."

"It leaves room for creativity and spontaneity." Vivi set her chin in her palm. "That's where the good stuff of life resides."

Laney snorted. "Unless you can't afford the good stuff, like vacations and travel."

Her derisive tone prompted David to kick her under the table. Vivi, however, seemed unaffected by the sharp remark.

"I could afford to travel more if I gave up my music lessons, photography classes, yoga, and so forth. It's just a matter of choices." Vivi sat back and flashed a self-effacing smile. "I couldn't work twelve hours each day like you all do. Then again, I was never the driven, academic type." Vivi winked at David, apparently in deference to the many times she lamented this fact to him. "Anyway, I'm a boring topic. Let's change the subject. Jackson, what did you guys do all day?"

"We went kayaking."

"Oh, jealous." Vivi's soft pink lips formed a pout. "I want to go kayaking, too."

David licked his own lips, then froze. *Quit it!*

"We'll go again later this week." Jackson leaned back and patted his stomach. "So tell us more about this party."

"Cat knows more about the details. Between rehearsing and drinking beer, I didn't pay attention to much else." Vivi turned toward Cat and smiled.

"John Slater's a Wall Street trader who has invited one hundred of his closest friends here to celebrate his thirty-fifth birthday. It'll be a catered affair—with the band, of course, and a DJ. We're all invited, courtesy of Vivi's efforts." Cat crossed her legs.

"What's the dress code?" Laney asked.

"Good question. I have no idea." Vivi laughed. "I'll ask tomorrow when I rehearse again."

David's muscles tightened. Each day she spent with Franco robbed him of opportunities to rebuild their friendship. God, why hadn't Cat told him she planned to bring Vivi?

"You have to rehearse again?" Jackson asked.

"Yep. And the next day, too."

"What kind of music will you be performing?" Hank asked.

"Mostly pop rock, a little indie rock. We whittled the set list down to what I knew." She popped her shoulders up as she grinned. "Short and sweet, just like me."

A collective groan turned into laughter. And although she projected confidence, David noticed Vivi nibble on her bottom lip. He then immediately wished he'd quit noticing her lips, and questioned why he couldn't stop staring at her.

Was it the year apart? Was it her indifference? The growing suspicion that it might be much more distressed him.

After clearing the dishes and cleaning the kitchen, everyone retired to the deck with a drink. David stood, leaning against the railing, staring out over the ocean while the wind ruffled his hair.

He listened to the slow thrum of the ocean, willing it to settle his thoughts, to remind him he had no right to interfere with Franco and Vivi. Hell, she was barely speaking with him, anyway. At that moment, her voice caught his attention, so he turned to face the group. Apparently she'd engaged them all in another of her silly games.

"If you were a dog, Jackson, you'd be a retriever!" Some of her wine slipped over the rim of her glass and dripped onto her lap. "Oops!"

David tore his gaze away as the liquid dribbled along her inner thigh.

"Why a retriever?" Jackson asked. "Big and messy?"

"Ha! Yes. But, you're a retriever at heart: exuberant, playful, and eager to please." She slapped his knee with the back of her hand.

He grinned and barked, "Woof, woof."

David chuckled under his breath. He then glanced at Laney, whose yawn indicated her boredom with Vivi's games. Had she been so humorless in Hong Kong? Then again, he'd been uptight, too. No wonder he'd been having trouble reconnecting with his family.

"Dare I ask?" Cat leaned forward curiously and speared Vivi with a warning look. "What kind of dog am I?"

"Oh, easy." Vivi smiled. "A Shiba Inu."

"I don't even know that dog." Cat's narrowed eyes challenged her friend. "Should I be insulted?"

"It's independent, bold, headstrong . . . and vocal!" Vivi eyed Jackson, and they burst into laughter while Cat sat back wearing a pleased expression.

The silly exchange reminded him of so many unproductive yet entertaining evenings with his family. Good times he missed and now wanted back in his life, along with Vivi.

When they returned to New York, he'd carve time from his schedule and reach out. They could rediscover their old haunts, check out the latest exhibitions, and people watch in the park.

"What about me?" Hank asked.

"Hmm. I don't know you very well, so I'd guess a Clumber spaniel: laid-back and devoted."

Hank smiled, apparently happy with his designation.

Vivi sank into her chair and chugged the rest of her wine, closing her eyes. No one seemed to notice or care he and Lancy had been left out of the discussion. Once again, he felt invisible. A disturbing trend.

"What about me?" He couldn't help himself; curiosity demanded to know how she saw him. Her eyes popped open with surprise, which made him grin. "I've never thought of myself as a dog, but now I must know my breed."

She hesitated, allowing the sudden silence on the deck to stretch out. The air crackled with electricity until she answered.

"A Doberman. Proud, aloof, intelligent guardian with a sensitive side."

Her reply caused his grin to stretch across his face. At least she still knew him. He had that going for him, anyway. "I can live with that, Vivi."

"Well, what about me?" Laney begrudgingly asked.

Once more, the night air vibrated with nervous energy. Jackson shot David what appeared to be a "good luck" glance.

"A poodle. Smart, elegant, and politely reserved."

Vivi's answer was kind and apt. When she'd first arrived, he'd fretted over the potential fallout of her meeting Laney. He wouldn't have predicted her relaxed acceptance, or her pursuit of an Italian photographer. He wasn't wrong often and didn't like when it happened.

In this case, he absolutely hated it.

"You know, you're very unusual, Vivi," Laney observed dryly.

"Thank you." Vivi smiled and closed her eyes again before resting her head against the Adirondack chair.

David grinned, doubting Laney intended her comment as a compliment. He glanced back to Vivi, curious. Did she still see herself as a thirteen-year-old misfit despite the years he'd spent convincing her of the remarkable person he'd always recognized her to be?

"What kind of dog are you?" he then asked her.

She lifted her head. Her violet eyes beheld him for several long seconds until her voice broke the mesmerizing effect of her gaze.

"A boxer . . . fun-loving, energetic, and loyal." Her eyes danced playfully, and he felt a hint of their old connection spring back to life. *Finally.*

"Perfect!" Jackson raised his beer in salutation.

"Thanks, Jacks."

At ten o'clock, Cat slunk away from the group with her phone in hand, probably planning to call that ass Justin. Although Hank and Jackson invited Vivi to join them for a night on the town, she declined. Instead, she remained outside, sipping her wine and stargazing. The look on her face hinted at some private joke she wouldn't share. David wondered whether she was daydreaming about Franco.

He closed his eyes, desperately wishing Laney would leave him alone with Vivi for a while. He told himself he just wanted a little private time to talk with his old friend. Time to work through the uncomfortable awareness of her he'd developed. Time to repair the damage he'd caused by neglecting her for too long.

Deep down he suspected he told himself lies.

Laney intertwined her fingers with his and rested her head against his shoulder. Normally he'd welcome her affection. Tonight it felt too possessive. She leaned close to his ear and whispered, "Let's go upstairs. I'm ready for bed."

"It's early," he murmured. "I'm not tired yet."

"Neither am I." She nipped at his earlobe.

He stiffened. Had Vivi noticed? No. She wasn't paying attention to Laney or him. In fact, unlike every other time since they'd met, he'd not once caught her watching him from a distance.

The recognition produced a sudden, profound sense of loss.

"Go on, then." He planted a light kiss on Laney's forehead as she rose to leave. "I'll be up in a bit."

"Good night, Vivi." Laney nodded before slipping inside.

David inclined toward Vivi and rested his elbows on his knees, clasping his hands together.

"I hope I didn't insult you earlier when I expressed concern over how you spent your day. I just worry you'll get hurt. Promise me you'll be careful."

Her brows climbed up her forehead, then lowered to frame her dancing eyes. "Thanks for your concern, David. I know I leaned on you over the years, but you don't need to worry anymore. I'm a big girl now."

"Maybe so, but I can't stop caring." He stared at his hands and frowned. When he raised his head, he held her gaze. "You know I always will."

"Of course. That's what friends do. We care." She placed her hand on his, and a sharp burst of energy reverberated between them. She withdrew it, as if she'd made a mistake, and sipped her wine. "Laney's waiting for you."

"I'd rather talk with you for a while. You haven't told me anything about what's been going on in your life. What's happening with your artwork? How are things between you and your father? Tell me about your latest adventure or favorite student from last year. I'll take anything, Vivi. Just talk to me."

He leaned forward again in his chair, elbows resting on his knees, as if praying for some response. She stared at the streak of moonlight lighting a path across the ocean before finally turning to glance at him.

"It's been a long, strange day, David. All I really want to do right now is zone out." She finished her wine. "I'm sorry, but I'm sure you can understand my need for space."

A sense of karma tempered his frustration. Perhaps he deserved a taste of the treatment he'd dished out for the past eighteen months. He'd withdrawn and shut down, and now the doors he'd closed weren't reopening easily.

"I understand." He hesitated. "Before I go in, can I ask if you've made plans for your birthday next month? I saw something recently about that Australian photographer you admire, Peter Lik, photographing a new series around New York. Maybe we could check out his gallery in SoHo and then kick around the neighborhood for the afternoon. We can browse all the little shops and street vendors you love so you can pick out a birthday gift."

Vivi went still, as if she were holding her breath. "That's a nice idea. Let's play it by ear, though, okay? Who knows what we'll both be doing in four weeks."

Her refusal to commit to any plans sent him a cold, clear signal—she intended to keep him at a distance. He'd acquiesce for now, but not forever. "I'll see you in the morning." He waited for a response. She faced him, wearing a serene smile that didn't reach her eyes.

"Sleep well, David."

Torn and unsatisfied, he conceded. "Good night, Vivi," he said on a sigh.

He gently squeezed her shoulder, allowing his fingers to linger a few seconds before he released her and went inside.

Chapter Eight

Muttering a curse thanks to another restless night, Vivi pushed the clock aside and glowered at the ceiling. Six o'clock. Why couldn't she sleep in like a normal person on vacation?

Across the room, Cat's chest rose and fell in a slow, steady rhythm. Vivi studied the framed picture of a vintage sailboat hanging on the wall. Several minutes passed before she gave up all attempts to relax. Dragging herself from bed, she schlepped to the bathroom to splash cold water on her face.

With her hands plastered on the vanity, she stared at the mirror. Naturally, her tangled mess of hair stuck out in six different directions. After several painful attempts to finger comb the unruly mass, she gave up and tucked it behind her ears as best she could. *Laney probably wakes up with perfect hair*, she thought. *Ugh!* Driving herself insane with comparisons wouldn't help.

Anyway, Franco liked her imperfect appearance. She brightened in anticipation of seeing him again. Between him and the upcoming performance, she'd lucked into some intriguing distractions.

She closed her eyes and imagined Franco's accent. Very hot! More than once she'd wondered why such a good-looking, mature man with an awesome career would find her interesting. Something must be wrong with him, and it would become apparent soon enough. She shrugged because she liked the diversion, in any event.

Satisfied her morning hair and breath were no longer lethal, she pushed away from the sink. Her light footsteps echoed in the open stairwell. When she reached the main level, the aroma of a fresh pot of coffee surprised her. Who else was awake . . . and whistling? Turning the corner, she bumped into Hank.

"Hey, you." She opened the cupboard and grabbed the largest mug available. "Why are you up so early?"

"Habit." He shoved his fingers through his thick hair, then sat at the dining table. "Anyway, I prefer the quiet before the storm, so to speak."

Trailing behind him, Vivi sat down and inhaled the coffee's aroma as she filled her mug. *Mmm, wonderful.*

"Jackson's still in bed?" She took a quick sip.

"He'll be sleeping for a while." Hank stretched his legs. "He got pretty drunk last night."

"I'm concerned about him. He doesn't look happy or healthy." Vivi blew out a long breath while thinking of her father's path of destruction. "I'm sorry to put you on the spot, but is he drinking more than usual?"

Hank twirled his mug around twice with his fingers, then he sighed in resignation.

"Yeah." Hank's eyes remained fixed on his cup. "He's been drinking a bit more since he and Alison broke up a few weeks ago."

"Why'd they break up?"

"He won't say, and I wouldn't mention it to him," Hank cautioned as he peered at Vivi from beneath his lashes.

She shivered at the possibility that Jackson might follow in her father's footsteps. "I can't watch another person in my life turn to alcohol to escape a broken heart. Maybe we should mention something to David?"

"That'll only make things worse. Maybe they were close before, but Jackson hasn't been happy with David lately." He rhythmically slid his fingers up and down his coffee mug. "Jackson's functioning well at work. And we're on vacation. Even you drank a lot last night. Let's give him a chance to work out his own demons."

Vivi grimaced. "Promise you'll reconsider speaking with David if you notice things continue to spiral downward."

Hank pushed his mug away, leaned back, and crossed his arms in front of his chest. "You put a lot of faith in David, although it seems he's wrapped up in his own life."

"That's the second unflattering comment you've made about him." Her jaw clenched. "Why do you dislike him so much?"

"I don't dislike him. I barely know him. All I know is he left town without so much as a backward glance, and Jackson feels abandoned by him."

Her chin withdrew as if avoiding a fatal blow.

"I didn't realize he owed *you* any explanation," she quipped. "I'm sure there's a good reason behind his unusual behavior. As for his family, he'd do anything if they needed him." She returned her gaze to Hank, whose mouth had twisted in disbelief. "Trust me, I know David."

"Okay, you know him better." He shifted his legs. "Sorry."

"Of course, I won't pretend his recent behavior hasn't hurt," she admitted.

Vivi yawned and rubbed her eyes. Uncomfortable with the conversation, she turned and studied the large work of art perched on the living room fireplace mantel.

Its massive frame housed an unusual oil painting of the beach house and bluff. The nonconforming proportions and wavy lines grabbed one's attention. In typical impasto application, brushstrokes spread thick layers of color on the canvas. Rather than choosing natural ocher and umber shades to reflect reality, she'd opted for vivid tints such as Vandyke brown, vermilionette, and viridian green, with the intention of making the painting shout love and warmth.

Hank leaned forward. "You like that painting?"

"I do." She smiled slyly. "What about you?"

"It's odd." He studied it another moment. "But alive. Does that even make sense?"

"Perfect sense." Her smile grew. "It's alive with love and memories."

"How do you know that?" Hank sat back and sipped his coffee.

"I painted it in high school, after my first visit here, and gave it to the family as a Christmas gift. David's mom understood it right away." Vivi leaned forward, chuckling to herself. "Everyone else probably thought I was drunk when I painted it."

"Were you?" Hank teased.

"Drunk with joy, maybe. It was the first real vacation I'd taken since my mother and brother were killed." She grimaced at the stab of remorse she felt any time she thought of them. Ignoring the heat creeping up her neck, she cleared her throat and continued. "When I got the idea to paint the house, I wanted to show how it felt more than how it looked. Back then I was in love with Van Gogh, so I mimicked what he did for olive trees and irises. Not very well, but . . ."

She suddenly remembered David's impressed response to her gift. Later that year, he'd bought her an expensive set of Winsor & Newton red-sable-hair paintbrushes for her birthday. He'd researched to find the very best set, made from the tail hairs of a male Kolinsky.

Cat sauntered into the room wearing a creamy silk robe trimmed with black lace, pulling Vivi from her thoughts. Like Laney, Cat never had a bad hair day. She was always stunning, even with sleepy eyes. In fact, her sleepy eyes only made her look more beautiful. If Vivi didn't love her, she could really hate her.

While Cat milled around the kitchen, Vivi noticed Hank watching her from the corner of his eye.

"What are you two discussing?" Cat poured herself a giant cup of coffee and joined them at the table. "You look like you're deep into some kind of conspiracy."

"No conspiracy, just talking about love and family." Vivi winked at Hank, who was now sitting ramrod straight in his chair.

David emerged from his room and jogged down the steps as Hank replied to Vivi. "A lot to be said for family, especially siblings. I love being part of a big family."

Hank's statement hung over the table. Vivi froze, knowing he intended his remark for David's ears.

"You're up early, Cat." David smirked as he filled his water bottle. "Want to come with me? Bet I can still beat you around our old loop." His hopeful smile echoed the one he'd worn last night, before Vivi had denied him a conversation that would've only fueled more of her useless desire.

"Maybe tomorrow."

"Okay." David wiped the disappointment from his face before inserting his earbuds and taking off for a run. When Vivi returned her attention to the table, she caught Cat covertly staring at Hank.

Hank and Cat continued to tread a polite, aloof dance with each other, yet were relaxed with everyone else. Maybe Vivi would have better luck getting to the bottom of that puzzler today.

"I don't have a big family, unless you count my crazy adopted family." She reached for Cat's hand, squeezing then releasing it. "What do you think, Cat? Do I happily share your burdens like a good sister would?"

"You're a great sister." Cat smiled affectionately, one of the few genuine smiles Vivi had seen from her all week. Justin's continued cell phone stalking was taking a toll.

It seemed as if everyone but Hank and Laney were battling demons this week. Vivi understood Cat's issues. Jackson's and David's struggles remained a mystery. Jackson's drinking, however, concerned her most.

Had someone intervened with her dad decades ago, his life and hers might not have fallen apart so spectacularly. The realization cast doubt on Hank's suggestion to give Jackson time to work things out alone. Involving David wouldn't exacerbate the problem. Then again, Vivi habitually miscalculated when it came to relationships—and David. Perhaps she should heed Hank's advice.

"Vivi, let's take a quick bike ride." Cat's voice interrupted her musing.

"Sorry. Not up for it." Then inspiration struck. "Hey, take Hank and show him some of the island."

"No, thanks." Hank interjected. "Last night Jackson mentioned chartering a fishing boat."

Cat erased her indignant expression with lightning speed. "Just as well."

He stood and nodded. "I'm going to shower."

As he padded away, Vivi cast a questioning glance at her friend.

"What?" Cat ground out.

Vivi swallowed the remaining sip of her coffee and placed the mug in front of her. "Nothing."

Cat groaned. "Well, I'm going to take a quick ride to work off all the extra calories I drank last night. Sure you won't come?"

"Nope. Unlike yours, my boss doesn't care if I gain weight!"

Once Cat left her, she searched out a deck chair and propped her feet up against the railing. The rising sun erased the last touches of lavender and pink from the horizon. She loved the hues of dawn and early evening skies. Every few minutes the colors changed and shifted, like sand art sliding into place.

Watching God's version of performance art furnished the first truly peaceful event of her trip. Drawing in a deep whiff of sea air, she savored the quiet.

A short while later, Jackson appeared at her side looking a little rough.

"Hey, buddy, what's up?" she asked. "Where's Hank?"

"Yow." He winced at her perky tone. "How 'bout turning it down to more of a whisper? Hank's on the phone."

Contrary to any good judgment, Vivi took advantage of the easy opening he'd supplied.

"Partied too hard?" Her blithe tone belied her unease.

"Is there such a thing, V?" A hint of remorse tinged his joke.

"You know I can't joke about drinking too much." She carefully concealed any guilt she felt from throwing her father's situation in his face.

"Sorry." He took a long sip of coffee. "I forgot."

"So, what's going on with this new hairstyle?" She fingered the edges of his hair, hoping the change of subject would relax him. "Honestly, I'm not sure whose hair is worse, yours or mine."

"What?" He tugged on his wayward locks. "You don't like it?"

"No. It overwhelms your face, like a lion's mane. You need a haircut, my dear." When he closed his eyes without responding, she continued. "It's not like you to let yourself go, or drink so much. Is everything okay?"

"I know you're ultrasensitive to the drinking, but I'm fine." He masked any trace of emotion. "We're on vacation, right? Can't I blow off some steam without being analyzed?"

He'd basically repeated Hank word for word. Faced with another closed-off St. James, she conceded. "Sure. As long as you remember that, if you want someone to talk to, you can trust me."

"Duly noted." He glanced out over the ocean. Although he avoided direct eye contact, he reached out and took hold of her hand.

His small gesture made her feel better. She clasped his hand with hers. Together they sat in companionable silence, each lost in their own thoughts.

A short while later, David appeared, clad in his sweat-soaked shirt, which clung to the corded muscles of his chest. Vivi's breathing fell shallow. She cursed her involuntary reaction to his presence.

He leaned against the railing, his eyes darting to their clasped hands and then to Jackson. One of his brows shot up. "You two look cozy."

Jackson rolled his eyes while Vivi widened hers. If she didn't know better, she'd swear David looked hurt. He speared Jackson with a nasty stare.

"Strike out last night and looking for consolation?" David rested his hands on his hips.

Jackson stood and stalked into the house without saying a word, but the biting remark stunned Vivi into sputtering.

"What's the *matter* with you?" she demanded once she found her voice.

"With me?" David asked incredulously. "What's the matter with *you*? Every time I turn around you're with another guy—Hank, Franco, Jackson—who's next, Vivi?"

Her eyes narrowed to slits in response to his insinuation. "Who *are* you? You *look* like David, but you *act* like someone I don't even know."

"That must be why you've been treating me like a virtual stranger since you arrived." He crossed his arms in front of his chest.

"Oh, that's rich, coming from you!" she scoffed.

"What's that supposed to mean?" His dark eyes widened.

Vivi's mouth dropped open. *The nerve!* "Are you kidding me?" Buried heartache and confusion blew the lid off her composure. "You basically withdrew from my life without any explanation. Now you show up and want to pretend nothing has changed?"

The hard lines of his face softened. Using his foot, he yanked her chair close to him and then squatted in front of her.

"I'm sorry, Vivi. My reasons for leaving had nothing to do with my feelings for you, Jackson, or Cat. You know me, so you *know* I never meant to hurt anyone. I even wrote to you about it."

Although his wild-eyed expression alerted her to be cautious, she didn't heed the warning. Her pain overshadowed any desire to comfort him.

"Don't lecture me about intentions. Nothing excuses your utter neglect. Maybe I'm not as smart as you, but I got the message loud and clear."

He jumped up and flung his arms toward heaven. "There was no message! I needed to be alone to work through something. Don't the years of being a good brother and friend count for anything? Hasn't loyal friendship earned me some right to expect you to cut me some slack?" He faced the ocean, gripping the railing while he clipped out, "So what now? I get no sympathy, no understanding?"

"Be happy, David. You no longer have to tolerate an unwanted *shadow* following you around." Vivi hugged her knees to her chest, like a child afraid to face an angry parent.

Yet some unfamiliar, ugly part of her rejoiced in hurting him.

"I'm not happy." He spun around, leaned over, and planted his hands on the arms of her deck chair, encircling her. "I don't like this distance, Vivi. It feels wrong on every level. Tell me how to fix it. I'll do anything." His eyes searched hers, imploring her for mercy. "And *I* never referred to you by that derogatory nickname. It's Jackson's little joke."

His proximity dazed her. She caught herself staring at his mouth, wanting. Abruptly, she tore her eyes away before he noticed. She frowned, unsure of what else to say.

"Tell me," he repeated, and then knelt down and grabbed her hand. "Please tell me how to make things right between us."

The contact heated her entire body. Damn him.

"What do you want from me?" She relished the feel of his gentle hold on her hand while struggling to comprehend her conflicted feelings of love and anger. "I haven't been unfriendly."

He shook his head. "You're not treating me the same. With everyone else, you're the old Vivi—laughing, playful, demonstrative. With me, you're reserved and cautious. You barely look at or talk to me." He rubbed his thumb against the soft skin on top of her hand, staring at it intently. "I miss you. I miss the way we were. The comfort of just being us." He hesitated. "Being with everyone now only makes me more aware of Mom's absence and the way things used to be. I knew it would be difficult to return, but I didn't expect everything to be harder. Especially not with you."

Vivi felt the pull of his gaze. His eyes had darkened with frustration and desperation. Empathy washed over her, yet she couldn't relent completely. Not while he withheld the reason behind his disappearance.

"You'll always have my friendship. But everything is different now. I've got my own life." She watched puzzling emotions play out in his expression. He loomed so close it grew hard to breathe. "You have Lancy. You don't need me."

His features pinched before settling into a slight frown. "I'll always need you," he whispered. "*Muñequita*, no one could ever replace you. Don't you know that yet? Our friendship is the most important one of my life."

Without warning, he pulled her to his chest. Her pounding heart felt like it would slam its way straight through her ribs. Only in her dreams did he ever need her . . . She was awake now. On instinct, she burrowed her face against his collar. Even though he'd arrived fresh from a run, she loved the smell of his skin.

Those loving words he'd spoken tempted her to comfort him. But if he truly meant all he said, then he wouldn't keep secrets. "Prove it."

"How?" he asked.

"Tell me why you took off. What happened with your dad?"

He flinched as if she'd slapped him. His face appeared haunted as he stood and started pacing like a caged animal. After a minute, he stopped and stared at the ocean, hands on his hips. She held her breath, sensing the waves of tension rippling off of him.

Finally, he turned on her wearing a grim expression. He reached out his hand to her. "Come with me."

Chapter Nine

David gripped Vivi's hand and silently led her partway down the rickety staircase leading to the beach. They stopped at a landing, where he deposited her on the built-in bench before leaning against the railing and staring at the bluffs.

Standing there on the stairs clinging to the edge of the cliff, he felt as if he were on the precipice of another turning point. If only he could see the outcome before jumping off.

Vivi had no idea what she'd asked of him, but desperation made him weak. Nothing less could explain why he'd ever consider telling her the truth. He closed his eyes, begging his mother to forgive him for breaking his promise. Technically he wasn't actually breaking his word. His mom had secured it to protect her family. And while everyone else considered Vivi part of the family, she was not and never had been.

She was not his sister. She was his best friend and more. She was . . . she was so many things to him she defied any label.

Ultimately, he needed her in his life. He'd hurt her by pushing her away, and now she no longer trusted him. This was his only option.

He didn't look at her when he started speaking. "Under no circumstances can you ever tell Cat or Jackson this information. I need your word, Vivi. No exceptions."

"I promise." She sat, alert, on the edge of the bench, hands on her knees.

"I mean it. You can't let even them know you know anything, either. You'll have to pretend—*to lie*—forever."

She nodded. Jesus, she had no idea what she was doing. He knew *exactly* how much keeping this news to herself would wear her down.

"Vivi, trust me, you'll regret this ultimatum. You can't fix what's broken with my dad. All this will accomplish is saddling you with my burden. I really don't want that. Is there no other way?"

Her eyes remained wide open, staring at him while apparently weighing his words.

"Maybe I can't change what happened, but I can help you, if only by being someone you can talk to. You say our friendship matters. You say you want me to trust in you again. Then you need to trust in me, too."

He hung his head, shoulders slumping. Before sitting beside her on the bench, he inhaled slowly. Once seated, he spoke without looking in her eyes.

"I went to Hong Kong so I wouldn't break a promise I made to my mother before she died." He glanced at her. "You know I visited her as often as possible those last months.

"One day, on my way to see her, I stopped at Starbucks for coffee. On my way to my car, I noticed my dad's Maserati across the lot, so I jogged over to surprise him. No one was more surprised than me when I caught him in a compromising position with a woman I recognized from our club named Janet."

Vivi's lips parted. "Janet? You mean, the Janet he's been dating this year?"

David nodded, closing his eyes to control the explosion of rage he felt any time he heard Janet's name. He suspected his dad never stopped seeing her but made it public only after an appropriate mourning period.

He opened his eyes to find Vivi staring at him, transfixed.

"I took off before he could stop me. When he came home, my mother overheard us arguing about what I saw. She learned about his affair before she died because of *me*."

David bent over and buried his face in his hands at the memory of that awful day. The only day he could recall having ever allowed emotions to overtake reason. If he had just controlled himself like usual, his mother could've died never knowing of her husband's betrayal.

"What happened next?" Vivi's question brought him back to the present.

"Instead of getting angry with him, she *begged* me not to tell Cat and Jackson. She was worried the news would tear the family apart after she died. I felt responsible for her learning of his deception, so I promised to honor her wish." He hoped he'd given her that much peace, at least. "The final weeks of her life were grueling for so many reasons. I was angry with my dad for his disgusting behavior, with myself for not protecting my mom, and with God, for taking her from me."

Reciting the events forced him to relive the pain anew. It ripped through him with hot, raw force equal to the day his mother died. He swallowed the lump in his throat, his voice rough as he continued.

"Once she died, I couldn't stick around and watch my dad play the grieving husband. It was too tempting to call him out as a liar and cheat. So I stayed away until I knew I could keep my promise. I've since realized I don't want Cat and Jackson to become disillusioned about our family, or marriage, like I have. Nothing can change the past, and I won't disregard my mom's wishes by tearing the family apart. It's the way I atone for my role in breaking her heart."

David suddenly turned to Vivi and crushed her head against his chest before resting his cheek on her forehead, the way he'd done so often. His hands groped the back of her head and shoulders as he squeezed her tighter than ever before.

His heart raced as a tremor slid through his body. Then he pressed a kiss to the crown of her head and then her temple. He closed his eyes, savoring the way her hands rubbed his back. The way she whispered soothing words, spilling slivers of light into the darkness.

~

Vivi held on to David with every ounce of her strength. They remained on the bench, rocking ever so slightly. Her own thoughts spun wildly, unable to process the fact that Mr. St. James had treated his amazing wife so horribly.

How could she look him or Janet in the eye whenever she next saw them? *Oh, God.* Panic began to seize her body. Tears mounted in her eyes as her muscles tensed. How would she keep this secret from Cat and Jackson? Surely they would take one look at her *and know.*

David had been right. She didn't want this burden. No amount of talking would ever make this right for him, and now she would have to live with this secret. Worst of all, she had no idea how to help him.

He eventually eased away and then wiped her tears with his thumbs. Holding her face in his hands, he stared into her eyes with such intensity it stole her breath. His gaze momentarily dipped to her mouth and something flashed in his eyes. "Vivi."

Time stood still. The breeze sweeping along the bluff seemed stronger. The crash of the waves below sounded ten times louder than normal. Her body tingled with heightened awareness. The charged moment—

"David? Vivi!" The wind carried Cat's holler down the stairwell before she appeared.

David abruptly released Vivi and sat back, turning his face away, presumably to regain his composure. Vivi, of course, couldn't think fast enough and simply looked up at Cat.

Cat hesitated, as if realizing she'd interrupted something private. Then, instead of leaving, she leaned against the railing. "Laney's looking for you, David."

He faced Cat, nodding. As he stood to leave, he glanced at Vivi, his eyes pleading for her to keep her promise. She tried her best to reassure him without words, but even she wasn't convinced she could succeed.

Once David left, Cat took the seat he'd just vacated. "Care to explain?"

"Explain what?" Vivi feigned ignorance, buying time to think.

"Well, we could start with what I just witnessed, and then talk about your attempt to play cupid, or vice versa." Cat arched one brow. "Your choice."

"I didn't play cupid." Lying had become an unfortunate habit this week, Vivi realized. But she'd rather talk about Hank than David right now. "I didn't want to go biking and thought Hank might enjoy it. Obviously, I was wrong."

"Don't push us together in some misguided attempt to get me away from Justin."

"Fine." Vivi held her hands up in the air. "I hear you."

"Seriously, Vivi. I'm already uncomfortable enough around him without your interference."

"Why on earth are you so uncomfortable with him?" Vivi tilted her head. "He's the sweetest guy."

Cat tapped her foot while she looked up toward the large shrubbery that blocked the view of their house from this vantage point. "Because a few months ago, during one of my and Justin's mini-breaks, I went to a small party at Jackson's and spent the night flirting with Hank. We fooled around a bit. Then two days later Justin and I reconciled, so when Hank called me, I ignored his calls. It was poorly done, I know. Let's just say I wasn't expecting to be face-to-face again here, or anywhere."

"Holy crap, Cat. I can't believe you didn't tell me all of this sooner!" Vivi ran a hand through her windblown hair. "No wonder you've both been acting so weird."

"Well, I really don't want to talk about it, especially here with him and Jackson lurking around," Cat uttered. "And besides, there's something more important to discuss."

"What?" Vivi snapped, hoping to avoid the inevitable.

"I think you know what." Cat wouldn't be cowed. "My brother."

"Jackson?" Vivi smiled sweetly.

"Ha, ha. Boy, aren't you a regular Ellen DeGeneres?" Cat affected the bored look she'd long ago perfected. "What's going on with you and David?"

Vivi sighed, attempting to match Cat's blasé attitude. *Please, God, help me keep my promise.*

"He's feeling alienated and assumed I'd be the most sympathetic listener."

She hoped her vague explanation would satisfy Cat without subjecting herself to a slew of personal questions. Questions she'd best not consider.

Because neither David's confession nor his tender words about their friendship made Laney vanish. No matter how much he cared for Vivi as his friend, he'd never shown any romantic interest. She couldn't continue reading into his words and actions, no matter how tempting.

"So were you?" Cat asked.

"Was I what?"

"Sympathetic." Cat frowned before twisting her body to face Vivi with a concerned expression. "Please don't get your hopes up again. Just because he's using you to mend fences with everyone doesn't mean he's going to dump Laney."

Vivi recoiled at the remark, unaccustomed to the blunt delivery. Using her? That's not at all how he'd made her feel. "I didn't assume he would."

She watched her friend's eyes roll upward before returning to meet Vivi's with compassion. "Vivi, you know I love you, but you've never faced the truth about your relationship with David. I've stayed out of it because it's so awkward for me. Now I have to speak up. Of course he loves you as a dear *friend*, but you can't keep hoping for more. Even *if* he were attracted to you, he'd be too wary of the complications stemming from all of our friendships. David's never been a risk taker. Surely you see that."

If Cat had taken a machete to Vivi's heart, it would have been kinder and quicker.

"Wow. I told you I'm not holding on to old fantasies about David." Vivi glowered to compensate for the tears she felt brimming behind her eyes. The past thirty minutes had blown the fuses on all her emotions. "But thanks for setting me straight."

"I believed you until I interrupted you two just now." Cat grasped Vivi's hand. "For the past few days it's been wonderful to be around you two and not feel awkward because he didn't return your feelings. I only worry what I saw just now might set you back. Please don't go there again." As if sensing she'd heaped too much on Vivi at once, she finished with a gentle tone. "I just want you to be happy, V. You know that, right?"

"I know." But Vivi had heard relief in Cat's voice, which hurt. Maybe it should be expected under the circumstances. Vivi rose from the bench. "I need more coffee. Want anything?"

"Nope. I'm good." Cat paused, then reached over and squeezed Vivi's hand. "We're good, right?"

Vivi nodded and watched Cat close her eyes and soak up the morning sun as if the whole world hadn't just been altered.

She walked away with uneven, halting steps, the ground beneath her suddenly feeling soft and yielding. Cat's searing observations rattled around in her head, summoning familiar self-doubt. And self-doubt wouldn't help her deal with David and what he'd revealed.

Learning the truth enabled her to forgive him for the way he'd pushed her away last year. He'd proven how much he trusted her, yet she couldn't let her imagination run wild with hope that his feelings ran deeper than friendship. And while she didn't want to turn away from him after what he'd shared, she also couldn't risk Cat and Jackson overhearing her talk to David, or becoming suspicious of her behavior and discovering the truth.

For the time being, David would have to rely on Laney for support.

Entering the house, she heard her text message notification ping. Her bedazzled phone stood out amid the pile of sleek smartphones on the counter. Franco's message confirmed he'd pick her up at one o'clock. Her speedy thumbs replied, *B waiting w/ bells on.*

The events of the week had stripped away the cocoon she'd always associated with the St. James family. A chill raced through her limbs at the thought of a life less involved with them, but maybe she'd overstayed her welcome.

Never before had she wanted to escape them all and regroup. Thankfully, Franco and the rehearsals provided a perfect cover. Once they returned to New York, she'd have time and space to process everything and figure out her next steps. *Just four more days.* She could manage until then.

While she poured herself a much-needed second cup of coffee, Jackson appeared in his bathing suit, carrying an empty cooler. He set it by the freezer and began to fill it with water bottles, beer, and ice.

"What's going on?" Vivi asked.

"I've decided we should go to Town Beach."

"Oh? Hank said you guys were going fishing."

"Nah. Changed my mind. I feel like being in a crowd today. I think there may be live music, too."

"A crowd, huh?" She grinned, hiding her strained nerves. "Or *girls*, Jackson?"

"Girls. Definitely girls." His dimples made a brief appearance, then Jackson slapped her thigh with the back of his hand. "Go get ready. We can eat lunch there."

"Gimme five minutes." She picked up her phone. "What about Cat?"

"I'll tell her now. Everyone's coming."

Darn it. It was a sorry state of affairs when sitting for final exams sounded better than spending time on the beach with her friends. She glanced at the top of Jackson's head, feeling a melancholy pang. Helping David mend all these relationships would take time and savvy. Today she'd simply look forward to Franco rescuing her at one o'clock.

Jackson slammed the cooler lid closed and stood up. He appeared unaffected by his earlier run-in with his brother, but Vivi couldn't stop herself from nudging him, for David's sake.

"Are you and David okay?" She watched him scratch his cheek and bend over to grab the cooler.

"Who knows? He won't tell anyone what the hell is going on with him." He grunted when he lifted the cooler. Vivi looked away, afraid he might see right through her. "He's unreachable these days."

"Maybe you could show him a little trust. Let him and your dad work out their own problems," Vivi suggested. "Just talk to him, Jackson. I know he wants to reconnect with you and Cat."

"Women talk about their feelings. Men don't." Jackson chuckled. "It'll work out in the end."

It's not that easy, she thought. She couldn't say more without raising his suspicion. Shrugging, she typed a second message to Franco, redirecting him to pick her up at Fred Benson's at one o'clock, and then went to change.

Twenty minutes later, everyone squeezed into the Jeep. Jackson and Hank sat in the front. David cast her a worried glance before climbing into the backseat with the boogie boards and cooler. Laney crawled onto David's lap and snuggled against him.

Vivi swallowed her envy by leaning forward and gently massaging Jackson's shoulders.

"All set?"

"Oh yeah." He patted her hand. "All set."

The car pulled onto the road to town, kicking gravel out from under its tires.

Chapter Ten

St. Jameses' House
Eleven Years Ago

Vivi settled into a lounge chair in Cat's backyard, surveying Jackson's high school graduation party. Floating candles illuminated the pool, pitching soft yellow light across its glassy surface. She knew those poor candles would be doused later when the guests would start tossing each other in the water—just like at David's party two years ago.

Tables and chairs, decorated with the Wilton High School team colors, stretched across the manicured lawn. U2's "Beautiful Day" blared from the patio speakers. Long buffet tables of food and beverages offered something for every palate. It was a picture-perfect party on an equally lovely day.

"Hey, you." David tousled her hair before sitting on the edge of her lounge chair.

Warmth spread throughout her body. David was maturing. His behavior and thoughts had always revealed an old soul, but now his body was catching up. Tonight he looked yummy in a crisp white shirt and navy flat-front shorts, and smelled just as good. Her eyes feasted on the flex of each muscle in his arms and calves whenever he moved. She envisioned him stripping off his shirt before jumping in the pool later. Swimming with Cat's family had become one of her favorite pastimes. Her cheeks flushed at her thoughts.

"Save me from these people," he said. "And tell me Cat's not turning into one of those girls."

Vivi followed David's gaze to where Cat was chatting with her fellow cheerleaders.

"Don't worry, she's still Cat. At least with me, anyway."

"Good." He waved off a dragonfly, muttering, "Three-hundred-million-year-old pest."

"Why do you know things like that?" Vivi laughed.

"I think it's interesting." He shrugged. "Speaking of interesting, let's go to MoMA for the *AUTObodies* exhibition. I want to see the antique Pininfarina and Ferrari Formula One racing car. There's also a photography exhibition of pictures taken in Astoria and other neighborhoods in Queens. Maybe we could grab sushi in the city afterward."

"Sounds wonderful!" Like a perfect date. She knew it wasn't, although she'd happily pretend. She'd playacted that role whenever they went for pizza and ice cream or caught a movie, although Cat and Jackson were usually with them, too.

"Great." He leaned forward and rested his elbows on his knees. "So, why are you sitting here alone?"

Vivi glanced over at Jackson, who was horsing around in the yard with his teammates and flirting with the prettier girls.

"I'm not a friend to most of these people." How embarrassing to admit aloud.

"Thank God! You're much more interesting than any of them." He shifted toward her and rested his hand on her ankle, mindlessly tracing circles on her skin with his thumb. She wondered if he realized how often he touched her whenever they talked. "But you're Cat's friend. You could hang out with her instead of sitting by yourself."

"I don't want to cramp her style, or Jackson's. Besides, everyone else feels like celebrating, while all I see are more good-byes. You know I hate good-byes."

When David opened his mouth to respond, he was cut off by voices calling his name. He held up his finger at them and then turned back to Vivi.

"It's not good-bye. It's just a change. There'll never be good-byes between us." He squeezed her hand before strolling across the lawn to stand beneath an old-growth sugar maple amid a circle of Jackson's friends.

Two years ago he'd been their lacrosse captain. Discerning the eager looks on the other guys' faces, Vivi suspected they were questioning him about college life and frat parties.

She shoved aside thoughts of David surrounded by a bevy of sorority girls. Although he never spoke of his girlfriends in front of her, she'd overheard Cat and Mrs. St. James mention a name or two. She pictured the type of beautiful girl he might date—tall, shapely, confident. Everything she was not.

Jealousy wracked her. Would she ever be more than his friend? As if sensing her thoughts, he looked up, caught her gaze, and winked before returning his attention to his friends. She loved summer. No homework struggles or cliques to avoid. And most importantly, David returned home. But come September, both he *and* Jackson would be gone. She frowned at the notion.

Her growling stomach motivated her to leave the safety of the chaise and wander in the direction of one of the buffet tables. Unfortunately, three of the nastiest girls from school stood between her and the food. Drawing a deep breath, she ducked her head and attempted to pass by unnoticed.

"Look at what the *Cat* dragged in," scoffed Janine, a graduating senior and former captain of the cheerleading squad. "Interesting outfit. Matches the purple streaks in your hair. It's almost as weird as you." Janine sneered with haughty delight. The other two mean girls snickered.

Vivi never liked Janine or her posse. The gang of them strutted through the halls of the school acting like their expensive clothes and haircuts made them better than others. But she wouldn't dare disrupt Jackson's party by creating a scene, nor would she subject Cat to an uncomfortable confrontation with members of her squad.

She valued Cat's friendship, especially knowing Cat's social life could've been much easier if she'd dumped Vivi once they'd entered high school. Cat was a beautiful, bold, accepted, and sought-after girl. Vivi, with her childlike figure and bargain-basement clothes, remained an outsider. Thankfully Cat wasn't shallow.

Fixing a serene smile on her face, Vivi said, "Excuse me, I'm just going to eat." She moved to her left to skirt around the small group. Janine stepped sideways to prevent her advance.

"Good idea. Maybe if you eat something, you might grow into a full-size person." Janine's snarky laugh sliced through the air.

When Vivi noticed David hovering at the outskirts of the group, her insides crumbled. Although she'd sometimes complained to him about her high school experiences, she never dreamed he'd witness her humiliation. Cornered, she took a deep breath and grinned through gritted teeth.

"Hi, David," cooed Janine. She ran her fingers through her silky blond hair and thrust her cleavage under his nose. "I've been hoping you'd come talk to me."

Vivi noted the stars in Janine's blue eyes and prayed her flirting wouldn't capture his attention. His eyes grazed the length of Janine with cool detachment and then he dismissed her as if bored.

"I came for Vivi." He turned his back on Janine when she gasped, then held out his hand to Vivi. "I'm starving. Come keep me company."

While steering her away from Janine's posse, he draped his arm over her shoulder and whispered, "Ignore her. Promise me you'll never change—not for anyone. You're absolutely perfect just as you are."

She practically floated across the grass as hot tracks of blood coursed through her body from the contact. Resting her cheek against the side of his chest, she briefly closed her eyes.

"You're the only one who thinks so."

He turned toward her and raised her chin with his free hand. In a deadly serious yet soft voice, he asked, "Who else matters, *Muñequita*?" He winked before bending down to plant a kiss on her forehead, and then dragged her to the buffet line.

No one else matters.

Chapter Eleven

Present Day

David rolled down the window, seeking fresh air for his tightened lungs. *Soham, Soham,* he mentally repeated, although meditating in the crowded car proved to be an exercise in futility.

His sister strategically positioned herself between Vivi and him like a human shield. Then again, maybe Vivi needed protection from his erratic behavior. He already regretted saddling her with his secrets, but he couldn't deny the small measure of relief he'd experienced from their shared confidence. During those moments on the bench, everything between them felt right again—better than right.

God, he might have even kissed her if Cat hadn't interrupted. Of course, Cat and Laney's presence provided icy reminders of why he could never act on his burgeoning feelings. Feelings he shouldn't trust in view of his screwed-up state of mind.

Glumly, he stared out his open window while the weight of Laney's presence pressed upon more than just his lap.

Jackson parked near the hub of activity at Fred Benson's. The humidity clung to David's skin when he stepped out of the car. He eyed the gray clouds gathering on the horizon with suspicion.

Laney tucked her hair under another oversized sun hat and then tossed David her beach bag. As always, she looked like a million bucks, wearing rhinestone flip-flops, an emerald-green cover-up, and a string bikini. It occurred to him that anyone who ended up with her would be spending a million bucks to keep her looking this way for the rest of her life.

He glanced back at his sister and Vivi. Cat's gigantic black sunglasses obscured much of her face. She chatted with Vivi, who looked distracted, which made sense given everything he'd just told her. A beach towel hung artlessly over her shoulders. Her shabby baseball cap shaded her face.

She'd never put much emphasis on her appearance. Unlike his sister and Laney, people sought her company because of her cheerful demeanor, not her looks. Still, she habitually managed to be adorable despite her lack of fashion sense.

The group strolled through the open pavilion and crossed its deck to get to the beach, passing by the band assembled near the steps. A wide array of rainbow-colored beach umbrellas littered the shore. Young children tore through the sand. Greasy aromas emanated from Rebecca's takeout concession area, completing the typical public beach experience.

Jackson's eyes scanned the horde, ostensibly to scope available women. His brother's juvenile behavior and heavy drinking this week raised red flags, but David reserved comment.

Jackson buried two umbrella poles deep into the sand. Laney settled herself in the shade of one of the generous orange canopies. David set her beach bag beside her. To his left, he noticed Vivi stripping off her shorts and T-shirt, revealing a barely there, tie-dyed string bikini. Suppressing the reckless urge to touch her, he sat beside Laney and closed his eyes.

Within fifteen minutes, the rest of the gang wandered off to join a volleyball game with a group of strangers. David remained with Laney, watching the others laugh and slap high-fives whenever someone got off a lucky shot. Vivi appeared to be holding up under pressure, which surprised him. After his confession, he'd half expected her to hover, make suggestions, offer solace. If he were being honest, he'd admit he craved her attention now. Contrary to his wishes, she seemed to be avoiding him even more than ever.

Maybe she needed distance to keep this secret. Or maybe she simply didn't care much about his feelings anymore. He rubbed his hands over his face to alleviate the sensation of staring into a fun house mirror. When he opened his eyes and looked back at the ongoing game, he realized they were all having fun, while he was not.

Suddenly, despite having no love for volleyball, he wanted to play. Leaning forward in his beach chair, he tapped Laney's arm. "Let's join the group."

She scrunched her nose. "It's so hot. Besides, I'm not athletic." Her eyes darted from his family back to him. "You go. I'm fine hiding under this umbrella."

The teams were evenly matched, so he couldn't include himself without creating an unfair advantage. Sitting back, he frowned and snatched a drink from the cooler.

While dragging a long pull from the bottle, he eyed Laney, wondering when exactly they'd fallen so out of sync. Looking back, he realized they hadn't spent much time going to movies, talking about books, or visiting museums. They'd discussed mergers and acquisitions, the law, and the business of the law. They'd done that and had sex. Pretty good sex, actually. But he knew little about her family or her past, her passions or hopes.

The realization that he didn't care to know more made him remorseful as hell. He needed to end things between them now that he suspected she wasn't being honest with him about her needs. Breaking up while maintaining an affable relationship at the office would require serious skill and planning. Definitely not something to undertake here in front of his family. He closed his eyes and breathed out through his nose before returning his attention to the beach.

When the volleyball match ended, the foursome wandered into the mild, rolling waves. Vivi screeched when the frigid north Atlantic sloshed against her legs. Rather than run out of the ocean, she dove headlong into a small wave. She popped out of the water, howling and shivering while wiping the water from her face.

David smiled. She'd always been an all-or-nothing girl. He should have guessed she would treat him likewise. For years she'd given him her all, and now she had nothing left.

His smile dissolved on that thought.

Hiding behind sunglasses, he watched Vivi riding Hank's shoulders while engaged in an intense game of chicken with Jackson and Cat.

The scene reminded him of playing the same game in the heated pool at his childhood home on warm summer evenings, surrounded by fireflies. His mom had served *piononos* or other delicious sweets they'd enjoyed. His team won most often due to his height advantage, meaning Jackson and Cat would be going under first. Yep, there they went, right into the deep blue sea.

Vivi fist-pumped the air above her head while laughing, then bent down to kiss the top of Hank's head and pat his shoulders. David's breath hitched and his fingers tightened around his bottle. He cast a chagrined glance toward Laney before loosening his grip and rolling his shoulders backward. Jackson and Cat regrouped for another round.

Seeing Vivi's thighs locked around Hank's head again made David's entire body tighten. He noticed her bite her lower lip, calling his attention to her fuller upper lip, which always looked a little bee-stung. *Kissable.*

Her wild hair clung to her shoulders, dripping water down her glistening skin. She looked like a tiny mermaid come to life—a living, breathing fantasy. He prepared to bolt from his chair and take Hank's place in the game, when he noticed a dark-haired man arrive and kneel in the sand, taking photos of Cat and Vivi. David sat forward, ready to go toss the camera in the water, then Vivi waved at the guy.

Franco.

Franco now had pictures of her in a tiny bikini. When David imagined what Franco might do with the sexy images, the vein in his neck began throbbing. He couldn't see Franco's face, but Vivi's beamed as she waded through the water to greet her new crush.

Watching her look at another man the way she used to look at him stole his breath away.

Then outrage replaced the hollow feeling in his chest. How could she so quickly brush aside everything he'd just told her and run off with this guy? He'd done as she asked—spilled his guts—and she still ignored him. For this guy. *This* guy, who was much too old for her, by the way.

David's fingertips pressed against the arms of his beach chair as he steeled himself for the forthcoming introduction.

"David, Laney, this is Franco." Vivi gathered her things, appearing eager to leave. "We're heading to rehearsal."

"Nice to meet you." David nodded politely while Laney said hello.

"You too." Franco smiled while keeping his eyes on Vivi.

The throbbing in David's neck shot to his temple.

He instantly disliked everything about Franco. And no, he didn't need more time to make his assessment. With the exception of misjudging his father, sizing up the integrity of others had always been his strength.

He knew men like Franco wielded their looks and easy charm to cast a wide net. That kind of guy only wanted to catch a few women long enough to satisfy his desires. Then he'd cut the women loose. Why didn't Vivi see how wrong he was for her?

"Okay, I'm all set." Vivi turned toward David. "See you all later."

"Bye," said Laney. "Oh, what about the dress code for the party?"

Franco donned another fucking cheesy smile. "I'm sure you'll look beautiful in whatever you choose to wear."

Laney flushed in response to Franco's bullshit flattery. David squeezed his eyes shut. How could Laney, a woman who was used to male attention, not spot a lothario? David knew Franco didn't have a sincere bone in his body, and he'd damn well make sure Vivi knew it before the week was through.

He opened his eyes in time to see Franco's hand slide down to the delicate curve of Vivi's back. Heaviness caved in on David's heart, but his gaze remained glued to Franco's hand. Then he shut his eyes again before panic completely swamped him.

He'd never before harbored romantic feelings for Vivi, if that's even what he was feeling. God, he'd gotten so turned around since his mother's death, he didn't know up from down, right from wrong. He needed to put a stop to these amorous sensations.

No doubt Jackson would be horrified by his newfound infatuation for their "sister." David could only imagine Cat's unfavorable reaction. Yet his stomach burned at the idea of Vivi with Franco.

Would she be with him if David hadn't brought Laney, if he hadn't distanced himself for the past year? Did it matter, since he couldn't even trust, let alone act upon, these strange new sentiments?

His eyes snapped open when Cat arrived and collapsed onto her towel, hiding in the shade of the umbrella.

"Cat, you guys undersold Franco's appeal," Laney said. "His accent—wow. He's handsome, too." She pointedly turned to David. "Good for Vivi."

"Yes." Cat's amused grin caught David's attention. "He seems interested in her."

Interested in adding Vivi as a notch on his belt, thought David. He'd left the country and, while he was away, everyone had gone mad.

Wedged between the two swooning women, he battled the sour feelings swarming in his gut. To escape the madness, he strode several yards away to where Hank and Jackson stood talking.

"Getting bored from sitting around and waiting on your lady?" Jackson teased when David approached.

"Asks the guy who's here without a lady of his own," David retorted.

"Touché, brother." Jackson's lighthearted smile elicited a slow grin from David.

"Why didn't Cat go with Vivi and Franco?" Hank asked.

"She didn't say." David shrugged. "Maybe she's planning on calling Justin. What's the deal there, Jackson?"

"Not sure." Jackson brushed sand off his thigh. "She never shares details."

No surprises there. None of the St. Jameses easily shared their private thoughts with others.

"Should we be concerned?" David pressed. "Why does she put up with that jerk?"

Hank tugged his earlobe, appearing to study David. It wasn't the first time he'd caught Hank observing him.

"Ask Vivi," Jackson suggested. "She's more likely to get at the truth than you or me."

"She wouldn't break Cat's confidence. Anyway, she's off with Franco." David raked his hand through his hair. "Do you think she's safe with him?"

"She's twenty-six and having a vacation fling." Jackson sighed. "She's fine."

Unconvinced, David rubbed his jaw and tried not to consider what Vivi's "vacation fling" might entail. His stomach clenched as the memory of Franco's hand on her back resurfaced. Once again, he noticed Hank's intense scrutiny. Instead of treating him as a rival, perhaps David should make him an ally in a campaign against Franco.

"Do you agree, Hank?" David asked.

"Pretty much." Hank cocked one brow. "I doubt he'll do anything to hurt her."

"Maybe not intentionally." David wasn't persuaded by their relaxed acceptance. Obviously neither of them saw the truth about the smarmy photographer.

Pressing the matter would just rouse their suspicions of his motive, so he dropped the discussion. He was on his own in any campaign to stop Franco's advances.

Three young women interrupted their conversation, jutting their hips and breasts out, playing with their hair, and giggling. When Jackson engaged in the flirtation, David excused himself and returned to his chair, but Laney was nowhere to be found.

He sat beside his sister, who quickly hid her phone back in her bag. *Justin again?* "Where's Laney?"

"The ladies' room," she mumbled.

"Oh." He watched his sister mindlessly brush sand from her towel, showing no signs of concern for Vivi. "Why didn't you take off with Vivi and Franco?"

"I'd rather stay here on the beach with all of you today." Cat reapplied sunscreen to her face and shoulders.

"What if Franco takes advantage of her?"

"Ha!" Cat laughed in his face and rolled over on her stomach. "Not likely."

"What's that mean?"

She propped herself up on her elbows and studied him.

"Vivi is the last girl in the world to find herself being used by any man."

"You sound certain." David leaned forward, resting his elbows on his knees. "What if you're wrong?"

"Well, I almost hope I am. Lord knows she wasted enough time saving herself for you all through high school. I thought she'd never have sex."

David sat stunned. Learning of Vivi's attempt to save her virginity for him awakened a primal sense of satisfaction. The temperature on the beach instantly jumped fifteen degrees. He buried his thoughts before his arousal became apparent to his sister and everyone else.

Cat smirked as if remembering something Vivi might have said, and then continued, “Thank God she met Alex during college, who finally convinced her of the benefits of having a real, live boyfriend instead of an imaginary one. Still, she takes things really slowly.”

“Too much info.” He reclined in his chair and summoned a memory of Vivi and him stretched out on his parents’ back lawn, stargazing and talking about her impending graduation. They’d lain side by side while laughing and reminiscing. At the time, he hadn’t felt anything remotely sexual. It had simply been . . . natural.

Now everything was changing. At least she wouldn’t become a notch on Franco’s belt—not today, anyway. Not ever, if he had anything to say about it. His headache subsided and the muscles in his shoulders softened.

“Perhaps. But you, of all people, better let her move on. Especially with Laney here.” Cat sat up. “It’s taken Vivi a long time to get over you. Thank God it’s finally happened. Can you imagine how awkward it would have been for all of us if you two had ever dated? Or worse, dated and broken up. It could’ve ruined everything.”

David’s soul absorbed the blow of his sister’s obvious relief, and of the confirmation she wouldn’t support them as a couple. He kept his expression blank as she continued voicing her thoughts.

“Ironically, if I’d known Laney was coming, I wouldn’t have brought Vivi. Of course, how could I have known, since you never mentioned she was in town, much less moved here?”

Ignoring her accusatory tone, he laughed to himself at his sister’s double standard. She shared no more about her private life than he did. Nonetheless, he didn’t wish to argue with her.

“Laney moved here because of her career. Trust me, if I had any big announcements in the works, you’d know.” He kept his eyes on Cat. “I don’t mean to shut you out. I’ve missed you. I take all the blame for this distance between us, but I want us to be close again, Cat.”

She tilted her head and met his eyes. "Are you happy?"

Had they been at a private lunch, or on a walk, perhaps he'd be a little more candid. However, Laney would be back soon, and Jackson and Hank might reappear at any time. This wasn't the time or place for sharing, so he evaded her question. "Are you?"

Cat shuttered her eyes and shrugged, then resumed a prone position on her towel.

"If I asked you about Justin, would you tell me anything worthwhile?" David pressed. "I've been watching you pretend to have everything under control these past days, but I can tell you're upset."

"You don't like him. I can tell." She turned her head to face him. "I doubt you can be objective."

"I probably can't be objective when it comes to you, that's true. I wish you'd let me in." He reached over and tugged her hair. "At least promise you'd come to me if you needed something?"

"Relax." She swatted his hand. "You always worry too much."

"That's not an answer."

"Yes, David, I'd come to you." Rolling her eyes, she grinned. "Satisfied?"

"For now." He smiled as she huffed and closed her eyes.

When Laney reappeared, she leaned down to kiss him on the forehead. He opened his eyes to find her green ones staring into his. She fingered his hair and let her thumb run along his jaw before taking her seat and picking up her book.

Her small gestures deluged him with contrition. He'd spent the past few days finding fault with her because of a knot of emotions involving Vivi. Both women deserved better.

Cat was right. He shouldn't interfere with Vivi's budding relationship when he couldn't offer anything in return. Surely this novel desire would fade—as soon as they spent more time together like always. Everything would go back to normal after a few months of daily life in the city.

And Laney deserved someone who could give her what she needed, which apparently was a lot more than he'd imagined.

When they returned to Manhattan, he'd find a way to let her down easily. Drawing in a deep breath, he gazed at the darkening clouds and willed himself to take control of his life without continuing to hurt the people who cared for him.

~

By late afternoon, the angry sky showered heavy sheets of rain onto the roof, and the torrential downpour resonated throughout the house. David welcomed the storm, which provided a perfect excuse to slow down and relax. As he listened to the dull roar overhead, he wished he were lying in bed with a good book. He couldn't recall the last time he'd enjoyed a lazy afternoon alone.

Then again, preparing dinner with Jackson had been a pleasant way to unwind. His brother whistled while cutting the garlic cloves and inserting those shards into the filet roast. David chopped onions, mushrooms, and parsley. He'd always found the rhythmic activity to be meditative. Afterward, he sautéed them with white wine and butter. The aroma of fresh herbs and garlic whetted his appetite.

Despite a tumult of emotion concerning Vivi, he'd salvaged a peaceful afternoon with his family, the first solid step toward repairing the damage created by his long absence. A long-forgotten feeling of hope sprouted in his chest.

He glanced around while he cleaned. Laney worked on her laptop in the living room, while Hank rested below. Cat was setting the table.

"I thought Vivi would be home by now. She must be eating dinner with Franco." Cat frowned. "I didn't consider how disruptive this gig would be when I suggested it."

"Text her," Jackson suggested.

"If she's rehearsing, she won't hear it." Cat placed the last of the silverware and then came to the counter. "Oh, well."

"Cheer up, sis." Jackson tweaked her nose. "You've got us."

"Yippee," Cat dryly replied, but the corners of her lips curled into a grin.

David's lungs tightened as he considered how much his mother would've enjoyed this occasion with her kids. He rubbed his hand over the tight spot in his chest and turned away from Jackson and Cat until his nose stopped tingling.

Minutes later, the front door opened just as a crack of thunder split the sky.

"Hi, guys, I'm back . . . and drenched." Vivi's chattering teeth punctuated her speech. "I'll be up to help once I dry off." The echo of her footsteps drifted up the stairwell.

David's mood instantly brightened, although he repressed a grin. *She didn't stay with Franco.*

~

After dinner and dessert, Vivi collected the dishes. "You all leave these. I'll clean up."

"Thanks, Viv." Jackson pushed back from the table.

Cat, Hank, and Laney followed Jackson to the living room. David gathered the glasses and trailed behind Vivi into the kitchen.

"I know we can't talk now, but I want to make sure you're okay. I feel like I should apologize for dumping everything on you this morning."

"*I* should apologize for putting you in an impossible situation." She cast a quick glance over her shoulder, toward the group in the living room. "Let's change the subject before we get caught."

"Good idea." He smiled as she opened the dishwasher door. "Seems like old times, us doing dishes."

"So it does." She grinned. "Even if I hadn't offered them an out tonight, I'm pretty sure Cat and Jackson would've found another excuse to duck out of kitchen duty, like when we were kids."

"Something you never shirked." David took the glasses from her after she rinsed them.

"Well, I had an ulterior motive." He watched the corners of her eyes crinkle with her smile. The water ran nonstop as she rinsed each plate and handed it to him to load in the dishwasher.

"Oh?" he asked, assuming she was referring to her former crush on him.

"Of course." Vivi stared out the window with a distant look in her eyes. "I had to stay in your mom's good graces so I'd always be welcomed back."

"And so you were," David said softly, remembering how much his mother had loved Vivi. How troubling to learn only now that for years Vivi had felt so insecure about her position within their family. "And here I'd always thought you'd volunteered to help because *my* company was so interesting."

Vivi's grin widened and she bumped his hip with her own.

"That, too, David." She plunged her hands into the soapy tub of water and began scrubbing the sauté pan. "So, I found several new pieces of sea glass in my luggage tonight when I changed out of my wet clothes. Any idea how those got there?"

"That was quick. I figured you wouldn't find those until the end of the week. That was the messiest duffel bag I've ever seen." He grinned. "I assume you still have that big jar of sea glass in your apartment, so when I saw a few pieces today on the beach, I stuck them in my pocket. A small token of appreciation for your discretion and friendship."

"Thank you," she said. "They'll make a nice addition to the collection. Obviously I haven't been doing much beachcombing because of the rehearsals."

"How'd it go today?" he asked, wanting to keep the positive momentum rolling. "You were gone a long time."

"We covered a lot of ground." She handed him the heavy pan to dry. "We'll do one final run-through tomorrow morning, and then whatever happens, happens."

David brushed a stray dollop of soapsuds from her arm, and then dried the pot while she wiped down the counters. When he finished, he asked, "Why didn't you ever mention your singing to me?"

She leaned against the counter and looked at her hands, laced together in front of her hips. He hung the dish towel to dry, keeping his eyes averted to give her time to speak. A cloud of tension and sorrow surrounded Vivi.

"I had my first voice lesson three days before we all learned about your mom's breast cancer. Her illness made my new hobby seem too frivolous to discuss. And then you left within days of the funeral . . ." She paused, leaving her accusation unspoken.

"I'm sorry, Vivi," he said softly. "I'm sorry for shutting you out for so long. I'm sorry for not offering any solace while we were both grieving my mother. And I'm sorry I took our friendship for granted."

"I know you are," she whispered while averting her eyes. He breathed a sigh of relief when he sensed his apologies finally pierced the invisible wall that had been separating them all week. Suddenly she waved her hand airily and grinned a little too brightly. "But now you're back, and tomorrow you'll be forced to hear my singing with your own ears. Please tell me you travel with earplugs."

"I doubt we'll need them. Jackson says you sing well."

"What does he know?" She smirked and, as always, shifted the focus off herself. "Anyway, should we get a game of charades going?"

"Maybe Cranium," David suggested, heartened by the familiar rhythm of their conversation.

"No way. Everyone but me is smart, so I'd only be a drag to my teammate."

"You know I hate when you say things like that, Vivi." David placed his hand on the back of her neck. "How many times have I told you? You're smart in every way that counts, regardless of your stupid grade-point average."

"Many," she conceded. "And *stupid* aptly describes my grade-point average."

"That's not what I meant and you know it." He threw his arm over her shoulder and rubbed his knuckles against her skull. Unlike the many times he'd done this before, tonight touching her ignited an irresistible urge to hold on, to take more. To take everything.

Slightly shaken, he forced himself to release her. "Don't wish to be different. If you ever changed, it would break my heart."

A faint blush tinged her cheeks.

"Thanks, David." She then tapped her finger against her lips. "So then, how about Pictionary?"

"Ah, now you're playing to your own advantage." He yanked his gaze from her damned soft lips. She was standing so close he could smell her vanilla-scented body lotion. He fought the impulse to close his eyes and inhale. "See how smart you are?"

She produced an exaggerated "aha" face.

"Who ever said miracles never happen?" She turned on her heel as she called out to the group, "Pictionary, anyone?"

Before she left, he grabbed her arm and whispered, "Meet me out front at midnight."

Her eyes widened. "Why?"

"Just dress warm and don't tell anyone. It'll be an adventure."

He released her and she left him in the kitchen, glancing back over her shoulder with a puzzled expression. When he finally followed her, he noticed Laney observing them with a troubled expression. *Shit.*

Chapter Twelve

Vivi crept out of the house and found David sitting on the stoop with two paint cans at his feet. He raised his finger to his lips to silence her, then handed her a flashlight and picked up the paint.

"What are we doing?" she whispered.

"Follow me." He grinned as she fell in step beside him.

It took her twenty seconds to realize they were headed toward the Painted Rock, a well-known tourist attraction situated near the St. Jameses' house. Vacationers routinely painted the small boulder on a whim. She'd seen it repainted more than once within a week during her former vacations. In her teens, she and Cat had once made it look like a giant smiley face.

"We're going to the Painted Rock?" Vivi asked. "When did you buy paint?"

"It's leftover house paint I found in the shed." He raised the cans to her eye level. "Interior white and something called Calypso blue—not much to work with. I'll count on you to be the creative director."

When they arrived at the rock, it resembled the American flag. The most recent artists probably created this graffiti over the past Fourth of July holiday. Funny no one else had changed it since then.

David pulled two old, stiff paintbrushes and a can opener out of his sweatpants pockets. "Here, see if you can do something with these bristles while I open and stir the paint."

"Yikes. Without vinegar or linseed oil, there's not much I can do." Vivi tried to manipulate the bristles with her hands. "At least they don't have old paint caked on them, but whatever we do will be streaky."

David stood over the open paint cans and put his hands on his hips. "Well, so be it. Now tell me, what can we do with white and blue paint?"

"Not much!" Vivi laughed until David grinned. Seeing him relax with her almost made the troubling secret worth knowing. "Okay, give me a minute to think."

He stretched out on the damp ground, propping himself up on one elbow, watching her as she circled the big rock. Once again, a hopeful smile tugged at his mouth and the corners of his eyes, although the sorrow beneath the surface lingered.

"Did you bring me out here to talk about your dad . . . about how to find a way to forgive him?" she asked. The night was oddly quiet except for the crickets' song humming around them.

"No. I only told you all of that so you would forgive *me.* There's no point in discussing it further." David's face contorted as he sat up and hugged his knees. "I've been drowning in old memories this week. For the first time, being here has been painful. Tonight I wanted to create a new memory instead of dwelling on the past." One corner of his mouth quirked upward. "As for why now, with you . . . well, for one, it's the only time we can spend together without everyone else being involved. Two, I hated being left out when you and Cat did this years ago. Three, who better to kick off new happy memories with than you, the person who's always pushing me to have more fun? I can't imagine what a crushing bore I might be if you'd never come into my life."

"Total stick in the mud." She lightly kicked the sole of his shoe and then turned back to the rock to hide the swell of emotion inside. She stared at the monument, searching for inspiration. Another minute or two passed before it came to her. "Okay, I've got an idea. First we have to paint the whole thing white."

"What's the idea?"

"Just paint, David."

Fifteen minutes later, the white rock appeared to glow in the dark.

"Now will you tell me what you plan to do with the blue paint?" David asked.

"Take a seat." She pointed to the ground before crouching down to paint a scrolled symbol resembling the script form of a capital letter *L* with an extra loop on the bottom-right swish.

"What are these?" David asked as she began painting another series of scrolled marks with curlicue tips on the other side of the rock.

"Zibu symbols of friendship"—she pointed to the first one, and then at the second—"and of beginning anew." She peered up at him from over her shoulder and smiled when his lips parted.

"I love them," he said softly, eyeing them more carefully. "They're perfect. Where did you learn about Zibu? I've never heard of it."

"Zibu symbols connect the love, inspiration, and healing energy of angels." Vivi stood up to stretch her legs, grinning at David's incredulous expression. "I forget the name of the woman who created them. She claims to have been visited by angels who explained their meaning to her after she started drawing them. I know, kooky, but you never know. Maybe it's true. Can't hurt, and they're pretty, too."

David removed his phone from his sweatshirt pocket. "Sit there beside the rock," he instructed. Vivi poked fun at her artistic choice by kneeling and folding her hands in prayer while looking up at the sky.

"Very funny. Now please look at the camera. I want a nice picture to remember this by." He snapped a photo of her beside each symbol and then shoved his phone back in his pocket. "Guess we can throw these old things away."

"Yes, they're useless." Vivi stood up and brushed the bits of stone and mud off her butt. "We should probably get back soon. Laney might get angry if she discovers our little midnight run."

David resealed the paint cans and then picked them up and began walking back to the house. "Don't worry about Laney."

"Well, she might get the wrong idea and make it uncomfortable for us to be friends." Vivi kept her eyes glued to the flashlight beam ahead of them as they crossed the road back onto the St. James property.

"She won't interfere," he said without looking at her. "Girlfriends come and go, Vivi, but you will always be part of my life."

"Oh." Her heart beat one thousand times in the following ten seconds. The old Vivi would read way more into that remark than he'd actually said. The new and improved Vivi focused solely on his words. If girlfriends come and go but she will always remain, then he clearly never intended to make her his girlfriend. "Still, it's better not to rock the boat. I don't want to cause problems."

David bent over inside the shed to put away the paint. He shut the doors and turned to Vivi as they reached the front steps. "Thanks for coming with me tonight."

"Thanks for asking." She sighed, quelling the tide of "what ifs" rising inside. *Stop it.* "Now I need to catch some sleep. Big performance tomorrow."

David grabbed her hand and kissed it. "Good night. Sleep well."

She padded down the steps to her room, exhausted by the extreme emotional swings of her day. Now, if only she could finally stop her heart from wanting more than the friendship he offered.

~

At the crack of dawn, Vivi realized mere hours stood between her and potential disaster. Seized with a touch of panic, she couldn't remember the titles of the set list, let alone the lyrics. The impulsive decision to perform with Disordered ranked on her top-ten list of harebrained stunts. Given her long list of exploits, that was really saying something.

Her stage experience consisted of a few dozen performances in the trendy, intimate setting at Winegasm in Astoria, where customers enjoyed supporting local musicians. Tonight would be very different from that venue, mostly because David would be watching. Franco and Laney were additional sources of anxiety, but David's opinion mattered most.

It's only nerves, Vivi repeated to herself. After all, yesterday's rehearsal went rather well. Everything would be fine. It would. Wouldn't it? Her hands bunched the coverlet up to her chin. She drew a deep breath in through her nose, held it, and then released it in one slow breath. When it didn't work, she repeated the ritual several times.

Hopeless.

Lugging herself from bed, she climbed the stairs in search of coffee and found Hank, David, and Laney conversing at the dining table. Once again, Laney was squeaky-clean and dressed for the day. *Of course.*

"Interesting hairstyle. Does it come naturally?" Laney's teasing couldn't suppress the hint of malice.

Perhaps Vivi hadn't imagined her becoming decidedly less polite last evening, or perhaps Laney had awakened in the wee hours of the morning and wondered where David had gone.

"Would you like the name of my stylist?" Vivi lifted her tangled locks with both hands and flashed a wicked smile. "Of course, not everyone can pull it off quite this well."

She noticed David scowl at Laney. Turning her back to hide her own nasty expression, Vivi meandered across the room to open the deck doors. She tipped her face toward the sun and grinned, knowing Laney's insults would provoke David's protective instinct. Beautiful Miss Smarty Pants would soon sink her own ship.

"You all set for the big night?" Hank thankfully interrupted the unpleasant repartee.

"Sure." Vivi feigned calmness. "One way or another, it'll be a night to remember. At the very least, the DJ will offer quality entertainment. Will you save me a dance, Hank?"

"I can't wait to hear you perform," David interjected. He grinned while holding her gaze. "I still can't believe I never knew you sang."

Before Vivi could respond, Laney shook her head. "*I* still can't believe you committed to this performance."

Whoa! Vivi's body stiffened and heated at the not-so-subtle insult. After burying her own feelings for days, she snapped.

"I lead with my heart, not my head." Vivi stared at Laney.

"Interesting strategy." Laney's smirk tipped Vivi over the edge.

"Laney—" David began before Vivi cut him off.

"Yes, I'm sure it's inconceivable to you—you'd need a heart to understand it." Vivi's nostrils flared. "But thanks for your vote of confidence."

David blinked in surprise. *Darn it.* So much for Laney sinking her own ship. Vivi grimaced at Hank before bolting downstairs. As she fled, she envisioned herself looking like a cartoon character, with steam spewing from her ears and trailing behind her.

Given her history as target practice for bitchy girls, why didn't she have elephant hide by now? In any case, she'd never understand what motivated girls with everything to be hostile toward those with less. If *she* had been born beautiful, intelligent, and graceful, she'd have used her gifts to lift others up, not drag them down.

She flung open the bedroom door, sending it crashing against the wall, before sagging onto her bed. At this point she couldn't care less whether her noisy entrance woke Cat.

"What's wrong?" Cat rolled over. "You look like you might eat me."

"Laney's unsheathed her claws," Vivi scowled. "She pushed my buttons and I bit back. I'm hiding until I'm ready to apologize." Regret had already arrived to crowd out her self-righteous indignation. She thrust her face into her hands, mumbling, "Can I blame it on my nerves?"

"What did she say?"

"Hmm . . . basically that I'm an ill-prepared idiot who'll probably humiliate myself tonight." Vivi's gaze drifted north. "Not that I needed anyone to point it out, mind you. It's all I've been thinking about for the past hour."

"I'm so sorry. You only agreed because I begged. It's messed up our trip, too." Cat frowned. "I'm not a good friend."

"Oh, shush." She faced her contrite friend. "You know perfectly well I always leap before looking. I could've put an end to it at any time. Honestly, it's been fun to sing with the band. And Franco's a bonus, although I've not yet spent time with him alone. He seems nice, though."

"I'll be glad to have you back tomorrow. And I know you'll be great tonight. If you forget some of the words, just smile and do a little 'la la la' kind of thing."

"Oh, yes, the 'la la la' trick. No one will notice!" Vivi groaned and fell back on the bed, lost in thought. One would never accuse Laney of being particularly friendly. Until this morning, she hadn't been cruel, either. "Laney's attitude toward me has definitely taken a negative turn."

Cat raised a brow. "Maybe she and David are having problems?"

"Why do you suspect that?"

"Duh! She moved around the world and no diamond ring." Cat shook her head when Vivi failed to make the connection. "Maybe she's feeling insecure and sees you as a rival for his affection."

"Oh, then please clue her in." Vivi laughed out loud. "There's no one less likely to be her romantic rival than me. If she knew how spectacularly I've failed to win his heart, she'd relax."

Cat nodded. Vivi felt the sting of Cat's thankfulness on that score, but the point was moot.

Following five minutes of sulking, Vivi extended her arm and pointed upward with her thumb. "Get up. I need moral support while I apologize."

Cat obediently followed Vivi upstairs and stood by her while she faced her foe.

"I'm sorry I snapped at you, Laney. I'm nervous about tonight." Vivi ran her tongue along the roof of her mouth to keep from biting it off. "But that's no excuse."

Laney glanced at David and then replied, "And I'm sorry if I undermined your confidence. It wasn't my intent."

Oh, right. Vivi nodded, struggling to keep her fist from landing squarely on Laney's nose. She glanced at David. A flash of frustration streaked through her limbs. Why was Laney the type of woman he wanted to date? Not that Vivi's opinion mattered one lick. Laney was his girlfriend, at least for now. Vivi would just have to avoid the woman as much as possible for the remainder of the trip.

"Shall we join Jackson and Hank on the deck before I have to leave for rehearsal?" Vivi asked Cat.

"Sure," replied Cat, who shot David an annoyed glare before going outside.

Jackson and Hank were discussing plans for some kitchen remodel. Vivi only gave them half of her attention. Her other half couldn't resist watching David and Laney through the windows. David pressed his lips together as he stared across the table at Laney, who was jabbing her finger at him. She contorted her face, then pushed away from the table and ran up the steps. Rather than follow her, David clamped his hands behind his drooped head and squeezed hard.

Given what she now knew about the severity of David's dilemma, Vivi couldn't stand seeing him endure additional suffering. She excused herself from the deck and slipped inside. He looked up from the table when she entered the room. For a heartbeat, their eyes locked like magnets as palpable energy passed between them. She slid the door closed behind her.

"I'm sorry, David. Did my tantrum cause you problems with Laney, or was it our midnight adventure that pissed her off?"

He shook his head, sighing, before he stood and approached her. His eyes assessed every inch of her face. He brushed a section of hair behind her ear.

"Don't apologize." He stroked her upper arms with his hands. Despite her vows to disengage, she still loved his touch. "And don't let her ruin your day, or your anticipation of tonight."

"Honestly, Laney's not the reason my nerves are on fire." She refrained from swaying into him. Always the pull. Always. "I wish I could be confident like you. You never sweat."

David's lips quirked upward. "You couldn't be more wrong. I second-guess myself often, especially lately."

"Present circumstances aside, I don't believe you for a second. But thanks for trying to make me feel better." She glanced at the kitchen clock and sighed. "I've got to change and head to the final rehearsal."

He clasped her hand, firing tingles of pleasure up her arm. "This band wouldn't have gone forward with you if you weren't up to it. " He raised her hand to his lips and kissed her fingers.

He'd often performed these tender ministrations in the past. Now it felt different. He held her hand, staring at her intently as if he wanted to say more. Jackson's burst of laughter on the other side of the window broke the spell. David squeezed her hand before releasing it and walking outside.

She left the house wondering what else he'd wanted to say.

~

Three hours later, the band completed its final run-through. Joe seemed pleased and thanked her multiple times. Vivi glanced around at the workers, who were scampering around putting the finishing touches on the tent and setting up the party supplies.

"Will you join me for lunch?" Franco asked as she hopped down from the newly constructed stage.

"Sounds great." She'd made very little progress this week in her battle to get over David. Lunch with Franco would be a step in the right direction. Plus, more time away from everyone meant less chance of accidentally exposing David's secret, and less opportunity for Laney to hurl more insults.

Franco suggested they return to Beachhead, which suited her fine. A girl on vacation could never eat too many lobster rolls. As before, they dined outdoors. Several flags on the porch snapped in the steady ocean breeze. If she closed her eyes, she could pretend she was on a sailboat.

After ordering lunch, Vivi launched into an interrogation.

"Do you have family in Italy?"

"My parents moved back two years ago. They live outside of Florence."

"Do you go home often?" She leaned forward, resting her chin in her hands. He mirrored her movement.

Up close, she noticed the golden highlights in his brown eyes. His dark lashes were short and thick instead of long and curled like David's.

"Probably twice a year. More if I'm on assignment nearby."

Vivi's mother's and brother's faces popped into her mind. If they had survived, nothing could've kept Vivi away. Heck, she even visited her dad at least once each month despite their difficult relationship. Then again, who was she to judge?

"I've never been. It looks so romantic in the movies. I'd love to go to Tuscany to paint someday." She momentarily checked out of the conversation and pictured herself on a balcony of an ancient stone villa with a red tile roof, overlooking a patio decorated with terra-cotta planters overflowing with ivy and flowers, sketching the rolling gold and green landscape.

"Music, photography, and painting." Franco grinned, bringing her back to the present. "A true artist."

"Not a great one, but I enjoy making art with my school kids." She smiled at the thought of her eager students. Of being covered in paint with them. Of their joy. "An easy-to-impress crowd. My favorite kind. In fact, maybe we should import them to the party tonight."

"Just accept the compliment." He sat forward. "Anyway, passion moves people more than skill where art is concerned, and you're obviously a passionate woman."

When he reached across the table to cover her hand with his, the dark flicker of desire in his eyes flustered her. She suspected he didn't have to work very hard to get most women into his bed. He'd soon learn she wasn't one of those women.

"Passionate about life." She withdrew her hand and sipped her soda. "I'm a big fan of nature walks, the movies, Indian food . . . well, all food, actually. How about you?"

Vivi continued to smile. If he didn't have any genuine interest in them getting to know each other, this would be their only date, because Vivi would never be his easy lay.

"Am I passionate?" He flashed a wicked grin. "I think so. Would you like me to prove it?"

"Poor Franco, setting yourself up for disappointment." She laughed so she wouldn't feel like his prey. "I keep warning everyone about the dangers of excessive expectations."

"I like your candor." He chuckled. "Relax. I'm just joking. I like you, so I'm not going to do anything to scare you away."

He liked her. How heartwarming. "So, let me travel vicariously through your experiences. Where is your favorite spot on the planet?" Vivi sat back. "I've never even been outside the U.S."

"Really?" His leaned forward, extending his palms across the table. "Maybe we can remedy that with one of my upcoming assignments. I can help you improve your landscape photography."

"I'd love a photography lesson! But maybe we could start in Central Park?" She sipped her tea, stalling. "So, back to my question. Where's your favorite place?"

"I can't pick one, although I prefer cities to places like this." He gestured out toward the island. "I need the buzz of people, traffic, lights . . . signs of life."

Vivi preferred nature's beauty—mountains, lakes, forests, and oceans. Of course, foreign cities with ancient buildings also held a certain appeal. She'd dreamed of sitting on the edge of the Trevi Fountain sipping espresso, then strolling through the Vatican and Sistine Chapel to look at Michelangelo's masterpiece.

In those dreams she was always with David, who would know as much as any docent about every place they would visit.

She looked across the table at Franco, disappointed by his vague answer. She continued questioning him about his family, friends, and hobbies. By the end of lunch, he'd neatly evaded her probing questions with breezy responses.

Although they'd laughed, and conversation was never stilted, she felt like she'd eaten a sugar-free dessert. A cheap imitation of something real.

Of course, this was her pattern. Meet a guy, get excited, then compare him unfavorably with David. Her muscles tensed. While Franco paid the bill, she rubbed the crease between her eyes and considered her fault-finding history.

Not again. There was nothing wrong with Franco. He'd been perfectly pleasant. No guy bares his whole heart and soul on a first date. She had to stop projecting too far ahead. Stop focusing on what was missing at the expense of what was available.

When he took her hand as they walked to the car, she didn't pull away. He'd be leaving the island tomorrow. Today would be about adventure and possibility, not doubt and worry.

~

When Franco drove up to the front of the St. James home, she noticed Laney's and Jackson's cars parked in the gravel driveway. Vivi fumbled with her seat belt latch while he reached into the backseat.

"Hang on." He brought forth a gift bag.

"What's this?" She picked through the tissue paper and discovered an ultrasoft jersey-knit halter dress in French blue, lavender, and white. "For me?"

"You mentioned you hadn't packed anything nice to wear to the party. I saw this in town and thought of you."

"That's so considerate." Her eyes widened in surprise. Wariness then spoiled her gratitude. "But I can't accept it."

"You don't like it?" He tilted his head, assessing her.

"I like it a lot. I mean, look at the colors!" She slid the silky-feeling fabric through her fingers. "Still, we barely know each other. You shouldn't buy me expensive gifts." She returned the dress back to the bag before handing it to him.

"I want you to have it." His mouth twitched and he kept his eyes on the bag.

Crap. Everything about his expression told her she'd insulted him. Vivi failed at many things, but boy, could she succeed at sabotaging happiness.

"Okay, I'll keep it." She reached over to touch his forearm. "It's pretty, Franco. You have good taste."

He smiled and looked at her again. "I'm glad you think so."

"I do. I really do." She squeezed his arm. "You're very sweet."

"I can be when properly motivated." He shot her a wolfish grin, which made him look anything but sweet.

Vivi laughed and kissed him on the cheek before waving him off. As he turned out of the driveway, she dashed inside the house.

"I'm back." Her bellow was met by silence. "Anyone here?"

She bounded down the steps, changed into a swimsuit, and then started down the cliff-side staircase. When she rounded the first bend, she saw the group below and picked up her pace.

"Hey." She laid her towel beside Cat's umbrella. David smiled at her. Laney barely looked up from her book. "Where are Jackson and Hank?"

"Not sure." Cat sat up and narrowed her gaze. "So, are you all set?"

"Yeah. It went well." Vivi curled her ponytail around her hand and drew it in front of her shoulder. "Of course, I suggested guests be forced to drink at least one shot of tequila when they arrive so they won't notice our mistakes."

"I'm glad you can joke." Cat slung back on her elbows. "I got worried when you took so long to return."

"Franco took me to lunch after rehearsal." She fidgeted with her hair as she recalled how she'd handled his surprise.

"Uh-oh. What's that look?" Cat studied Vivi's face. "Did something happen?"

David's gaze fell on Vivi, too. Their focused attention made her twitchy. She shrugged while sifting sand through her fingers.

"He bought me a dress to wear tonight."

"Ooh la la." A knowing smile graced Cat's face. "That's interesting."

"At first I told him I couldn't accept it." Vivi scrunched up her face. "I could tell I'd hurt his feelings, so I kept it."

"Why couldn't you accept it?" Laney piped up.

Vivi snapped her head toward Laney. "We don't know each other well. Lunch was our first real date. It seemed too personal, under the circumstances."

"It's a present from a handsome man, not something sinister." Laney placed her book on her thighs and crossed her arms. "Just enjoy it."

"I don't want to create any expectations." Vivi frowned.

"You're overthinking it. He bought you a gift. He didn't hand you a hotel key and a condom." Laney rolled her eyes and resumed reading, oblivious to Vivi's stunned reaction.

"If you're not comfortable, give it back," David interrupted.

Laney lowered her book, pinning David with a derisive glare.

"How interesting, David." She narrowed her gaze. "Perhaps I should've declined the gifts you've bought me instead of assuming you bought them as tokens of affection."

"Don't twist my words, Laney." His snappish tone made Vivi gulp. "If Vivi's uncomfortable, she should return it." He tilted toward Vivi, his hand stretching across the sand toward her leg. "You've always trusted your gut. Don't stop now."

The temperature on the beach couldn't compete with the caustic showdown between David and Laney. Apparently they hadn't resolved the argument they'd begun at the breakfast table.

Despite Vivi's efforts to be gracious, each day of this trip kept getting harder, not easier. The lies, half-truths, and mixed signals were taking a toll on her peace of mind. Although she'd love for David to dump Laney, she didn't want to be the source of their problems.

"Maybe I'm overreacting." Vivi forced a smile. "It's a pretty dress. He said he bought it because I'd mentioned not having anything to wear to the party. It was really thoughtful, actually."

Cat's silence didn't fool Vivi, who knew her friend was biting her tongue. Finally, Cat stood and fixed her eyes on Vivi's. "Let's walk."

Once they'd moved away from the couple, Vivi asked, "Did you figure out what's going on with them?"

"I've no idea. Laney's been on a tear all day. I might feel bad for David if I weren't still a little peeved with him." Cat snickered. "Karma's a bitch. Apparently one from Chicago."

Even if Vivi hadn't known the truth behind David's absence, she wouldn't have taken pleasure in his misery.

"Not nice, friend." Vivi batted Cat's arm, then walked in silence for a few yards. Careful not to raise too much suspicion, she said, "It's obvious David wants things to get back to normal with you and Jackson. Can't you just throw him a bone? Talk to him."

"He avoids direct questions." Cat waved her hand in disgust. "Such a lawyer."

"Whatever is going on between him and your dad, they have to sort it out. Don't let it affect your relationship." Vivi clasped her hands behind her back and stared across the waves.

Had she said too much? God, three more days and nights. She'd never survive all the tension! For the first time ever, she wished for vacation days to pass quickly.

When they returned to their towels, Laney was gone. Cat looked at her brother, awaiting some explanation. "What's going on with you and Laney?"

"Please, Cat, don't grill me now. I've been on the defensive all day." He returned his attention to his book, shutting down any further discussion. Cat gave Vivi a "told you so" look, then tipped up her chin before gathering her things.

"Well, if I'm going to party tonight, I think I'll get a little beauty rest." Cat started toward the steps, carrying her towel and water bottle. "Vivi?"

"I'll be up in a minute." Vivi hesitated, drawn to David despite everything. She knew eventually her broken heart would mend, and their friendship was a rare gift worth keeping.

She sat down and stretched out her legs. "Do you want to talk?"

"Actually, I have a little good-luck token for you in case you get nervous tonight." He handed her a slip of paper he'd withdrawn from inside the back cover of his book. "It's not so extravagant as a new dress, but it's from the heart. Mind you, it's an abridged version, and not perfect for the occasion. I hope you'll get *my* meaning."

"Thanks, David. That's sweet." Vivi unfolded the note and read the abbreviated sections of the poem he'd copied.

"The Singers"
God sent his Singers upon earth
With songs of sadness and of mirth,
That they might touch the hearts of men,
And bring them back to heaven again.
. . .
These are the three great chords of might,
And he whose ear is tuned aright
Will hear no discord in the three,
But the most perfect harmony.
—Henry Wadsworth Longfellow

"Oh, gosh." She looked at his grinning face. "Jeez, talk about pressure. Touch the hearts of men?" She chuckled. "Leave it to you to quote Longfellow. You couldn't have just gone with a four-leaf clover or something?"

"No. It had to be this. I'll never stop trying to get you to appreciate the classics." He squeezed her ankle. "The meaning of the actual poem isn't fitting, but these lines are a reminder that the power and beauty of song isn't about having a perfect voice. I don't even need to hear you to know your voice will reflect your generous spirit, and so it *will* touch the hearts of men, even if you hit an off-key note or skip a word or two."

"We'll see if you can look me in the eye later tonight and say that without laughing," she teased to dispel the urge to launch herself into his arms. "I appreciate the sentiment. Thanks." She refolded the note, holding it in her hand. "So, let's stop talking about me and tell me what's going on with Laney. You know I feel responsible after the way I lit into her this morning."

He shook his head. "I can't talk about Laney with you, Vivi."

"Why not?"

"Because . . ." His brows furrowed as he rested his book on his thighs. "Because it feels weird to discuss our love lives. We've never done so before, not once in thirteen years."

"Well, there's a first time for everything." She wore an overly broad smile to convince him, if not quite herself, that she had moved past her old feelings.

"I don't want to. I like the way we've always been—inside our own bubble where the rest of the world sort of disappears." His wan smile reflected the melancholy note in his voice. "And I really don't want to hear the intimate details of your relationship with Franco, or anyone else for that matter."

"Why not?" The words flew from her mouth before she thought better of them.

David swallowed hard and shifted uncomfortably in his beach chair, looking everywhere but at her. His gaze followed the gull that had swooped down and flown out over the glittering sea.

Time slowed. So did her breathing.

Seconds that seemed liked hours ticked by before he finally answered with a tight voice. "I just don't."

Her palms smoothed the sand around her legs while she tried to compose her thoughts. These kinds of exchanges were why she'd held on to hope for far too long. Frustration shot through her, making her angry—whether at him or herself, she wasn't sure.

"Really? So you'd rather retreat and pout, and let everyone else squirm in discomfort than open up about Laney?" She pointed her finger at him. "You think I can't handle it because of how I always felt before? Well, I can now."

"Maybe *I* can't, Vivi." He rubbed his hands against his thighs without making eye contact. "Please let it go."

A moment of silence passed before Vivi let out a long sigh. Much as she'd always love him, she'd moved beyond the point of begging David for anything.

"Fine. But don't complain to me about the changes in our relationship and then shut me out whenever *you* decide something is off-limits. You can't have it all ways and only on your terms. We can be friends, or not. Let me know once you decide." She grabbed her towel and stormed off before he responded.

Well, that didn't go as she'd hoped. Seemed nothing ever did.

She clutched the poem in her hand as she climbed the stairs, as if pretty words alone would make everything better.

~

At six thirty, Vivi stood in front of the mirror. Cat had insisted on applying Vivi's makeup, claiming she needed to wear enough to be seen from the stage. Now Vivi barely recognized the face staring back at her. She braided two small sections of hair at each temple and let the rest hang wild and free. It looked decent at that point, but in this humidity she would probably resemble a Chia Pet by nightfall. Shrugging to herself, she slipped into her new dress and stepped back to take a look at the final product.

Oh no!

"Cat!" She clutched at the halter, then pushed and prodded her bra straps in every direction. "There's no way I can wear a bra in this dress."

"Nope. No bra." Cat finished buckling the belt of her own crimson wrap dress. "It's lined, right?"

"Barely. And I never go braless." After removing her bra, Vivi swayed her body and moved her arms around, frowning. "I'm going to jiggle the whole time I'm performing."

Cat's devilish grin widened. "Well, now we know what prompted Franco to buy *that* dress."

"Oh, God." Vivi bugged her eyes out and crossed her arms in front of her chest. "I should change."

"Hell no!" Cat's hands clamped onto Vivi's shoulders. "Stop hiding from men. Embrace your sexuality. Embrace Franco's attention. Act your age and have fun. In ten years, gravity will make it impossible to look decent in a dress like this, so enjoy it now."

Taken aback, Vivi uncrossed her arms and stared at herself again. Maybe Cat was right. She had been hiding behind ratty clothes for as long as she could remember. Squaring her shoulders, she drew a deep breath and followed Cat upstairs.

Hank whistled when the girls entered the living room. Jackson threw down the magazine he'd been reading and flashed his dimples.

"Let's go." He clapped his hands together and winked at Vivi.

"Where's David?" Cat glanced at the light emanating from the top of the stairwell.

"They're running late. I think Laney's giving him a hard time." Jackson cast Hank a sidelong glance and smirked. "They'll be along in a little while."

"Seriously?" Cat huffed and shook her head. "She's pulling this now, when we're all supposed to be going out together?"

Vivi played with the hem of her dress to hide her disappointment. Despite her nerves and their recent spat, she'd wanted to share her singing with David. Now he'd probably miss it. In her heart, she knew Laney had purposely forced David to choose, and his choice hurt more than she wanted anyone else to see.

"Let's go." She flashed a sheepish grin. "Before I chicken out."

"I'm looking forward to your performance." Hank slung his arm around her shoulders. "I know you'll be great."

"Thanks." She patted his hand. "Great would be nice, though I'll settle for decent."

"I think the men will be so distracted looking at you, they might not even hear a single note." He twirled her around. "Does that make you feel better or worse?"

"I'm not sure." Inwardly, though, his words pleased her. She'd never before been the kind of girl men noticed, not in a good way, anyhow.

Halfway to the car, Vivi remembered her purse and ran back inside to grab it. As she turned to head out, David hurtled down the steps.

"Vivi." He halted in front of her and reached for her hand. "I want to wish you luck. I promise I'll be there as soon as possible. I'm not going to miss the show."

Then suddenly his eyes darkened as he studied her outfit.

"Franco bought *this*?" His jaw ticked as his eyes lingered on her chest.

Her cheeks pinked in shame, then Cat's words echoed in her mind. *Stop hiding from men.* Embracing that message, she straightened her posture.

"Yes." She twirled to show off the back of the dress, or rather the lack thereof. "Fun, right?"

Unlike Hank, David offered no compliments. Rigidity, from the firm set of his mouth to his clenched fists, was his sole response.

"Well," she said, "I've got to run. Thanks for the well-wishes." Before he said another word, she dashed out the door.

Chapter Thirteen

David stared at Vivi as she receded into the evening. He'd never seen her face so made-up, or her lips smothered in shiny pink gloss. Her new dress swung around her thighs while she trotted toward Jackson's car. The ribbons of the halter ties trailed down her spine.

She looked like a gift-wrapped sex toy—one quick tug and the dress would fall around her ankles. Franco's clear motive burned a hole through David's brain.

Watching his family drive away filled him with angst. Guilt over his increasingly possessive impulses regarding Vivi made him capitulate to Laney's games tonight. Now he'd just let Vivi go off to be ravaged by some player. He slammed the front door closed and stalked upstairs.

He pushed open the bedroom door. "Let's set this all aside until tomorrow. I don't want to miss the whole show."

Several lit candles projecting flickering light around the room stopped him short. Laney sat straddling the corner of the bed wearing only black lace underwear.

"Actually, I thought of a better way to channel our frustration." She leaned forward with her palms pressed together on the mattress between her thighs, pushing her full bosom front and center.

"Wow, you change gears quickly," David stalled. Sex was the last thing he wanted right now. An unusual and disturbing reaction.

Bent on seduction, Laney rose and reached out for him. She cupped his face with her hands and kissed him, but he felt antsy, not tempted. She tugged him onto the bed. Within seconds he disengaged.

"Not now, Laney." Zero interest. "It'll be rushed."

She propped herself up on her elbows. "You'd rather run off to a party of strangers than make love with me?"

"Don't pull that crap." He sat up, annoyed by her manipulation. "We've been planning this evening with my family for days. I want to hear Vivi sing. Afterward you and I can resolve these issues and think about sex."

"Sex." She muttered as she sat on her calves. "In Hong Kong you never had any problem making time for *sex*. This week you've been distracted by other things, other people."

"Don't make me feel bad about making up for lost time with my brother and sister."

"Don't forget Vivi. You're making up for lost time there, too, aren't you?" Laney crossed her arms.

"You know what, I'm not letting you bait me into another argument now." David inhaled slowly while walking toward the door. "Right now we can get a quick drink before the party, or not. Either way, I won't defend my desire to reconnect with the people I love."

"Oh, so there are some people you love. You can say the word, it seems." Laney slid off the bed and lifted her dress off the nearby chaise.

David's self-reproach diminished his anger by a small margin. Clearly he'd been completely wrong about Laney's lack of interest in hearts and flowers.

"Laney, I'm sorry you're upset, but can we please put it aside until tomorrow?"

"Fine." She slipped on her sandals. "But this conversation isn't over, David, not by a long shot."

"Don't I know it," he mumbled to himself. Hell, nothing was going according to plan, and he didn't like unplanned outcomes.

~

David escorted Laney to Hotel Manisses for a private drink. They sat at a tall bar table beside a brick wall, giving them a full view of the lively bar. Yet neither the dynamic atmosphere nor any topic of conversation shook Laney loose.

Other couples were sharing drinks or meals, whispering to and touching each other. All around him, David noticed normal people laughing together, enjoying their vacation. Not him. He'd made one misstep after another, culminating in the present standoff with his soon-to-be ex-girlfriend.

"Tell me the truth, David." Laney set her chin in her palm. "What's really between you and Vivi?"

"Thirteen years of close friendship." It wasn't exactly a lie.

"You never mentioned her to me before, yet you've been preoccupied with her since she arrived. You look for any excuse to steal a few minutes alone with her."

"I'm trying to reestablish my relationship with her, just like with Jackson and Cat. Our friendship is . . . different, but it's always been platonic." David knew his defensiveness wouldn't help his argument. He also knew he didn't want to have this conversation in public.

"Either you're lying to me, or you're lying to yourself." She sat back in her chair, frowning. "Maybe both."

"Please drop the inquisition." David dragged his hand through his hair for the millionth time that day. "Can't we just enjoy a drink and go to the party?"

Laney simply crossed her arms and stared at him.

He mentally threw his hands up at her unwillingness to set aside her own anger. Glancing at his watch, he saw the band had started playing thirty minutes ago. Determined not to miss the entire show, he paid the tab and escorted Laney to her car.

By the time they'd arrived, the sky was growing dark. He couldn't determine much about the property, but light shone from every window of the large home. Cars were parked all along the driveway and on parts of the yard. David squeezed Laney's small car into a space not far from the front of the house.

Music drifted through the air. He listened, unable to discern the song or Vivi's voice from where they stood. He reached for Laney's hand out of habit. Naturally she withheld it and began walking away. He kicked the gravel in frustration and then caught up to her as she strode toward the backyard.

They both momentarily halted as they rounded the corner of the house. John Slater knew how to throw a party. Thousands of white lights were strung throughout the massive tent. Tall cocktail tables sat along the perimeter of a parquet dance floor, each one draped in dark table linens and topped with a hurricane candle arrangement. Separate bars were set up in the two far corners of the tented area. The guests were dancing, chatting, and drinking.

David's gaze hovered over the crowd until he caught a glimpse of Vivi as the band finished its song. A grin spread across his face just before he spotted Cat, Jackson, and Hank on the right side of the tent. He weaved through the crowd to reach them, dragging Laney behind him.

"How's it going?" he asked Cat just as the twang of guitar strings and heavy drum beats erupted onstage.

"Great!" she shouted.

The thumping music pulled his attention back to the stage. Vivi stepped up to the microphone. He moved sideways to gain a better view through the crowd. She swayed to the beat and pasted a sly smile on her lips before crooning the beginning of Tristan Prettyman's "My Oh My."

His eyebrows scaled his forehead in surprise. Vivi's voice was as unexpected and soulful as everything else about her. He stood mesmerized by her sultry stage presence and bluesy vocals.

As the crowd clapped along, David's heartbeat matched the rhythm of the song. Just like when he'd first seen her on the dock after so long apart, observing her onstage cast her in a different light. She was the same, yet different. And damn, her sexy voice stirred unbidden desire.

The band announced its final song, one in which Vivi provided harmony. He calculated he had about four minutes to sneak away to share a private moment with her after the show.

Cupping his hand behind Laney's ear, he asked, "Would you like a drink? I'm going to get a beer."

"Fine." She shrugged. "White wine, please."

Her cool demeanor hardly registered with him as he took off in search of Vivi. Skirting along the edge of the crowd, he drew closer to the stage as the music ended and the band took a final bow. From a distance, he watched her jump down from the platform, straight into Franco's arms.

She didn't see David, who stood a few feet away, obscured by other guests. He watched her lips break into a dazzling smile in response to something Franco whispered. Chills radiated down his spine when Franco curved his hand around the nape of her neck and kissed her, a kiss she returned.

Air rushed from David's lungs as if he'd been karate kicked in the chest. The force of his jealousy sent him stumbling backward, his thoughts scattering, while a deep ache unfurled in his heart.

He'd convinced himself they could never be together. He still believed it. But for the first time ever, he realized one day, maybe very soon, she'd belong to someone else. Someday she'd brighten another man's life instead of his. And whoever that man was, he might curtail Vivi's friendships with other men, including David.

Worst of all, David would be forced to witness her lover at major events and holidays, because Vivi would always be part of his family. He'd never considered how it would feel to lose his place in her life.

Now he knew.

It was crushing.

In a haze of depressing thoughts, he tottered to the bar to order some drinks. When he returned to his family, Jackson tilted his head inquisitively.

"What's with the scowl?" Jackson asked, raising his beer in the air.

"Nothing." David handed Laney her wine. The image of Vivi kissing Franco replayed. He hated the imprint it left on his heart. "Just fighting the crowds."

"*Hey!*" his sister shouted, hailing the arrival of Vivi and Franco, who were now holding hands.

David wiped his face clear of any emotion, but his body stiffened of its own volition. He could barely look at Vivi. Franco's victorious grin was the worst. When he noticed Franco's thumb gently rubbing the top of Vivi's hand, his stomach clenched again.

"You were awesome." Cat embraced Vivi. "Just awesome!"

Cat rocked Vivi back and forth before passing her to Jackson, who lifted her off the ground. Hank planted a quick congratulatory peck on her cheek while David witnessed the entire scene unfold from a distance, wishing he could disappear.

Everything he thought he knew about himself, his life, and his needs was disintegrating. Once again, he felt like a stranger in his own family. He'd closed himself off for so long, now he didn't know how to come back.

Laney elbowed him, waking him from his hazy thoughts. Vivi appeared to be awaiting a response, but he hadn't heard her question.

"Amazing, Vivi." He smiled, withholding from touching her. He couldn't risk it. Not with Franco, Laney, and everyone else watching him. "You were magnificent."

"Thanks," she said. Although just inches apart, he felt the distance between them widening. "I'm glad you caught part of the show."

"Me too." Damn, the air felt close and hot. His jaw ached from grinding his teeth.

Salvation arrived in the form of the DJ, who started off his set with a pounding Usher dance tune, silencing David's thoughts.

Vivi looked at David as if she were expecting something more from him. For a split second of pure insanity, he considered picking her up, tossing her over his shoulder, and running off. When he remained stoic, she turned to Franco.

"Do you dance?"

"*Sì.*"

David watched them vanish into the crowd. A spinning disco ball bounced light across the congested tent. He watched his sister head to the center of the floor with a stranger. Next, Hank followed a cute girl into the crowd.

Needing something to take his mind off Vivi, David held out his hand to Laney, but she declined his invitation. Apparently she wasn't finished punishing him. He'd lost track of his infractions by this point.

Fuck it. Defiantly, he ground out, "If you're intent on punishing me, I may as well do something to make it worth your while." He grabbed Jackson's arm and tugged. "Let's go find something stronger than beer."

~

By midnight, the crowd had begun to thin. Empty glasses and crumpled napkins laid discarded on the tables under the tent. David had spent a majority of the evening tossing back drinks with Jackson and covertly spying on Vivi as she danced, flirted, and enjoyed the party with Franco, Cat, and dozens of others.

He'd thought the alcohol would be a good distraction. But no amount of whiskey could numb him to the fact that he was losing one of the most important relationships of his life.

When he noticed Laney and Cat waving them over, he and his brother crossed the floor on unsteady legs. The ladies announced their desire to go home. After thanking the host, the group strode across the lawn in search of their cars.

Along the way, David realized Vivi wasn't with them. He'd barely spoken with her all night. If she'd noticed him keeping his distance, she hadn't seemed to care. Thinking of Franco touching and kissing her made him feel like throwing up.

"Where'sh Vivi?" he slurred.

"She's not ready to leave." Cat shrugged. "Franco will bring her home later."

"Oh no!" He slammed the top of the car with his hand. "He'll use her. Or what if he's too drunk to drive?"

"Look who's talking! Laney better have the keys." Cat rolled her eyes and snapped her fingers to get Jackson's attention before pushing him into the car. "Vivi's a big girl, David. She'll be okay."

Cat and Hank climbed into the Jeep. Laney stood on the driver's side of her car, glaring at David over the rooftop. Already in the doghouse, he had little left to lose. He held up his hand with all five fingers stretched wide.

"Back in five."

"I'll come with you," Laney said.

"No. Wait here."

He jogged toward the tent—possibly zigzagging. He couldn't be sure. Within a minute, he saw Franco, who was standing very close to a pretty brunette.

"Where's Vivi?" David refrained from clocking the womanizer in the face.

"Inside. She'll be right back," he answered before returning his attention to his friend.

David strode toward the house and surprised Vivi as she came through the back door.

"Hey." She smiled. "I thought you all left."

"Not without you." He grabbed her arm and pushed her back into the house. "Let's go."

"David, I'm staying." She shrugged loose from his grip. "I'll be home later."

"No, you're not." He noticed her react to his harsh, if slightly garbled, tone.

"You smell like whiskey!" Her blue eyes widened. "Are you drunk?"

Maybe. That was beside the point. To avoid a public argument, he tugged her into a bathroom and pinned her against the door.

"You're not staying here, dressed in nothing, with that jerk." His thoughts were as jumbled as his words sounded. "You could end up dead or worse." Worse than dead made no sense, but he couldn't focus.

He planted his hands on the door, just above each of her shoulders, bracing himself for a fight. He'd become accustomed to arguing with Laney, so he could withstand whatever Vivi threw at him.

Rather than fight with him, she softened. "Don't worry, David. I won't do anything stupid."

He didn't want her understanding. He wanted to battle—to release his anger at her for making him feel this way.

"You barely know him. See him tomorrow, but come home now." He leaned his forehead against the door. His mouth settled an inch from her ear. *Mmm*. Her hair and skin smelled like flowers. "Please. Don't make me crazy. Come home."

"Make you crazy?" She rested her hands on his chest to gently push him away. "How am I making you crazy?"

"You're slipping away." He fingered a lock of her hair between his thumb and forefinger. While toying with it, he murmured into her ear. "You're pushing me away. I can feel it, and it's driving me crazy."

A short silence ensued.

"I'm right here," she whispered.

He felt his breathing change, and hers fell shallow, too. He drew his head back to catch her staring at his lips. Her pupils were large and dark. Magically, all the noise, people, and background faded away, disappearing all around them, leaving them alone in their private cocoon.

"Vivi," he said, sliding a glance to her mouth just as she licked her lips. "Vivi." His voice sounded husky to his own ears.

He'd been eyeing those lips all week. Without further thought, he uttered, "Kiss me," and then sucked her pouty lip between his own. He nipped it gently with his teeth, making her gasp. When she didn't pull away, he slid his tongue into her sweet, hot mouth.

His fingers trailed down from her jaw to the base of her neck, where he felt her pulse racing. Her reaction elicited a groan of pleasure and sudden heaviness in his groin. He deepened his kiss. Her hands tenderly touched his face before threading through his hair. Pulling back, he kissed her eyelids and the tip of her nose before reclaiming her mouth.

She shivered in his arms, sending him up in flames. His erection grew insistent and hard as he wrapped his hands around her waist and lifted her. She clamped her legs around his hips. *Vivi.*

"I want you," he ground out between kisses on her mouth and neck. "God, I want you, Vivi."

She mewled and clung to him, melding her body against his. Despite his frenzy, her gentle touch moved deliberately, exploring him. It felt so good.

So damn good.

He stumbled around the small bathroom, eventually setting her on the vanity. He felt drunk, but not from the Jack Daniel's. Her taste, smell, and feel intoxicated him.

His hands slid down her bare back before coming under her breasts. He brushed his thumbs against the flimsy halter top and felt her nipples tighten. She moaned and arched into his caress, sending his emotions careening over the edge.

A growl resounded in the back of his throat as he tucked the tip of his thumb under the fabric of the halter. He nudged it aside, but then a sudden bang at the door stilled them both. Wide-eyed, they both stopped breathing when Laney's voice rang out.

"David, Vivi, are you in there?"

David stared at Vivi, blinking, his mind confused. Before he reacted, Vivi answered.

"It's me, Laney."

"I heard moaning. What's going on?"

"I'm not feeling well." Vivi's face drained of color. "Too much excitement."

"Where's David?" Laney demanded.

Without skipping a beat, Vivi replied, "Probably looking for you. He stormed off after I refused to go home." She met his eyes without blinking.

For a strained second, no one spoke.

Laney broke the silence from beyond the door. "Okay. See you tomorrow."

David remained fastened to Vivi in a mix of passion, panic, and wonder. She wriggled free of his hold and fixed her dress before sliding off the vanity. He held on to her arm, but she stiffened and looked away.

"Hold on." He rubbed his face with both hands and shook his head. "God, just wait a second. We'll talk tomorrow. Come home now. Please, Vivi."

"No." She bore her cold, dewy eyes into his, every trace of desire wiped clean from her gaze. "You go home with your girlfriend. I'm staying." She smoothed her hair with her hands. "Please, leave me alone."

"Vivi," he started, unable to form a coherent thought.

Before opening the door, she directed him to hide in the bathtub. "Wait an extra minute."

She cracked the door open, peered into the hall, and then disappeared from sight, taking his heart with her.

His erection hadn't fully subsided, making it awkward to stalk out of the house and back to the car. Miraculously, Laney hadn't yet returned. She must be searching for him in the tent. Maybe she'd believed Vivi's lie. He hoped so because he didn't want to have the big breakup talk in front of his family.

Remorse washed over him for what he'd done. He'd reduced them both to being liars and cheats. If he wasn't careful, he'd hurt everyone he cared about and be left with nothing, not even his self-respect. He'd become like his father—his worst fear come true.

Laney returned to the car in a black mood. "Did you get lost?" At least her wry remark was an improvement over her earlier silence.

"Sorry." He couldn't look at her, still feeling flush from kissing Vivi. Irrationally, he felt pissed at Laney for interrupting. He'd behaved abominably, and yet, given the chance, he'd probably do it again.

And then some.

"Me too." Laney started the ignition and backed out of the turnaround.

He wasn't sure whether she'd intended to apologize for her bitchy behavior, or merely remark on the lame state of his own. Worse, he wasn't sure he cared. He closed his eyes to escape, but couldn't.

He was stuck.

And Vivi was with Franco.

Chapter Fourteen

Keep it together. Keep. It. Together. Vivi slipped down the hall and ducked into a bedroom. Closing the door behind her, she set one hand against it and bent over at her waist, gasping for air. Tears threatened to spill from her eyes.

She turned, leaned her back against the door, and clapped her hands over her mouth to smother the sob stuck in her throat. Slowly, she slid her bottom down to the floor, then hugged her knees.

When Panzer appeared out of nowhere, she yelped. He whimpered and sniffed her, licking her cheek.

Minutes passed while she hugged and petted the dog. His was the most peaceful company she'd enjoyed all week. He stayed with her, apparently sensing her pain, as her thoughts spun. Had David left? Did Laney hear them? How would she face them in the morning? What would Cat think? Vivi shook her head to clear each thought, only to face another onslaught. Guilt, shock, joy, and shame commingled. With each passing second, the creases in her forehead deepened.

Thirteen years! She'd spent thirteen years fantasizing about David, imagining his kiss. In none of her countless dreams did those kisses end with her alone in the dark.

On the floor.

Unhappy.

She dabbed her eyes with the base of her palms before swiping her runny nose with the back of her hand. Gross, but she couldn't care less. A choked laugh escaped her throat as images of other teary moments, on the floors of high school bathrooms or house parties, drifted through her memory. She was pretty sure she'd used her arm as a tissue then, too. Some things never changed.

Her breathing resumed a normal pace as her shock wore off. Once calmed, she replayed the bathroom scene.

David's eyes had been filled with longing and tenderness. He'd desired her. He'd initiated those kisses. It had been everything she'd ever wanted until Laney intruded.

Shame gushed forward, swamping her. How could she kiss another woman's boyfriend—even if he should have been hers from the beginning? She had no right. Good girls—nice girls like Vivi—didn't steal another woman's man. Not even when that woman deserved it.

But David had kissed her. Of course, he'd been shit-faced drunk after having lived under tremendous strain for months, which explained why he trapped her in the bathroom and mauled her with kisses. Kisses that made her knees go weak. Kisses that set her body aflame. Kisses that promised the ever-elusive love she craved.

Once again she'd been the fool, and now she had no one to talk to. Cat wanted David and Vivi apart, and so she wouldn't be receptive to the discussion. Jackson would rip into David if he learned what had happened. And although Hank seemed to be a good listener, this incident would only prove him right about David's self-centeredness.

She'd have to handle it on her own. "You're the only one I can cry to, Panzer." She scratched behind his ears, recalling the many dogs she'd shared her secrets with throughout the years.

Resting her head against the door, she realized a private pity party wouldn't help matters. Heaving a sigh, Vivi dragged herself off the floor.

She leaned against the white wicker dresser, gazing into the mirror hanging on the wall behind it. Hopeless. No amount of finger combing could fix her now. Licking her thumbs, she swiped the mascara smudges from under her eyes. Even in the dark room she could see her frazzled appearance. What would she tell Franco?

Then panic struck. What if David was right about Franco's expectations? She couldn't even imagine kissing Franco again while the taste of David's lips lingered on her own.

Drawing a deep breath, she blew it out slowly and spoke to her reflection. "You can do this." Then she bent down to pat Panzer's head. "Wish me luck."

The brisk night air helped revive her once she stepped outside. Franco stood several yards away, talking with two friends. She hoped he didn't expect an explanation as to why she'd been gone so long. They weren't officially a couple. No promises were made. In fact, they'd only just shared their first real kiss tonight. Who knew how many other women he might be seeing?

Dizzy from the round of unanswerable questions, she smacked her own head with her open hand. Now wasn't the time or place for any confessions. Satisfied with her decision, she meandered over to Franco.

"Vivi?" His mouth fell open. He excused himself from his friends and led her a few steps away. "What happened?"

Darn it. Her freakin' open-book face gave her away.

"David and I . . ." She rubbed her forehead, then looked him straight in the eye. "David and I argued."

"About what?"

"He wanted me to leave." She paused. "It got heated."

"Did he try to force you?"

Force her? Hardly. She'd thrown herself into his embrace with every ounce of heart and soul at her disposal. Of course, that's not what Franco meant.

"No." Vivi chewed her lip. "It's all good now. Let's forget it. Who were those people you were talking with?"

Franco tucked a lock of hair behind her ear. He raised her chin with his fingers. "Should I take you home?"

"No! Let's go dance, or get a drink or something."

He shook his head. "I don't think so. Your mood is ruined, so let's not pretend. I'll take you home."

"The party isn't over yet," she protested.

"It is for you." Franco sipped from his glass before looking at her. "I'd like to get to know you better, but I'm not interested in wasting my time. I think your heart is engaged elsewhere."

Vivi couldn't tell another lie, so she laughed. It started with a giggle then exploded into yawping laughter. The more quizzical Franco's gaze became, the harder she laughed. He crossed his arms but then grinned at her obvious breakdown. Eventually, she wiped a stray tear from her cheek and settled herself.

Placing her hand on his forearm, she said, "Oh, Franco. I wish I hadn't wasted years pining after a man who never wanted me. Yet I did, and I can't honestly say I'm done, although I desperately want to be." Sighing, she nudged closer to him. "Can we maybe spend some time together in New York? Casually. No strings, no promises? If nothing else, I'd like to be friends."

"*Sì, bella.*" He tugged her into a warm hug. His cologne smelled sexy as she nestled against the hard muscles of his chest. For an instant, she wondered how different her life might be if she'd never met David. "Now I'm taking you home."

~

"Hey, sleepyhead, wake up." Cat chucked a pillow at Vivi. "What time did you come home?"

Vivi blinked, confused by her surroundings. Her breath caught as those few erotic moments in the bathroom with David swept through her memory. Shaking her head to erase them, she stretched and avoided Cat's stare. Now she had two major secrets to keep.

"I didn't stay much longer than you." She risked a glimpse at Cat. "You were zonked when I came in."

"The party rocked. I overdid it with the drinking and dancing. I hope no one tags me in any Facebook photos. I can't deal with Justin, or my agent, grilling me about my every move." Cat grimaced. "You must feel great after killing it last night! We should check YouTube to see if anyone posted video of the band. Maybe you should hit the road with them again soon."

"Ha, ha." Vivi rolled her eyes. "Band life isn't for me. But it was totally fun, for *one* night."

"Vivi LeBrun, Rock Star!" Cat's hands outlined an imaginary marquee as she giggled. "I don't know, I think you should reconsider."

Vivi sat up. Her body felt like she'd gone several rounds with Manny Pacquiao.

"So, anything interesting happen with Franco?" Cat's eyes danced with curiosity. "Confession time. I'll keep your secrets."

Yikes. Vivi doubted it. In fact, Cat might have a stroke if she learned about the steamy make-out session with David. It sucked not to be able to confide in her best friend about how all her dreams almost came true.

"I didn't sleep with him, if that's what you're asking." Vivi winced at Cat's disappointed reaction. "We're going to get together in New York." Seeing Cat's skeptical expression, she volunteered, "We kissed."

Of course, it hadn't compared with David's sensual kisses. Vivi shivered at the memory. Unfortunately, Cat mistook the cause of her reaction.

"Ooh, that good, huh?" Cat's feline smile appeared. "Okay, so there's some promise here. Progress."

Vivi merely nodded, unable to blatantly lie anymore. The number of fibs she'd indulged this week exceeded her limit. It wasn't worth it. She was uncomfortable and couldn't keep track of who knew what.

"Shall we get breakfast?" Cat stood and stretched before pulling up her covers.

Oh, God. She doubted she could face David or Laney just yet. Vivi's stomach turned over and her skin became clammy.

"Are you okay? You look sick." Cat's concern made Vivi feel worse. "Did you drink too much last night?"

"I'll be fine." She pulled herself out of bed. "Let's go out to breakfast, just the two of us."

"Why?"

"We haven't spent much time together this week. Plus, I don't like being the center of attention. I'd rather avoid everyone this morning." Would Cat buy her cover story?

"Fine." Cat shrugged. "Get moving. I'm starving."

Unfortunately, they needed to borrow Jackson's car, which meant going upstairs to get the keys.

"There she is, Miss Superstar." Jackson grinned and pointed at the table, which was loaded with bacon, scrambled eggs, bagels, and juice. "Sit down. We made you breakfast."

Hank pulled out a dining chair and gestured for her to sit.

Crud. Naturally fate would punish her for lying. The story of her life. She forced a tight smile and sat at the table. At least David and Laney were still asleep. Picturing them wrapped up together in bed put a frown on her face. She straightened her shoulders and flashed another phony smile.

"This is unexpected, although you're making me uncomfortable." She unfolded a napkin on her lap and avoided eye contact, fearing they'd all see the truth about everything if they looked in her eyes. "All I did was sing."

"Hell, V. What a kick-ass party." Jackson sat beside her and chugged some OJ. "Besides, you were awesome. If you get bored with teaching, you could hit the road," he teased before tugging on her hair.

"With my fan club of three? I'd end up even more broke than I already am." She laughed at the thought, which felt good. "But thanks for the compliment. Now, however, let's change the subject. I hate being the center of attention."

"Yeah. That's how I know you're not really my sister." He shot a look at Catalina, who had the grace to chuckle.

The lighthearted banter eased Vivi's nerves. After a few bites of the greasy breakfast, her stomach settled. Amid the chatter, she mentally repeated the words *I think I can*, willing herself to become like the little blue engine in one of the children's books her mother used to read aloud.

The memory of her mother's embrace and soft voice momentarily blinded Vivi, who was unaccustomed to pleasant memories from her childhood. *Quit dreaming.* She had neither a mother nor best friend to turn to today. Robotically, she spread strawberry cream cheese on her bagel.

David's bedroom door squeaked open, pulling her from her haze. Vivi froze. Her stomach then fell to the ground, which prompted her to move.

She bounded from her seat, drawing a cockeyed stare from Cat, pushing through the dizziness that threatened to fell her.

"I feel sick. Need some fresh air. I'll be back in a bit." She slipped out through the glass door, fled across the lawn, and disappeared down the rickety steps.

She stopped on the landing where David had revealed everything the other day. With the cliff to her back, she sat and let the sun warm her face while trying to block out the pained sound of the gulls' cries.

Leaning forward, she rested her hands on the railing and lowered her chin onto them. An enormous bumblebee hovered over the flowering shrubs near the staircase. The fat bee didn't have problems. Vivi wished she could sprout wings and join him, collecting nectar and spreading beauty throughout the world.

She stared out over the ocean. Its immensity often put her own problems in perspective. Today the horizon offered no comfort. She bent over with her arms wrapped around her waist, wishing she could throw up and feel better.

It was just a kiss. It didn't mean anything. Oh, she wished it meant everything. It never would. David probably woke up filled with regret, if he even remembered last night at all.

With her eyes closed, she hugged herself harder and thought about Franco. At lunch yesterday she'd considered him a bit superficial. Then last night he showed compassion.

Other women fell for the bad boys, but kindness had always been Vivi's Achilles' heel. Maybe once she returned home to her normal routines, she would take a stab at a second date with Franco.

That still left two more nights here with David and Laney. Somehow she'd have to face them. More importantly, she'd have to salvage some type of friendship with David, if not to honor their shared history, then at least for the sake of her relationships with Cat and Jackson.

"Vivi." David's voice sounded tentative.

She started and then dropped her head.

He sat next to her, turning his back toward the ocean so he could face her. Gripping the bench with his hands, he leaned back slightly to stretch his legs out in front of him. Their bodies were mere inches apart, yet Vivi felt as if they were sitting on either side of a high-voltage fence.

"I'm glad you got home safely," he began. "I couldn't fall asleep until I heard you come in."

Her head snapped toward him. Everything and nothing whipped through her mind in a jumble. Why was he suddenly so attentive? Did he mean anything he said last night? What was happening with him and Laney? She stared at him, unable to give voice to any of her thoughts.

When he reached for her hand, she reflexively pulled away. Self-defense. If he touched her, she'd either slap him or collapse against him and never let go. He winced and inhaled the salt air.

"I'm sorry about last night." He rubbed his face with his palms and then rested them on his thighs. He stared up at the cliff tops before looking at her. "Seems I'm apologizing to you every day this week. Actually, I've behaved badly toward you since my mom died."

He covered his eyes with his hands and shook his bowed head. Still, she couldn't respond. Her heart thumped hard against her chest. It hurt.

"This thing with my dad has really messed me up, Vivi. I hate the fact that I can't seem to get control of it, or myself." David shifted his position and faced her, looking somber. "I think we should talk about last night, and why it happened." When she didn't reply, he asked, "Are you so disgusted now you can't even stand speaking with me?"

Vivi heard the heavy sound of her uneven breathing. Her throat felt strangled. Breaking eye contact, she stood and leaned against the railing. Once at a safe distance, she reined in her thoughts, took a big breath, and set them free in a tumble of words.

"When your mom died, I gave you space, assuming you'd eventually turn to me the way I'd always turned to you. Then you left us all without looking back. When Cat told me you came home, I couldn't wait to see you, even though you never bothered to find time for me. Then, at the docks, you blindsided me with the news of your girlfriend. I knew then that nothing I'd ever hoped for or believed had been true."

Her eyes filled with tears, but she continued to speak through her tight throat.

"I pushed through that disappointment because I thought, if nothing else, we'd always remain great friends. Your friendship has meant so much to me. I know it couldn't have been easy to have always been careful with my feelings. I'm sure you were pressured by your family to be patient, even when I suffocated you—"

"Vivi, you didn't—" David interrupted.

"Let me finish, please. Despite my clingy ways, somehow we built this incredible friendship. I know you care about me, and I believe *you* believe everything you've said this week in your campaign to reconnect. But surely you see nothing is the same now. Not our friendship, not you . . . and not me. We've changed. I'm honored you confided in me about your dad. I'm so sorry for what's happened, and I'm most sorry for how it has changed you, and us.

"Maybe last night you were grasping for what's been lost. But there's no going backward. No stolen kiss can recover what's gone. It was a mistake, and we both know it. At least it didn't go too far. Nothing has happened that can't be overcome. So let's start fresh and create a new friendship. We'll see each other in New York sometimes, just like I see Jackson. Before we know it, everything will settle and be fine. You can work through your problems with Laney. I'll get back to living my life with whoever comes along. And once in a while we'll see each other."

She inhaled through her nose. "We can do this, David." She laughed at herself. "Well, of course, *you* can do this. You already have. I guess what I mean is *I* can do this, and you don't have to feel guilty about anything. We'll forget all about our little indiscretion. Maybe someday we'll even laugh about it."

Unloading her feelings provided a rush of relief. To speak the truth finally! A grin split her face. "Oh, David, I already feel so much better. You have no idea. Thanks for listening."

"You didn't give me a choice, did you?" He rose to his feet and stepped toward her. "Now it's my turn. And I have a lot to say. Things I need to tell you."

Surprising herself, she shook her head. "No." She didn't want apologies, or to hear him repeat what a "special friend" she would always be—the label that had kept her clinging to fantasies far too long.

His chin withdrew. When he opened his mouth to respond, Vivi covered it with her hand. He grabbed her waist while waiting for her to remove her hand. His touch heated her body like a furnace.

"Just let it go." Keeping her hand over his mouth, she rested her head against his chest and breathed in deeply, savoring their embrace. "Please. Please don't say anything." She felt him close his mouth, so she withdrew her hand and backed away, loosening his fingers from her body.

He looked grave standing there staring at her. "Vivi, wait. You don't understand."

Her eyes welled up, so she backed away. "I'll see you later." Spinning on her heel, she started up the steps without looking back.

I did it. It's done. I'm okay. She inhaled several cleansing breaths and started across the lawn. Wiping away a tear from her eye, she squinted up at the house. Oh, fudge. Laney stood on the deck staring at her through venomous eyes.

Had David confessed to her? She pleaded with God to make Cat, Jackson, or Hank appear and spare her a confrontation, but God wasn't granting wishes to dishonest women today. With great effort, she lumbered up the steps to meet her foe.

"Good morning, Laney." Vivi flashed a benign smile and tried ducking inside the open door.

"Hold on, Vivi." Laney crossed her arms. "We need to talk."

"Do we?" Vivi halted in the open doorway, preserving a quick escape route. "About what?"

"David."

"What about him?" Heat crept up into Vivi's cheeks and ears.

"I'd like you to back off." Laney fastened her with an accusing glare.

"I'm sorry, what are you talking about?" Vivi leaned against the doorjamb for support, certain her knees might give out at any minute. Her indignity was undercut by the fact that she believed she deserved every bit of the anger Laney was about to unleash.

"Let's not play games. I'm not an idiot. I can tell something is going on between you and David. I know you have a long history, and I can guess you probably had a big crush on him for years. But it isn't fair to exploit his desire to reestablish his family relationships for your own benefit. Besides, he's here with me, Vivi. We've been together for seven months." She crossed her arms. "You've had years to win his heart, and failed. You seem nice enough, although you're really not his type."

Vivi should be sputtering. Instead, laughter bubbled up from her chest. "Trust me, Laney, no one knows that better than I do." She should've turned to go, but something made her want to fight back. Maybe the memory of David's panting in her ear triggered something vengeful. Maybe it was nothing more than jealousy. She didn't know; she didn't care. Spinning back on her heel, she said, "But you know, you're not his type, either."

Laney's eyes widened before her features twisted into an ugly knot. "You have no idea what you're talking about. Our relationship is perfect."

"Really? Then what's got you so worked up?"

"Your games are ruining our vacation." Laney's eyes narrowed. "You're playing on his sensitivities. He told me he cares for you deeply *as a friend.* So again, I'm asking you, please don't interfere now when he and I are close to making a significant commitment. I don't know what happened between you two last night, but it's me he sleeps with every night. No one else."

"Sex isn't love, Laney. I suspect you know that or you wouldn't be feeling so threatened." Vivi pushed off the doorjamb, now fully enraged. "I know David better than anybody. Trust me when I tell you, you really are *not* his type."

"I am exactly his type. We're equal in intelligence, ambition, looks, and refinement. Unlike you and him, we're perfectly matched."

"After all this time, you still don't know him at all. It's almost sad." Vivi stepped closer to Laney. "You have to 'feel' David, not 'think' him. Since we've already established you lack much heart, you'll never be able to touch his."

"I'm a thousand times closer than you'll ever be."

Suddenly Vivi noticed Laney blanch, so she glanced around the deck. Without realizing when it had happened, they'd gained an audience. Cat and Hank stood just inside the open door. David was standing, slack-jawed, behind Vivi.

Vivi's eyes squeezed shut. How much had everyone heard?

"What's going on?" David looked like he might smash something to bits.

Laney turned her rage into tears. "Vivi says you'll never love me because I lack a heart. She's not as sweet as she appears to be, is she?"

Vivi's eyes flew open in protest. Before she could speak, David stormed toward Laney.

"Upstairs, now." His clipped tone brooked no argument. Without sparing a glance at Vivi, his sister, or Hank, he ushered Laney inside. Seconds later, they disappeared from view.

"What the hell was that about?" Cat asked.

Vivi felt her mouth open and close. Defeated, she shrugged. "She thinks I'm trying to steal her man." Moments ago she'd delivered the best speech of her life to David. Now she'd blown it to hell by baiting Laney.

"Vivi?" Cat tilted her head, eyes wide. "I thought you were over him."

Her concerned tone nearly brought Vivi to tears. Riding to the rescue as always, Hank broke the tension by joking, "Well, Vivi, you sure do put on a good show. Singing, drama . . . what's next? Save me a seat, will you?"

His green eyes offered understanding. *I could kiss you*, she thought, then stifled a laugh at how utterly inappropriate her response was under the circumstances.

Despite utter emotional exhaustion, Vivi forced herself to laugh. "Perhaps I could get a job working for Ringling Brothers."

Through the ceiling, terse voices caught everyone's attention.

"Maybe we ought to leave the house to give them some privacy," Vivi suggested.

"I'll grab Jackson and meet you both outside," Hank offered.

~

After a long day in town and a late dinner, Vivi, Cat, Jackson, and Hank brought two bottles of wine and several hurricane lanterns outside. A warm breeze skimmed over them as they settled into the deck chairs. Despite the disconcerting day, listening to her friends' idle chatter soothed Vivi's battered soul.

"I wonder if David saw Dad's e-mail yet," Cat said to Jackson.

"It'll be the icing on the cake of his shitty day." Jackson puffed his cigar. "He won't be happy, that's for sure."

"Why would he be unhappy about your dad getting remarried?" Hank glanced from Cat to Jackson. "Doesn't he like Janet?"

"We don't know what the problem is." Jackson flicked his ash and gazed out to the sea. "Neither Dad nor David will tell us why they don't speak anymore. I'm sick of it."

Vivi sat in her chair, feeling near the edge of some kind of breakdown. She could only imagine David's reaction to his dad's announcement today. Hostility. Anguish. Outrage. All were too weak to describe what he must be feeling. And if he refused to accept the marriage, it would widen the rift between him and his family.

She desperately wanted to help. She wanted to *tell*, but she wouldn't. Yet she had to do something. "David had a rare bond with your mom. Maybe he's angry about your dad dating again and that's why they're not talking," Vivi volunteered.

"Hell, Vivi. We *all* miss Mom. But she's dead. My dad deserves to move on. He's getting married and David's got to wrap his head around it. Janet's a little young, but I don't think she's a gold digger." Jackson guzzled his wine and placed the empty glass on the deck beside his chair. "She's got a lot in common with Dad. They're happy. Besides, David and Dad's fight began before Janet came on the scene."

Oh, Jackson, you're so wrong.

"David's never been irrational. He must have a good reason for this stalemate. Maybe you could give him the benefit of the doubt?"

"Guess I'm not surprised to hear you defend him, even after all this time." Jackson inhaled deeply and then turned to look across the sea. For once her lifelong love of David came in handy. No one suspected anything else to be the root of her attempts to mend fences.

Conversation remained subdued, leaving Vivi's mind free to drift back to David. He'd texted Jackson just before seven o'clock. Apparently he'd decided to take the ferry with Laney and asked Jackson to bring his clothes back to New York for him on Sunday.

Vivi had no right to be disappointed he'd gone with Laney. She'd made her peace with David that morning. She'd meant every word at the time. The chance to be a different kind of woman and friend seemed like the mature response.

Unfortunately, the truth grew clearer as day turned into night. And the truth was she had wanted him to choose her. He hadn't, and it hurt. Her foolish heart would never learn. After all this time, she remained as sappy as a thirteen-year-old fool in love.

Then, magically, David appeared in the living room.

"Yo, I thought you left," Jackson called through the screen door, stopping David.

"Well, I'm back." His disheveled hair and clothing revealed exhaustion as his empty gaze slid past everyone. "Going to bed." Like a phantom, he vanished, retreating to the safe haven of his room.

Vivi bit her lip, dying to comfort him, knowing she'd have to wait for a more private time and place. Oddly, in the midst of her anxiety, she realized he'd returned without Laney. Something small and warm broke open in the deepest recess of her heart, where she stored her most fervent hopes.

An inappropriate grin tugged at the corners of her mouth. What might tomorrow bring?

Chapter Fifteen

St. Jameses' House
Five Years Ago

David dried himself off and then wrapped his towel around his waist. Christmas weekend with his family had been relaxing, but tonight he'd return to the city. He fished around inside his suitcase for his last pair of clean underwear.

While dressing, he glanced out his window and noticed Vivi's car parked in the driveway. He'd expected her to arrive earlier this afternoon. Cat had been engrossed in modeling her new clothes and texting her friends, so she'd never mentioned what kept Vivi detained.

At least she was here now, so he'd enjoy her company at dinner. Between his seventy-plus-hour work schedule and her busy senior year of college, they'd not been in touch as often this past semester. He missed her breezy e-mails, which no longer flooded his in-box.

While buttoning his shirt, a flurry of activity outside caught his attention. On closer inspection, he saw Vivi wipe her eyes before opening her car door. Without thinking, he banged on the windowpane. Her head snapped up. He waved, shrugging his shoulders in question. She barely smiled, then blew him a kiss and hopped into her car. His brows furrowed as she drove away.

Downstairs, he observed a pile of artfully wrapped boxes with elaborate bows sitting on the kitchen counter. Across the room, his mother opened the oven to retrieve the turkey.

"Here, let me." He grabbed the oven mitts from her and hauled the heavy roasting pan onto the stove. "Where'd Vivi go?"

"Home. She stopped by to deliver those." She gestured toward the packages before mixing a roux for the gravy. "Are you disappointed?"

He masked his emotions with a nonchalant shrug. "Well, I haven't talked to her in a while and was looking forward to hearing her crazy stories. My life's become rather dull lately."

His mother produced an odd smile. "Mmm. I see."

"Guess I'll have to settle for your company instead." David winked before kissing his beautiful mother's forehead. He knew he'd been blessed with a close-knit family, which he credited largely to his mother's abundant and unconditional love. "It's just as well, since you've always been my favorite lady."

She patted his cheek. "You've always been my sweetest child."

Soon after dinner, David packed his bag, grabbed his unopened gift from Vivi, and said his good-byes.

"You're leaving early," Jackson lamented.

"Some of us are expected at work early in the morning." David envied his brother's self-employed status. Unlike David, who preferred playing things safe, Jackson followed his gut. After two years spent working for a well-known construction company, he'd started his own small contracting business. In mere months, he'd cobbled together an impressive crew and secured three whole-house renovation jobs in Fairfield County.

"So quit your candy-ass career and come work for me." Jackson chuckled, eager as ever to spar with his big brother.

David wasn't in the mood for games. "Uh, pass. Thanks."

He kissed his mother and sister good-bye, slapped Jackson between the shoulders, and hugged his father.

Once alone in his car, he drove straight to Vivi's. Something was off. She'd never missed Christmas dinner with his family before.

He pulled into her driveway. Light streamed from the living room window of the dilapidated 1950s ranch home, casting an amber glow across the snow-covered lawn. He'd dropped her off dozens of times over the years, but she'd never invited him in. He suspected she didn't want him comparing her home with his family's large center-hall colonial.

Tonight, however, he didn't care what she wanted. He sensed she needed him. He shut off the ignition and headed up the walkway. A bitter wind nipped at his cheeks, filling his nostrils with the metallic smell of a New England winter night.

When the door opened, David came face-to-face with Mr. LeBrun, who looked pasty and miserable. Mr. LeBrun narrowed his eyes as if finding his way through a haze. "You're that St. James kid."

"David, sir," David replied. "Merry Christmas."

Mr. LeBrun stood in the doorway, letting the cold air rush into the house, when David heard Vivi's voice call out. "Dad, close the door!"

She appeared behind her dad, wearing flannel pajamas decorated with moose on skis. "David, what are you doing here?" She turned to her father. "It's okay, Dad, I've got it." After he wandered away, she looked down at her clothes and sighed. "Obviously we weren't expecting company. Is everything okay?"

"That's what I'm here to find out." He stepped forward. "Can I come in?"

Resigned, she shrugged. "Sure."

He almost tripped over the broom and dustpan lying in the middle of the living room floor in front of a toppled Christmas tree. Broken ornaments were strewn throughout the room.

Before he could ask any questions, Vivi's dad started to unscrew the cap of a bottle of whiskey, sending her into a panic. "No, Dad." She dashed to his side to wrest the bottle from his grip. "Water. Only water."

"Dammit, girl. Let go." He yanked at the bottle, but her grip was firm, causing him to stumble.

David caught him before he hit the ground. "Steady."

Vivi wouldn't meet David's eyes as she took her father by the arm and led him to his bedroom. "You need rest. Please go back to bed." She glanced over her shoulder at David and whispered, "Thank you."

While he waited for Vivi's return, he spied a half-eaten grilled cheese sandwich on the coffee table. *Some Christmas dinner*. Acid churned in his stomach and he swallowed the lump in his throat. Why was her life so damned hard?

When she reappeared, her cheeks were red, which only made David angrier about her circumstances.

"What happened here?" he asked, gesturing toward the tree.

Without warning, tears sprang from her eyes. She knelt to clean the mess.

"Last night my dad got so drunk he fell into the tree and started throwing up. When he passed out, I couldn't wake him, so I called nine-one-one. We spent the night in Norwalk Hospital, where they pumped his stomach and kept him on an IV. He had alcohol poisoning." She sniffed and wiped her eyes with her arm. "We got home this afternoon and I got him into bed so I could deliver the gifts to your house. He woke up an hour ago, hungry and irritable. Now I need to clean this mess and take the tree outside. But I can't lift it by myself." She began crying in earnest. "Some of these ornaments were from when my mom was alive. Now they're all gone." Tears streaked down her cheeks as she swept up the shards of glass.

David crouched beside her and cradled her against his chest. Kissing the top of her head, he murmured, "Don't cry, *Muñequita.* I'm here. I'll help." He rubbed her back as her shoulders shook. "Shhh, shhh, shhh. Please don't cry."

Forty minutes later, they'd rescued the few unbroken ornaments and untangled the lights strung around the branches. David hefted the tree up and out of the house. When he came back inside, Vivi had thrown away the last of the trash.

"Thanks, David. I'm sorry to drag you into this mess on the holiday."

"Why didn't you call last night? I hate thinking of you spending Christmas Eve alone at the hospital." His jaw tightened as he envisioned her being terrified her father might die. Not that the man offered any comfort, but without him she'd be truly alone.

"I'd never ruin your holiday with my problems."

"None of us would have minded. If we'd known what happened, you wouldn't have been alone."

"I'm too tired to argue," she said on a sigh. "I'm sure you have better things to do, too, like go home and rest."

He surveyed the dismal living room with its worn furniture and rugs. Somehow she normally managed to maintain a chipper attitude despite these conditions. Her fragile appearance belied a core of steel.

"I'm not in a rush." He went to his coat and retrieved a shiny red box from the inside pocket. "Besides, I brought you something."

Her face lit up for the first time since he'd arrived. Warmth spread through him as he watched her open his gift: two tickets to Broadway's revival of *Les Misérables.*

She squealed and bounced on her toes.

"I heard you tell my mom you've never seen a Broadway show. I got you an extra ticket so you could take Cat or another friend."

Her smile consumed her face. In those ridiculous pajamas, she looked like the proverbial kid at Christmas.

"Super! I know the perfect person to ask."

"Oh?" Curiosity spurred him to ask, "Who?"

"A great guy. Really nice, smart . . . thoughtful."

Vivi'd never mentioned other guys in her life before, so he'd simply assumed there weren't any. He was debating whether to ask a follow-up question when she rose up on her toes, grabbed him around his neck, and buried her face into his collar.

"Will you come with me?" Her breath brushed against his skin.

"Absolutely." He smiled and lifted her off the ground, pleased to have brightened her holiday. "Merry Christmas, Vivi."

"Thank you." She squeezed him a little tighter.

He placed her back on the ground and kissed her forehead. "My pleasure."

Chapter Sixteen

Present Day

With his knees pulled to his chest, David curled up in the window seat next to the living room fireplace and pressed his head against the cool glass. Wrung dry by the past twenty-four hours, the stillness of the dark house felt comforting.

When he returned from his unplanned round-trip ferry ride, he'd intentionally skirted questions about Laney, and avoided all discussion about his father's announcement.

Earlier that day, he'd stared at the horrifying save-the-date e-mail in disbelief before he vomited on the dock. His stomach muscles contracted every time he thought about his father's plans to marry Janet. Janet—the most despicable, heartless home wrecker on the planet.

His father's announcement ripped open the wounds that had only barely begun to heal. His father loved *her*? Chose *her* over his mother? Over him?

That whore poisoned his father, making him turn his back on everything he'd supposedly valued. His marrying her before resolving things with David came as another gross betrayal.

The fact that his father knew David wouldn't expose the secret gnawed at him more rabidly than ever before. A test more fraught with potential disaster than the most difficult law school exam he'd taken. Somehow he'd live by his own code, no matter how this wedding provoked him. He envied Cat's and Jackson's ignorance, but he wouldn't deprive them of it, either.

Perhaps it should be enough to know his silence shielded them from the painful truth. However, tonight it didn't suppress his fury.

He'd hidden in his room this evening seeking solace. Although exhausted by all the recent events, he couldn't fall asleep. Perpetual fucking limbo. That's what his life had become.

Hushed footsteps interrupted his train of thought. Through the shadows, he saw Vivi going into the kitchen. Watching her pad around in the dark to fetch a glass of water reminded him of the many times he'd bumped into her late at night when she'd stay at their house. She hadn't changed much over the years, in size or personality. Yet everything about her looked different to him now.

For the past eighteen months, he'd busied himself to block out his anguish. His blind determination had left him little time to miss Vivi. Then, the instant he saw her again, their entire history rushed to the forefront.

Like watching a favorite movie, he'd revisited their years of friendship, the way she'd made him feel like a superhero, the silly things she'd done to make him laugh at life. Then he'd gone and badly mishandled his taboo attraction in a fit of drunken idiocy.

No matter what his feelings for Vivi might be, he knew what they couldn't become. Nothing had changed in that regard. Cat's objections were clear, and the other obstacles remained. Thank God Vivi had prevented him from unloading his confused feelings earlier today.

Spilling his guts would've only complicated everything for both of them. And anyway, she'd confessed the change of heart he'd been sensing all week—her desire to lead a life less involved with him. The role reversal might be amusing if it didn't gut him so much. Another painful truth he'd have to accept. He prayed his longing would pass soon.

He understood little about women, and even less about love, but he'd felt the rush of lust before and it always passed.

"Don't you know it's dangerous to skulk around houses in the dark?" he asked as she gulped down her drink.

"Oh!" Her hand flew to her chest, then she set her glass on the counter. "Jeez, David. You startled me." She blew out a breath before finishing her drink. Afterward, she crossed the living room and sat on the end table near his alcove. Her presence filled the air with unpredictability.

"What are you doing?" She folded her hands in her lap and crossed her ankles. Moonlight streamed in through the window; its beams reflected in her eyes. Her relaxed posture contrasted with the turmoil of the past twenty-four hours.

He remembered her words from earlier. *You have to "feel" David, not "think" him.* Is that how she'd always known him so well? Could she feel him, even now? If so, she should be running away.

"Can't sleep."

"Welcome to my world," she snickered.

Silence stretched between them. He glanced back out the window. When she didn't leave, he looked at her once more. A somber expression replaced her grin.

"David, I'm sorry for what I said to Laney." Her face pinched. "It was selfish to speak as if I knew how you felt."

"It's not your fault." He wished he could've scoffed at Laney's accusations this afternoon, but he couldn't truthfully deny all of them. He hadn't made love with Vivi the night before, but he'd wanted to. He winced at the memory. "I'm sorry she's upset, but the trouble between us existed before you said a word."

"If that's true, then why did she move to New York?" Vivi's expression proved she had second thoughts about her question.

"In Hong Kong, things between us had been easy. Exactly what I'd needed, under the circumstances. I'd assumed it would continue in New York along those lines. I was wrong. She wants more from me than I have to give." On the dock, Laney had thrown down the gauntlet, ordering him to get his shit together before he crawled back to her. Well, hell, that would just be never. "I suppose I should've paid more attention to her signals and discouraged her from expecting a bigger commitment."

Despite his best intentions, he'd obviously hurt Laney, and that knowledge ate at his gut. Now he'd return to New York in two days and finalize the breakup, which meant he faced the uncomfortable prospect of working alongside a pissed-off ex-lover.

"She must've been pretty upset," Vivi said. "Did she drive back on her own?"

"I offered to drive her home out of concern for her safety. She refused." Laney's martyrdom, however, annoyed him more than it made him feel guilty. "She texted once she got back, so at least that's off my mind tonight."

"Oh." When he said nothing, she sighed. "Obviously you're upset about your dad's plans to remarry."

If Vivi pushed him, he'd end up fighting with her, or worse, crossing the clear lines between them. He had to shut down the conversation.

"I don't want to discuss it." His sharp tone sent a clear warning, which she promptly ignored.

"It must hurt to see him move on, especially after what he did." Her eyes filled with compassion. "But I've given it a lot of thought, and I think your mom would want this, David."

"Oh?" Her naive remark ignited his sarcasm. "Why would you think so?"

"Because despite his mistakes, she loved him. The fact that she forgave him and made you keep this secret proves that, doesn't it?" Her bemused expression surprised him. "She wouldn't have wanted him to spend the rest of his life alone."

"As you know, I doubt she expected him to be alone," he sneered. "Let this go."

"Please listen to me. I've got some experience dealing with life's misfortunes, you know," she said. "Don't lose another year or two fighting against something you can't control. You need to find a way to accept what's happened and what's coming next."

"Accept it?" He snorted. "Accept seeing Janet at every birthday, holiday, wedding, and other family event *for the rest of my life*? Accept watching Cat and Jackson support this depraved situation? Let them grow close to her while pushing me further out of their circle?"

"It doesn't have to be that way. Not if you find a way to forgive your dad."

"I can't. And neither would Jackson or Cat if they knew everything. They'd want nothing to do with him or Janet. Trust me on that point." He both envied and resented their ignorant bliss, their memories of their "perfect" family. "I know you're trying to help, but you can't, Vivi."

"I've never known you to be a quitter, David. Saying you can't accept it is a cop-out, and we both know it."

He faced her, setting his feet on the cool wood floor.

"I'm in no mood for a lecture. It's not what I need or want tonight."

"What do you need?" she asked, wide-eyed.

Her open, direct gaze drew him in, as always. He paused, fighting against the pull of her empathy. Another battle he'd lose.

"Things I can't have." Desire unfurled as he noticed her bare arms and legs extending out from her formfitting sleepwear. Prickles of awareness traveled along his spine. What he needed right now was her beneath him.

"I don't believe that for a minute." She smiled as if he were foolish. "You've never thought anything lay beyond your reach."

"It's different now and you know it. I've made promises that preclude me from speaking the truth." His body leaned toward hers.

"Satisfying myself would hurt others." His eyes dipped to drink in her lips as they parted.

"Oh." She sat still, but he heard her breath become shallow.

Their eyes locked. His body tingled. He shoved himself deeper into the alcove to break the spell.

"Maybe the consequences wouldn't be as bad as you think." She stood hesitantly, then sat on the edge of the window seat.

"If I tell Cat and Jackson the truth now, they'd never accept Janet as their stepmother. My mother's worst fear would be realized once *none* of her children wanted to be a part of Dad's new life."

As things stood, David was the only one alienated. He needed to honor the promise that had given his mother peace of mind during her final weeks.

Besides, what he really wanted right then was to make love with Vivi—and that could yield equally detrimental consequences for both of them.

"You should go back to bed." He noticed her dilated pupils. Every part of his body snapped to attention as she closed the distance between them. He cleared his throat. "Stay away from me, Vivi. I can't be trusted, especially tonight."

"Can't be trusted?" Her confused expression frustrated him.

"Yes. Hasn't my behavior this week—*last night*—proven I'm far from being okay? I don't trust myself. I can't control my fucked-up emotions. Hell, half the time I don't even understand them."

Her eyes widened when he cursed. "I want to help. Please let me help you."

He stared at her, warring between grabbing her and pushing her away. "You can't help me, Vivi. Please walk away from me before I hurt you, too."

"I can't leave you like this"—she bit her lower lip and gestured around the room—"alone and brooding in the dark."

They sat mere inches apart. His body burned to touch hers.

"You should listen to my warning." Unable to stop himself, he raised his hand and traced her upper lip with his fingers.

When her tongue flicked against the pad of his thumb, he sucked in his breath. Consent? He didn't even stop to ask before he captured her lips with his own. She opened up to him and dug her hands into his hair.

God, she felt good. *Amazing.*

He devoured her mouth. Every muscle in his body tightened as he yanked her onto his lap and ran his hands along her back, pressing her closer without stopping to breathe.

His lips moved along her jaw to the spot just below her ear. He nibbled. She trembled.

He whispered, "Stop me, Vivi."

Before she answered, he kissed her again and growled in response to her touch. A low moan escaped her lips as he kissed her neck and shoulder. His conscience screamed, but he couldn't let go of her.

"Tell me to stop," he pleaded.

She kissed his temple and cheek before lifting his chin to kiss his mouth with those perfect lips. *Mmm.* He traced them with his tongue, tasting them once more before plundering the wet heat inside.

She twisted around in his embrace until she sat astride his lap. His drawstring cotton pants did nothing to conceal his growing erection. When her hips rocked against him, he shuddered. "Upstairs."

She wrapped her legs around his waist as he rose and cupped his hands under her flawless little bottom. He started carrying her toward the steps, but fumbled behind the sofa. Her legs released his waist and her feet hit the floor without her breaking their soul-stealing kiss.

A minute passed before he pulled his hands from her hair and led her up the steps at a near run. Closing the door quietly, he scooped her up and threw her onto his messy bed. Her swollen lips and dreamy eyes beckoned him. No one had ever looked prettier curled up in his sheets than she did just then.

White noise roared in his ears as he crawled on top of her and kissed her everywhere. His frenzied hands explored her body. Overwhelming desire made him feel like an untried puppy.

"God, I want to be inside you already," he confessed between kisses. "I don't think I can wait and make this good for you."

"Don't worry, I'm not experienced enough to know the difference," she teased. "Unless you count my fantasies."

He drew back and stared at her. The possessive feeling he'd experienced on the beach two days earlier reared again. "Not helping."

He bent over, willing himself to slow down, and kissed her gently. She mewled and ran her hands under his shirt, sending him spiraling out of control again. As he worked his way down to her shoulder and breastbone, she said, "Besides, if it happens too quickly, the perfectionist in you will insist on a do-over until you get it just right."

For the first time ever, he laughed out loud in the middle of foreplay. God, she knew him well. He shot her a look. "Maybe I'll need multiple do-overs."

That shut her up. He raised the hem of her shirt to kiss her abdomen. She sank her fingers into his hair. He licked the center of her stomach as he raised her shirt. Her skin smelled like vanilla and tasted just as sweet. She lifted her arms in anticipation of him removing her tank top.

While on his knees, he shrugged off his own shirt as he stared at her perky breasts, which were slightly upturned, just like her nose. Her rosy nipples were fully aroused.

"You're beautiful, Vivi," he said before he lowered his head to take one into his mouth. His eyes fluttered open and closed. He was torn between wanting to watch her respond and drowning in his own bliss.

She arched her back and inhaled sharply. Using his hands and tongue, he fondled, bit, and pinched her until she squirmed beneath him. Her fingers drew lines down his waist and tugged at the draw-string of his pants. Without breaking contact with his mouth, he raised his hips and she used her feet to disrobe him.

Skin to skin, Vivi felt feminine and soft despite being fit. Her flesh broke into goose bumps with each stroke of his hand or tongue.

"Mmm," she purred.

Her knees fell apart as he reached between her legs.

"God." He looked down the length of her. "You're so ready."

"I've been ready for you forever," she said as she kissed his chest.

"Jesus . . . I really can't wait." He bit her shoulder and thrust himself home.

She gasped. He kissed her hard and began a slow withdraw. She dug her hands into his hips.

"Wait," she breathed. He looked into her glassy eyes.

"Did I hurt you?"

"No." She looked at him in wonder. "Now we're finally as one."

Air raced from his lungs as he gazed in her eyes, which revealed endless stores of love. It gripped his soul and undid him.

As one. They'd always shared an innate understanding of each other. Now their bodies moved in unison and, for the first time in a very long time, he felt at home. It scared him shitless.

Her hips rolled forward, scattering his thoughts.

"I knew you'd feel this good," she murmured before closing her eyes and lifting her spine off the mattress.

Her inner muscles squeezed him, urging him to move.

"Tell me where to touch you," he uttered. "What excites you?"

"You do," she whispered. "No hands needed."

When he looked at her quizzically, she said, "Everything you do and say excites me."

Passion and affection fused within him. He pushed her arms above her head and kissed her as he began to meet her rocking hips with his own. He struggled to maintain control with easy, steady movements while he watched her. Her unpracticed, yet thoroughly erotic, touches enthralled him. His heart pounded in his chest as he nipped at her face, shoulder, and breasts.

As his pace increased, he worried he might break her tiny frame, which didn't seem capable of withstanding the punishing tempo. She bit her lip and moaned, lifting her hips to meet his. "God, yes, David. Don't stop!"

He couldn't stop if he wanted to, which he didn't. Everything blurred. He was dizzy with ecstasy.

"Oh! Oh, David. Yes, yes." Her muscles contracted around him as her body shuddered beneath him. The sight and feel of her orgasm triggered his own. Each cell in his body seemed to explode simultaneously. A string of expletives burst from his lips. Before he blinked, he spilled deep inside her.

For an instant everything went dark, then he woke from his haze. His face lay buried against the side of hers. He spent a moment enjoying the feeling of her hands softly caressing his back.

So much mine.

He kissed her neck and thrust himself in deeper, needing to feel closer. Then it hit him.

"Oh, shit, Vivi. I forgot a condom." He propped up on his elbows to look at her, stunned. "I've never forgotten before."

"It's okay." She stretched her neck to kiss him. "I'm on the pill."

He narrowed his gaze. "Why?"

"My cycle is irregular." She blushed. "The pill makes life predictable."

"There are other protections to consider."

"I'm not worried. If you always wear one, then you're safe. I know I am. We're all good." She smiled and ran her hands through his hair, letting her finger slide down his forehead to rub the frown line between his eyes. "Don't stress and ruin everything, okay?"

He kissed her again. "Okay."

He withdrew from her and rolled onto his back, dragging her alongside of him. Her fingers traced the lines of his chest. Closing his eyes, he relived the unforgettable orgasm.

Had it been so incredible because he hadn't been wearing a condom? Doubtful. His connection with her ran far deeper than he was prepared to consider or admit. Foreboding collided with his pleasure as he realized, despite his warnings and her consent, he probably wouldn't escape this night without some regret. But regret could wait. Right now he'd enjoy his time alone with her.

Peace settled over him while laying with her in the dark. Her soft breath brushed against his skin as she ran her hands along the planes of his torso. Since they'd met, he'd thought of her as his *muñequita*—one he wanted to protect.

His sexual desire for her this week still shocked him. Had absence made his heart grow fonder, or had he simply been blind all those years? Why'd she have to fit so perfectly against his body?

If David were convinced they could last a lifetime, he might risk everything. Yet how could he know that now, when these feelings were so new, and when his faith in love was shaken? The stakes were too high, and the likelihood of a breakup too great.

She'd harbored a crush on him in the past. But her idealized vision of him didn't match reality, even if she wouldn't believe him. He could never make her happy long-term. She'd grow to resent his time commitment to work. She'd become bored with his staid emotions.

She believed in everlasting love, and since he no longer did, he doubted he could be the man to give her the kind of commitment and family she deserved.

So they would share one single night of passion. He'd content himself with memorizing every second of it so he could enjoy it again in his daydreams.

"David?"

“Hmm?” He caressed her shoulder and threaded his fingers through her hair.

She rested her chin on his chest. “More.”

“More what?” He pushed her wild hair away from her eyes.

“More you,” she said before nibbling on his jaw.

He briefly hesitated, sensing the more time they spent intimately, the harder it would be to let go. Then her hand tickled his inner thigh and chased away his better judgment.

Chapter Seventeen

David's tender kiss sent Vivi's heart rate soaring once more. She was living out her fantasy. And reality eclipsed her dreams. He was absolutely perfect in every way, from the musky scent of his skin and its salty taste, to the firmness of his touch. For more than a decade she'd waited for his eyes to cloud with desire for her, and now they did.

I'm so happy. Please let it last.

"Is this my do-over?" He kissed her nose, cheeks, and eyelids.

"Yes." She giggled and reached between his legs.

He grabbed her wrist, dragging her hand away. "Oh, no. *My* do-over, my pace." He kissed her, drawing her upper lip into his mouth.

His gentle hands swept over her arms and down the length of her waist, then ran up her stomach to her breasts. She watched his eyes darken as he took her into his mouth. His tongue flicked and teased her, making her body writhe and twist to pull him closer. She wanted him inside her already, so she drew her legs around his hips and tilted her pelvis in invitation.

"Not yet," he growled while pushing her legs down. "Slowly."

"Now, David," she moaned.

He looked at her and arched one brow. "Patience."

When his mouth found her abdomen and headed south, her body shivered in anticipation. She stared at his shadowed, beautiful face and bit back the words *I love you*. Those words coiled in her mouth like a spring waiting for release. But even in a state of bliss, she knew if she sprung them on him too soon, they'd destroy the fragile bud that was taking root tonight.

"Be still, Vivi," he commanded before his head sank between her thighs.

She squirmed and gripped the sheets as he explored her with his tongue and fingers. "David," she rasped.

She heard a rumble from his chest, but he didn't stop his relentless teasing. His right hand came up to play with her breast while his mouth assaulted her, leaving her panting shamelessly.

"Oh, God."

He broke away just long enough to whisper, "Come for me, baby."

And she did. Her body quaked uncontrollably and she moaned in satisfaction. She'd barely recovered before he slid on top of her.

"I love how you respond to me," he murmured while kissing her. "I don't know which part of you I like kissing most."

"Don't discriminate," she replied. "You keep on testing until you figure it out."

He smiled just before his expression turned hungry. Then he was inside her again, stretching her mercilessly. The slight pain somehow enhanced her pleasure.

"You feel so good, Vivi." His warm breath heated her neck as he tightened his hold on her.

Her body couldn't take much more. Every nerve tingled with sensation overload. David somehow seemed to remain in complete control. Determined. He alternated slow and quick thrusts, bringing her close to the edge and then whisking her away, only to drive her back over it again. Granted, she had limited experience, but he was beyond amazing.

She loved him with every part of her being. How could her feelings not heighten his every touch? And now she knew he loved her, too. He must, or none of this would've happened between them. Surely he felt as awed by their lovemaking as she did.

His hungry groan drew her attention back to their bodies. He flipped onto his back, keeping himself buried inside her while he pulled her on top. His skin glistened from perspiration, emphasizing the corded muscles in his chest and abdomen. The intensity of his gaze and the fullness of his luscious mouth excited her.

She sank down, taking him even deeper inside. His control slipped. He gripped her hips, then reached for her breast. He pulled her down to suck her nipple into his mouth again while driving himself deep inside her.

"David, don't stop," she panted. "Don't stop."

Teasing subsided as she rode him hard and quick. They came together, their bodies shaking. He swore again, which made her feel powerful and sexy. She collapsed on top of him.

Lying in the dark, she listened to the sound of his heartbeat thudding in her ear. Strong and steady, just like him. Her beloved David.

She closed her eyes and absorbed every detail of the moment, each one like a tattoo on her heart. His arm lay slung over her shoulders while he tucked his other arm behind his head. She couldn't tell if his eyes were open or closed, and wouldn't risk being separated from his body for even an instant to check.

Her fingers traced a capital *I*, the shape of a heart, and a capital *U* on his chest. He stopped breathing for an instant. No, she felt his breath against her hair. Perhaps she'd imagined it. His hand came to rest on top of hers. Neither said a word.

Minutes later, she giggled softly.

"What's so funny?" He stretched his neck to peer down at her.

She raised her chin to face him.

"I'm imagining Jackson's and Cat's reaction to all of this. *Shocked* is not a strong-enough word."

He didn't smile. In fact, she saw a thousand conflicting emotions race through his eyes in the span of five seconds. He raised her hand to his lips and kissed it, then frowned.

"I didn't think we'd be sharing this with them." His sober expression made her stomach fall to the floor.

"You want me to lie?" Her body stiffened.

"I want this to be our private memory. Something intimate and special only we share." He paused, then stroked her arm. "I don't want it debated, dissected, and joked about by my brother and sister from now until eternity."

All the heat drained from her body. She felt disconnected from the setting while she processed his intent. *Stupid, Vivi. Stupid, stupid, stupid.* Tonight hadn't been the beginning of their love affair.

For him, it had been a whim. For her, a mistake.

An enormous, brutally painful mistake.

Her ears buzzed louder than a chainsaw. She moved mechanically, unable to focus on him or anything else in the room. She needed to escape before she cried, hit him, screamed, or did anything else to further humiliate herself—if that were even possible. Pulling away from the warmth of his body, she searched for her clothes in the covers. He gripped her arm.

"Where are you going?"

She couldn't meet his eyes. Shrugging out of his grasp, she sprang from the bed as if it were on fire before she bent over to retrieve her discarded pajamas. The chill of her bare feet on the cold floor helped shake her from her haze.

"If Cat wakes up, she'll wonder where I am." She pulled her tank over her head. "I should go."

"Hold on. Don't rush off." He sat up. In her peripheral vision, she saw him extend his arm to her as he spoke. "Let's make this last a little longer."

Her throat closed while tears collected behind her eyes. Thank God for the dark room. She shook her head in silence, eager to flee.

"Vivi, look at me." She heard a twinge of remorse in his voice. His pity only heightened her anguish.

From across the room she faced him. Her heart squeezed at the sight of him sitting naked where they'd been so intimate. Flashing a weak smile, she dashed for the door. "Bye."

He called her name again as she turned and ran. She tiptoed downstairs without slowing.

Once on the ground level, she dropped to her hands and knees, curling into a ball. His scent clung to her body. She listened for his footsteps, but he hadn't chased after her. It was done.

They'd destroyed their friendship. He'd tried to warn her away tonight. Of course, she'd ignored him. *Please let this be the last of my punishments.* Now another big secret threatened to damage her friendship with Cat and Jackson.

Hiding the truth mere hours from now, with David lurking around, would be unbearable. She had to leave right away before anyone realized she'd gone. In a day or two, she'd start to put the pieces of her heart back together and face the world. By morning? Not possible.

One final lie would be required to explain her abrupt departure, but she had to do whatever it took to get away.

Drawing a deep breath, she entered her bedroom noiselessly. Cat was in a deep sleep, as usual. Moonlight slipped past the edges of the shade, illuminating Vivi's corner of the room. Her suitcase lay on the floor—clean clothes inside, dirty ones piled next to it. For once her slovenly habits would pay off. Gathering her belongings would be quick and quiet work, without drawers to open and close.

She glanced at her watch and raked her hand through her hair and over her face. Only three o'clock. The first ferry wouldn't depart the island for five more hours. If undisturbed, Cat might sleep in late enough to make it impossible for her to storm the harbor and drag Vivi back. Vivi would have to leave the house before seven in order to avoid questions and confrontations. It wasn't much of a plan.

She dozed in and out of fitful sleep during the following hours. Shortly after six, she awoke again. Although the ache in her body weighed her down, fear of discovery pushed her out of bed.

Moving like a cat burglar, she changed into clean clothes, threw her other clothes in her bag, and crept from the room. She stopped in the hall bathroom to brush her teeth and splash cold water on her face. Once she calmed her shaky hands, she twisted her hair into a ponytail, then she started for the front door.

At the top of the first half flight, she reached for the doorknob. She paused, her body paralyzed. Doubt took root as she considered that fleeing might only raise suspicion. No, she must go. But if she left without any word, everyone would worry.

Texting would wake Cat, so she nixed the option. She glanced up the stairs to the main living area. David slept only yards away. Pain momentarily crippled her as she pictured him asleep in the bed where they'd made love mere hours ago.

Like a rabbit on guard, she listened for any sounds. Nothing. No signs of Hank, the other early riser in the group. Could she risk it? Placing her bag by the door, she sneaked up the steps.

She eased open a drawer and withdrew a pen and notepad. Without any thought, she wrote:

So sorry. I had to go. Don't worry. Will call later. Love, Vivi

P.S. I assume Cat can come home with David, so I've taken the rental car. Sorry for any inconvenience.

She dropped the note on the counter and tiptoed back to the front door. Holding her breath, she clicked the deadbolt open. No one stirred. Slipping outside, she pressed the door closed and scurried across the yard. The heavy bag banged against her thigh as she ran down the driveway and out to the Painted Rock.

Once she reached it, she burst into tears. She sat atop the stupid symbols she'd painted with David—symbols that failed to live up to their meaning—and glanced at her watch. Six thirty. She looked up the number for a taxi service on her phone and called for a ride. Dark gray clouds had rolled in overnight, threatening rain. Thank God she was leaving; being trapped indoors all day with David might well have killed her.

Hopefully the rain would wash away the paint on this rock and erase all evidence of that night. She'd never paint that rock again. In fact, she'd probably never return to the island, at least not with this family.

Tears ran down her cheeks at the private admission that her own impulsive behavior might cost her the family she'd come to love. He'd warned her. Begged her to leave him alone. Would she never learn to think before acting?

The next twenty minutes may as well have been twenty years. Ironically, the beginning and end of her trip shared a certain symmetry: on both occasions, she felt like throwing up. When the cab arrived, she tossed her bag in the backseat and slammed her door closed.

By quarter past seven she was sitting on a railing sipping coffee at the harbor. When her phone rang, Cat's name popped up on her screen. If she avoided the call, Cat would come searching for her. Steeling herself, she answered with a chipper tone to fool her friend. "Hey, you're up early."

She slapped her hand over her mouth when Hank's voice replied, "I saw your note and wanted to make sure you're okay."

"Hank? Why do you have Cat's phone?"

"She left it charging in the kitchen. Now, tell me what's going on."

Vivi heard the concern in his voice. She hadn't actually promised David she'd keep their secret. But telling everyone would jeopardize her relationships, and his. Fudge. She'd been so busy getting out of the house unnoticed, she hadn't given any thought to a credible reason for her hasty departure.

"Vivi, talk to me. Everyone else is asleep, so I'm alone."

"I needed to leave, Hank. I just . . . I just feel responsible for stirring up trouble between David and Laney. It's humiliating. David looked so dejected when he came home last night, I couldn't face him today. Please don't tell them all the truth, though. I'm going to say my dad needed me. It's best this way. Please." She held her breath, hating herself for making Hank complicit in another one of her lies.

"Okay. Relax. Your secret is safe with me."

"Thank you." Vivi's fierce grip relaxed. "Meeting you may've been the best part of this trip, Hank. Really. I hope we keep in touch back in New York."

"You bet. It's been a real pleasure for me, too. Take care now."

Vivi put her phone away and finished her coffee. Hank had been so sweet to go along with her silly plan to fool everyone into believing she was over David. She wanted to find a way to repay him one day. Just not today.

Cars had begun to line up at the dock. Exhausted parents struggled to entertain their children while awaiting the call to board the ferry. A wistful smile crossed Vivi's face as she watched one father hoist his toddler onto his shoulders.

Her own father had never been playful, or maybe he had been when she was young. People said her dad was a happy man before the accident—a man who loved his wife and two young children. Her scant early-childhood recollections weren't reliable. Most were based on photographs, or stories her father had told her during his lucid moments. Any real memories of things prior to the accident had apparently been deleted without backup.

Hostility festered as she considered how her dad's subsequent behavior had affected her entire life. Years of neglect—of his being consumed by his own grief—had conditioned her to give much more than she ever demanded in return. Shame and fear had made her tolerate the abuse, expect it, even believe she deserved it.

Until now she hadn't realized how much that dynamic had spilled over to all of her relationships. How could she expect anyone to love and respect her if she didn't love and respect herself enough to require equality in her relationships?

She'd been punishing herself since the day she walked away from that crash. Well, no more. Hank and Franco were happy to give her time, attention, and effort. Never again would she allow David, or anyone, to use her as a friend of convenience.

With each passing minute, her nervousness eased. Soon she'd board the ferry and put this trip behind her forever.

Chapter Eighteen

David lingered at the corner across the street from an old stone cathedral. A brilliant sun blazed in a cloudless sky, yet he felt no heat—no temperature whatsoever. He watched the attendees, all dressed in black, filing out of the church's open doors.

Since his mother's death, his muscles constricted any time he crossed paths with a funeral procession. This time was no different, except he felt inexplicably drawn to this particular occasion. But why?

He needed to go to Vivi. She'd be waiting for him. As usual, the thought of seeing her lightened his mood. He turned to leave, then caught sight of Catalina and Jackson amid the mourners. Unease set in. His hasty steps carried him across the street as if he'd been floating.

"Why are you here?" His gaze moved from his brother to his sister.

"Why weren't *you here?" Cat's angry eyes scorched him. "Why are you dressed so casually? Don't you care at all?"*

Bewildered, he wondered if his father had died and he'd somehow not known. That couldn't be right. Something was off—and terribly wrong.

Jackson lowered his brows scornfully before shrugging dismissively and wrapping his arm around Cat. "We'll miss her, but she's with Mom now."

"Who?" David's voice resonated impatience. "Who will you miss?"

His brother's and sister's apparent disdain irked him.

"Vivi, David," Cat choked out. "Vivi's dead."

David's eyes snapped open just before he bolted upright in bed. A chill swept through him, but his labored breathing settled once the nightmare faded. Falling back to his pillow, he flung his forearm across his eyes. Thank God. A world without Vivi would be bleak.

With his eyes closed, he curled his body into a fetal position, hugging the pillows. He buried his nose in them and inhaled her scent, which lingered in the bed. *Sweet Vivi.* The memory of her naked body tangled in his sheets aroused him. If he didn't smell her perfume, he might believe last night had also been a dream—a fantastic dream.

He'd never have anticipated the best sex of his life would be with his childhood friend. The tiny girl with tremendous heart. The intensity of his persistent desire surprised him. An unexpected outcome.

One he doubted would diminish any time soon.

Once he returned to New York, the demands of his profession would help push the memory of last night from his mind. He'd just been assigned to another prominent transaction. The details would dominate his time and attention. *Shit.* He winced at the thought of working with Laney on the deal.

The near future looked grim, especially the immediate challenge of hanging out with Vivi today as if nothing had changed. No matter what he'd told himself or her, everything between them was different now. His body throbbed as he envisioned her asleep in a bed downstairs. Was she awake and thinking of him?

He scowled, remembering how she'd torn out of his room last night like Cinderella at midnight. Perhaps her point about Cat finding her bed empty rang true, but it had seemed sudden.

Ending it quickly, however, might have been for the best. Like ripping off a Band-Aid. Better their friendship suffer a temporary setback than she risk everything for him when he was too lost and broken to think clearly.

He stretched and glanced at the clock. Seven twenty. Vivi might be in the kitchen making breakfast now. His pulse quickened. Then he felt ridiculous for panicking. He'd negotiated with some of the toughest lawyers on the planet; surely he could maintain a poker face around Vivi for twenty-four hours. The only real question was whether she could do the same. Then a second question popped into his head: Could he keep from seducing her tonight?

Dammit. He was in trouble.

A quick run would ease his nerves; it always did the trick. He tied his shoelaces and blew out a deep breath. When he descended the steps, Hank looked up from the kitchen table.

"Good morning, Hank." David glanced around.

"Feeling better today?" Hank straightened in his chair. "Yesterday was pretty lousy."

"It was," David replied. "I have a better perspective this morning."

"Too bad Vivi didn't feel the same." Hank studied David, as if expecting a certain reaction.

"Oh?" David fiddled with his iPhone, trying to act indifferent. "What gives you that impression?"

Hank tossed a piece of paper across the table. "She's gone home."

David's lips twitched despite every effort to keep his expression blank. He scanned the note, although his eyes couldn't focus on the words with everything around him turning black.

She'd left without saying good-bye.

To get away from him? Probably. He'd hurt her, exactly as he'd warned her he would.

Overwhelming desire had hijacked his judgment last night. Now a sense of panic threatened to do so again if he didn't get control of himself. Though lost in thought, he gradually became aware of Hank's scrutiny. With effort, he relaxed his posture and studied Vivi's note once more.

"No explanation?" He rubbed his hand against the back of his neck. "Maybe it's her father. He gives her no peace."

"Is that right?" Hank's voice revealed sarcasm.

Not only had Hank buddied up to Vivi all week, but he'd been studying David, too. Hank's gaze felt intrusive, and David never liked being in the hot seat.

"You've been judging me all week and I'm sick of it." David crossed his arms. "If you have something to say, then spit it out."

"Chill, David." Hank steepled his fingers. "I'm just trying to figure you out. I mean, you seem to care about Jackson, Cat, and Vivi, yet you aren't really there when they need you."

"Maybe it looks that way to you. Whether or not anyone believes me, I am doing what is best, just as I've always done. They might not admit it, but they know I'm always here for them."

Hank shrugged. "If you say so."

David wondered if they'd all confided these thoughts to Hank, or if he was drawing his own conclusions. He wouldn't ask. Hank didn't appear to be the kind of guy to betray a confidence. David might never know the answer, but he knew one thing for certain: no way would he defend himself to Hank. He tossed the note back on the table. "Cat will be disappointed."

The kitchen clock read seven thirty-five; twenty-five minutes remained before the ferry left. If he sprinted, he might make it to the harbor in time. "I'm on my way out for a long run. Be back in an hour."

He inserted his earphones and jogged down the steps, dismissing Hank and his conjecture.

Once outside, he dialed Vivi's cell. No answer. He stood in the middle of the road and glanced at the darkening sky. Three and a half miles to the harbor. He'd end up stuck in a downpour. He hesitated, considering his options. If she stayed, he'd be too tempted to get her alone again.

Everything would be easy if it were only sex. But last night he'd been captivated like never before. He wished he could trust these feelings. Wished he could be the man to make all Vivi's dreams come true. Wished he believed they could withstand whatever Cat and Jackson threw at them, along with all the other obstacles couples face.

Regrettably, he'd lost all faith in happy endings when he caught his dad with Janet. And without more certainty about the outcome of a romantic relationship with Vivi, he couldn't let her jeopardize her relationship with his entire family. He'd have to hold back, to let go of fantasies that they could build some lasting love.

Sorrow gripped him. Whether today or tomorrow, next week or next year, the result would be the same. He should let her go now.

But something coaxed his feet to move. His sluggish pace broke into an all-out run.

He reached the harbor at five past eight. The ferry churned through the water several hundred yards offshore. *Goddamn it!*

He'd run two women off the island in an equal number of days. *One hell of a record*, he thought grimly.

Standing on the shore, he watched the increasing distance between Vivi and him. He called her phone again only to be sent to voice mail. Apparently physical distance alone wouldn't satisfy her.

He stood in the middle of the parking lot, uncertain of his next move. Minutes passed before the charcoal sky began spitting fat raindrops on his face. Frowning, he looked up at what probably wouldn't be a passing storm. Not what he needed now, but probably what he deserved. In the absence of thunder, he decided to head home rather than take cover in town.

On a good day, the ascent from town to the cliffs made the run home a hearty challenge. Today, it plain sucked. Within minutes, his soaking clothes clung to him. Wet socks and soggy shoes rubbed against the backs of his ankles, causing blisters to form by the time he returned home.

He stepped inside the house and sneezed in the air-conditioned space. Trotting upstairs with the intention of bypassing the group and taking a hot shower, his plans were derailed by his sister.

"Did you know Vivi left?" Cat asked.

"Hank told me before my run." Had Vivi taken Cat's call? Perhaps she wasn't avoiding him; perhaps her phone was dead. "Have you spoken with her?"

"Just hung up. Her dad left some disturbing messages last night, but she hasn't been able to reach him this morning." Cat crossed to the coffeepot and refilled her cup. "I'll bet he got drunk, mumbled a bunch of garbage, then passed out. No doubt he'll be fine, yet he found a way to ruin her vacation."

Though plausible, David doubted the explanation. Now he had confirmation that Vivi was, in fact, avoiding him. She fabricated this excuse about her dad, just like she had when David had blown up over the paella.

Her father hadn't ruined her vacation—David had. Another reason to hate this version of himself.

"I'm going to shower." God forbid any of them noticed the sickening emotions roiling inside him.

Thankfully, the hot water relaxed some of the tension in his neck and shoulders. Dried and dressed for the day, David returned to the kitchen to make breakfast. Jackson had joined Cat and Hank in the adjacent living room. Rather than seek their company, David ate alone at the counter.

He'd deal with Vivi later. First he had to finalize the end of his relationship with Laney. What he'd experienced with Vivi only underscored the hollowness of what he shared with Laney.

He almost resented now learning he might not be satisfied with the type of relationship he'd previously found comforting, especially when the one that felt so much better was taboo.

David stirred his coffee while remembering the look in Vivi's eyes when they'd made love. Seeing that love staring back at him again had been the sweetest victory. Even now, he felt drawn to her despite her absence.

What in the hell was he going to do with these feelings? And how would he salvage their friendship? Jesus, he'd fucked everything up.

Jackson's hand clamped onto his shoulder, breaking his daze.

"How are you today?" Jackson appeared genuinely empathetic. He plopped onto the stool next to David. "Between Laney and Dad, I'm sure you're having a rough one."

David gaped at his brother, having completely forgotten about his father's impending wedding. *How is that possible?* He set his spoon aside and sighed. "I'll survive."

Jackson nodded and flashed a sheepish grin. "Not really another option, is there?"

The simple statement of fact sank David's heart. He had no options. He'd been sleepwalking through his life lately, waiting to feel better. Instead of controlling his situation, he'd let it control him, which hurt the people he most loved. Defeated, he shook his head. Jackson set his elbow on the counter and leaned his jaw against his fist.

"Are you ever going to let us in on your beef with Dad?" he asked.

"No." David's sharp answer came quickly. The image of his mother's pleading face flashed through his mind, strengthening his resolve. "I'm sorry it bothers you. I wish it didn't."

"I barely recognize you, David," Cat called out from the sofa, her large eyes filled with concern. "I believe you think you're doing the right thing, but it feels wrong to me. You should've stayed and grieved with us instead of running away. Even now you're only half-present."

"I'm sorry, Cat." David sighed and dropped his head to his hands. "I love you both. That doesn't mean I'm not entitled to some privacy with respect to my personal problems, whether they involve Dad, Laney, or anyone else." *Vivi.*

"You're the same as Dad," Jackson muttered. "Tight-lipped. Closed off."

"I don't particularly appreciate the comparison, Jackson." David shoved his mug aside. No insult could have hit him harder. "Trust me, I'm nothing like Dad."

"So I take it you won't be attending his wedding?" Jackson sat back, arms crossed.

"You assume correctly." David refused to be the first to break eye contact.

"Are you pissed he's not still mourning Mom?" Jackson leaned forward. "I know it hasn't quite been two years, but doesn't he deserve another shot at love?"

David reminded himself of Jackson's ignorance regarding the timing of their father's "love" affair with Janet. His mother's voice rang in his ears. *"Don't tear everyone apart, David. Please! You'll only bring more pain to everyone. Let your brother and sister keep their memories of our family intact."*

He held his tongue. Seething at the injustice of the situation, his outrage rolled off him in ripples, like heat waves.

Jackson stood up, shaking his head. "Hell, someone in this family should be happily in love. You, Cat, and I sure aren't having any luck."

"Hey," Cat chimed in from across the room. "Speak for yourself."

David snapped, his recent disappointments and mistakes bringing him to his knees. Like a cornered animal, he came back biting. "Guess what? I don't give a fuck what Dad does. I'm just not interested in being any part of it."

Jackson's head jerked. "Very nice. Mom would be real proud of you right now."

The final straw. David swept his hand across the counter, sending several magazines and a napkin holder to the ground. Rarely did he lose his temper. God, it felt damned good.

Cat gasped, sitting stiff as a statue beside Hank, who looked as if he were deciding whether or not to intervene.

David barked, "You have *no* idea what you're talking about. Much as I would love to enlighten you, I can't." Rising from his seat, he continued, "If you want to paint me as the bad guy, go ahead." He glanced at Cat, then returned his attention to Jackson. "This is going to be a long day. I'll leave you all alone and catch up on some work."

As David started up the steps, he heard his brother's mocking voice and turned to face him. "Yes, walk away." Jackson's hands went to his waist. "You're real good at that."

David had never before wanted to strike his brother, but it took all his concentration not to punch him now. He glanced at Cat, who now hovered at the edge of the kitchen, twisting the bracelet she was wearing around and around.

"Why would I confide in you when you've already judged me guilty?" David glowered at his siblings, then stomped upstairs and slammed his door closed.

The bedroom walls shook as though they might come crumbling down around him. Standing alone in his room, he privately acknowledged they'd already collapsed.

~

Hours later, David shoved the asset purchase agreement in his briefcase. He'd been unable to concentrate on seller representations and warranties because he'd been constantly checking his phone for a message from Vivi. She'd continued avoiding his calls all day.

What the hell had happened between two and seven this morning?

He tried reading in bed, then tossed the book aside after he'd read the same paragraph three times. He paced the floor, stopping once in a while to stare out the windows at the ocean. Finally, at three o'clock, Vivi responded to his multiple messages via an e-mail.

David,

I've never been anyone's one-night stand. To be yours hurts more than I can say. Most humiliating is your need to hide it from everyone, like a shameful secret. My rose-colored glasses blinded me to the truth, but now I see it. You simply aren't the man I thought you were. Please stop calling.

His hands trembled. *You simply aren't the man I thought you were.* He reread her message twice, blinking repeatedly.

How could she say that? She knew how much he'd always cared for her. He'd proved it for years. He'd confided in her this week. He'd *begged* her to stop him to make sure she didn't feel pressured.

Then he'd crossed the line.

A selfish impulse, perhaps, but he hadn't been malicious or misleading. He'd explained why they should be discreet, and it had nothing to do with shame. Now it seemed she planned on completely cutting him out of her life.

He envisioned her sitting alone at the harbor this morning, and then felt sick. How could he have expected her to disengage her own heart when he was having such trouble doing the same?

He'd been greedy and selfish, indulging his own desire with the barest provocation. After a decade of protecting her from pain caused by others, he'd now inflicted the worst heartache.

David had never before known such self-loathing. Had his father felt even one-tenth of this emotion during the past eighteen months?

Ironically, David now needed the very forgiveness he couldn't give his own dad.

He threw his phone aside and fell backward on the bed, unsure of how to respond. No matter what she believed at the moment, she wouldn't have the last word.

Chapter Nineteen

The following afternoon, Jackson dropped off David and Cat at the Stamford, Connecticut, Metro-North train station. Sixty minutes remained to try to make some reparation with Cat.

"Should I expect the silent treatment for the rest of the trip?" He sighed as he slid in the seat beside his sister.

"I thought you preferred it to talking." She glanced at him, looking concerned and displeased. "I know I was a bit preoccupied this week dealing with Justin's calls, but you . . . you were like a yo-yo. Your outburst yesterday—that was a real first."

He stared straight ahead, then briefly closed his eyes. "I'm sorry I've upset you. I know you don't understand me, but between Laney and Dad," he began, omitting any mention of Vivi, "I hit a wall. I honestly don't know where to go from here."

"Look, it doesn't matter if *we* don't happen to think Janet's the catch of the century. Dad's clearly in love with her." She grabbed David's hand. "As much as we miss Mom, she's gone and life has to go on. Don't you want Dad to be happy?"

David could feel his jaw clenching while he used every ounce of energy to keep himself in check. His sister made it sound so easy. Did he want his dad to be happy? Did he? "I don't know what I want."

It was the most honest answer he could give.

"Well, I do. I want us all to be happy. I want us to be a family again. I wish you did, too."

"I do, Cat. That's what I'd hoped to rebuild this week with you and Jackson. But other things got in the way."

"Speaking of which, what *are* you going to do about Laney?" Cat turned toward him, trying to read his expression.

"End it."

"Just like that?" Her eyes widened.

"Just like that. When it's not right, it's not right." He hoped his tone would get her to consider ending her own relationship.

They both fell silent for a while. He swayed in his seat as the train rattled along the tracks toward Grand Central Station. Staring out the window at the buildings along the track, he cursed to himself.

A now-familiar hostility unfurled inside, which he traced back to his father and their fight weeks before his mother died. David had never before let anger and disgust peck away at his soul like a vulture on a corpse.

If only he hadn't caught his father with Janet. If only he hadn't confronted him within earshot of his mother. If only his mother hadn't extracted the promise.

At the time, his father had blamed David for hurting his mother with his outburst. Never mind the fact that there wouldn't have been an outburst without the adultery.

"David," Cat said, "I hope you can resolve things with Dad before whatever's going on eats you alive."

David dropped his head to hide the desperate fury he felt burning in his eyes from merely considering extending an olive branch. Meanwhile his father had never once asked for forgiveness, or thanked David for keeping his mouth shut.

He felt the walls closing in on him, which made him resent his mother for putting him in an impossible position.

The instant the thought occurred, it choked him with guilt.

"Home again, home again, jiggety-jig," Cat sighed as the train came to a stop in Grand Central Station.

As they stood in the taxi line, David thought about the two women he needed to speak with today. Laney would be expecting him. She'd be stuck waiting a few more hours, because he wanted to see Vivi first.

He and Cat shared a silent taxi ride from Grand Central to their neighborhood. The condo he'd bought near her building to be closer to her hadn't made anything between them easier.

Another failure to add to his list.

He dropped her off first. When the cab pulled up to his building, he felt utterly depleted.

"Mr. St. James." The doorman nodded.

"Hey, Bill." David forced a smile. "Can you hold on to my bag until I return? I'll be back in an hour or two."

"Sure." Bill placed the bag behind the counter and waved as David raced outside to hail a cab to Queens.

David stood on the busy Astoria thoroughfare, surveying the drab brick apartment building he'd helped Vivi move into years ago. She'd been so excited about her awful little studio. It represented freedom from her dad, though, which he'd assumed explained her euphoria. Of course, the little storefronts and trees aligning the streets gave the area a friendly neighborhood vibe. It suited her.

He pressed the security buzzer, shoved his hands in his pockets, and waited to hear her voice. When she didn't answer, he glanced at his watch. Had she gone out for lunch? His own stomach rumbled at the thought.

He jogged across the street to a Greek diner and ordered a gyro.

Sitting at a narrow counter running along the plate glass window, he ate his greasy sandwich and watched for Vivi. Each time he envisioned confronting her, his mood vacillated between worried and antagonistic. One minute he wanted to reassure her, the next he wanted to rip into her for how her comments had gutted him.

When he spotted her approaching her building, he froze.

Showtime.

He threw twenty bucks on the counter and bolted out the door. His legs moved awkwardly, stiffened by anxiety. He came up behind her as she stopped to retrieve her keys.

"Vivi." He clasped her arm.

Startled, she stared wide-eyed at him. He held her firmly, with no intention of releasing her. Being near her—touching her again—turned his brain to mush.

"Let go, David."

"We need to talk." Even to his own ears, he sounded like a caveman.

"No, we don't." Her defiant attitude set off alarms.

Vivi had never before simply refused him. She'd never looked at him like something unwanted on the bottom of her shoe. Anguish and anger seized control of his muscles.

"Don't do this," he said. "We have to clear up some things. One way or another, Vivi, you will hear me out."

"You're hurting my arm." She stared at his hand until he released her.

He hovered beside her, refusing to let her slip inside without him. A breeze lifted a section of her hair, sending a whiff of citrus his way. Despite his irritation, he envisioned burying his hands in her messy hair and kissing her hard. He shook his head and frowned, but then leaned in closer. He couldn't help himself.

"Back up so I can open the door, please." She sighed, oblivious to her effect on him. "Five minutes, David. Five."

"Fine."

As she put the key in the lock, he noticed how her baggy paint-spattered overalls consumed her tiny frame. My God, she looked like a waif who just lost a paintball tournament. He grinned. "Where'd you go dressed like that?"

"Sorry I'm not in Prada." She shot him a cold stare. "Designer clothes don't last long in an art studio."

"Jesus, Vivi, I wasn't criticizing." He followed her into the building, wondering if he'd destroyed the caring, sweet girl he knew.

When they entered her apartment, her keys landed on the minuscule kitchen counter with a bang. Her studio, littered with art supplies and dozens of knickknacks from children, made him feel claustrophobic.

Her unpacked duffel bag lay on the floor beside her bed. He couldn't tear his eyes from her ruffled white down comforter, or stop picturing her tumbled in those sheets. His body vibrated as mixed emotions paralyzed him once again.

"Go ahead." She faced him. "Get it over with so we can both move on."

He wrung his hands while he paced back and forth, searching for the right approach. He was a lawyer, dammit. He knew he could persuade her to reconsider her position as long as he kept his feelings in check. Winning an argument required divorcing oneself from all sentiment.

Yet he couldn't do it.

"I got your e-mail." His grave start seemed to bore her. She needed a push. "You were unfair, Vivi. I didn't use you, and I'm not ashamed of what happened. I warned you to leave me alone. You chose to stay. Now I'm the bad guy? Not the man you thought?"

Not his most articulate speech. Who could blame him when he was torn between wanting to shake her and wanting to throw her onto the bed to make love again?

"Warned me?" Her eyes narrowed. "Maybe you did. But you can't honestly believe I understood your 'I might hurt you' dilemma to involve having sex with me."

"How could you not? We were discussing it right before I kissed you. I literally begged you to stop me before it went too far." The facts supported him. His logic couldn't be defeated.

She rolled her eyes at his reasoning.

"My God, David. You're either a complete jerk or really, *really* stupid about love." She squinted in disbelief at his speechless gape. "Even if I had understood—which I did not—did you truly think I could've stopped myself? I've loved you for a dozen years and more. You've known it just as long. You knew I could never say no to any chance you might return my feelings. If it didn't mean anything to you, then you should have been the one to stop it." She shook her head. "Instead, you took advantage of my trust, then got embarrassed and insisted on sweeping it under the carpet."

"It's not like that, and you know it. Being with you meant a lot to me, Vivi. It was very special. I am not embarrassed that we made love. Quite obviously I *wanted* to be with you, but that doesn't mean it was the right thing for us to do. If I took advantage, it wasn't intentional. My head has been fucked up for months, which you well know. I'm certainly not in a place where I can have a healthy relationship with a woman. Not even with you." He ran his hand through his hair, then softened his voice. "I'm just trying to protect you—protect both of us—from destroying everything."

"There's no protecting us from that, David," Vivi snapped, crossing her arms. "What happened has pretty much guaranteed it."

"Only if you let it." He drew a deep breath and stepped closer to her. She receded slightly, which stopped his advance. "Why can't it enhance our friendship, Vivi? My God, I felt closer to you than ever before. And that's saying a lot, considering how important you've always been."

"Never quite important enough." Her quiet tone cut him to the quick. His mouth opened, but he couldn't think of what to say next.

He paced in a tight circle, speechless, thoughts in a wild spin. "How can you honestly make that crack to me . . . *to me* . . . after the friendship we've shared? Jesus, I just confided my worst nightmare to you a few days ago to prove how important you are to me. Apparently that's not enough for you. How many tests do I have to pass to win back your friendship?"

She closed her eyes and slouched. "I don't know. So much has changed between us, even before the other night. We can't go back to what was, and you don't want to move forward to something more."

"We could never be a couple, and deep down you know all the reasons why. Cat and Jackson would freak out, for starters. But that's child's play compared with what would happen when we broke up. You'd feel awkward with my family . . . not to mention how I'd mourn the loss of our friendship." He reached for her. "Don't you see? It's better this way. Just one night, without promises or unnecessary pain."

"Too late. There's already pain. And why are you so sure it couldn't work out? Because I'm not sophisticated like Laney?" Her false bravado couldn't hide the lack of confidence revealed by her remarks.

"No, Vivi. I've always liked you exactly as you are, and you know it." He set his hands on her shoulders. "That's only half the battle. For God's sake, even you must admit most relationships fail, no matter how much people like each other when they begin. With our differences, we'd barely have a chance."

"More lame excuses." She shrugged away from him. "Besides, your mom and dad were different as night and day, and they were married for thirty years."

"Ha!" He snorted. "You just proved my point. Obviously theirs was not a perfect marriage. God forbid we'd end up like them."

"Just stop." She sat down and set her forehead into her palm. After a deep sigh, she looked up at him. "Please leave me alone now. Why is our friendship suddenly so important to you anyway? Just go back to Manhattan and pretend you're still in Hong Kong."

The floor beneath him sank as if he were standing in quicksand. In eighteen admittedly selfish months and one memorable, if stupid, decision to take her to bed, he'd burned through all their goodwill.

"I can't believe you'd shut me out now, after everything that happened this week. After everything I told you. After all the times I was there for you with your dad, now you're walking out on me when I need help with mine." His hoarse voice choked out his final words. "I'm tapped out, Vivi. You have no idea how leveling it is to have everything you believe about someone you love turn out to be untrue."

David briefly closed his eyes and shook his head while a shiver traveled the length of his entire body.

She had to see his rationale. Maybe she'd even be sympathetic due to the magnitude of what he'd confided in her. Surely, at least, she'd understand he hadn't used her the other night.

Her fingers fiddled with the pencils on the table while she considered his last remarks. But when she looked at him, he saw no compassion in her eyes.

"You're wrong, David. I know exactly how it feels to find out everything you believed about someone is false, because you're just like your dad. You've basically betrayed one woman with another. You're keeping secrets to protect yourself, or your image, or whatever. Funny you can't forgive him, yet you expect me to forgive you."

"I'm nothing like my father!" Her insult ripped through his heart. "I'm not married to Laney. We don't share children and a life. She hasn't sacrificed anything for me. And besides, we were essentially broken up when I acted on my feelings for you."

"*Essentially* broken up?" Vivi shook her head. "Laney moved her life to be close to you. Maybe you didn't take vows before God, but you owed her better than you gave, David."

Her words stopped him, scattering his thoughts before he could defend against her twisted rationale. He'd failed to convince her. With nothing left to lose, he tried guilt. "If you think I'm as selfish as my father, then you've never known me at all."

"That's exactly what I'd already admitted in my e-mail. You're neither loyal nor selfless. And you're a coward."

"A coward? Why? Because I prefer to preserve a long-term friendship rather than roll the dice on a risky love affair?" He stood defiantly while she stared. He bit back a scream, settling for something less than a shout. "So you'd risk your relationship with Cat and Jackson, and our friendship, on the *chance* of love?"

"I'd have risked anything for your love, David." Her answer came quick and direct, then she looked away. "But not anymore."

She stood and clasped her hands together in front of her hips. "I've heard you out. We disagree. You should go now." She turned away from him, then glanced over her shoulder. "I'm sorry I can't feel much sympathy for you now. I will keep both secrets—ours and your dad's. You can count on me for that much, anyway."

His world went black. Perspiration beaded on his forehead and his eyes stung.

"Vivi, your friendship means everything to me." He crossed the room and came up behind her. "I don't want to lose it."

"Of course you don't. Who would willingly let go of someone who gives everything and asks for nothing in return?" She turned toward him, her arms wrapped around her waist. "For years, your attention convinced me I was unique and lovable. I savored every minute we spent together, and in return I gave you absolutely everything I had to give.

"Instead of turning to me, you disappeared and cut me out. Now you've come back as someone I don't recognize. I've tried to be supportive, to defend your recent choices, but I can't do it anymore. Not after the other night. Now *I'm* tapped out, too."

"Don't say that." He hugged her to his chest and kissed her head, though she remained rigid in his arms. "If I took our friendship for granted while I was away, it wasn't because I don't care. Jesus, Vivi, our night together was exceptional. Better than with any other woman. Please believe me. I never wanted it to hurt you. Tell me, at least, you know how much you've always meant to me."

"If you care at all, then you'll leave me alone. And you're wrong about something else. This isn't just about forgiveness, David. It's about self-respect." She tipped up her chin. "I'm done groveling for scraps of affection from you, from anyone. You can't give me what I want, so let me go."

"I can, Vivi. I'll do better as a friend, I swear it." Her breath grazed the skin on his arms. "Just tell me what you want."

"Everything." She pushed free from the embrace. "I want everything."

"Everything or nothing?" He sighed. "You're being unfair."

"Life's never fair. I've learned to adapt, and you will, too." She turned away. "Please leave, David. You've worn me down. I don't want your company. I don't want to think about the past, or why you want to blame everything on your dad, or anything else you've said."

He stood, motionless, searching her eyes for any mercy. None.

"Just *please* go."

Chapter Twenty

St. Jameses' House
Nineteen Months Ago

Mr. St. James opened the door, looking more imposing than ever. Unlike his wife, his handsome features were austere. Countless interactions hadn't made Vivi much more comfortable than the first time she'd met him. Even now, she referred to him formally, while years ago she'd begun to call his wife by her name, Graciela. Vivi's heart warmed at the thought of her pseudo-mom.

"Hi, Mr. St. James!" She flashed him her best grin and stepped forward to enter the house.

He unexpectedly blocked her entry.

"Today's not a good day, Vivi." Despite his stiff manner and firmly set mouth, he appeared flummoxed.

"But she's expecting me." Vivi held out the book she'd been reading to Graciela each week since she'd been confined to bed. "It's our reading day!"

"She's not up to it today. I'm sorry."

A lump swelled in Vivi's throat. Cat had estimated two months before Graciela would pass away. Had her condition taken a turn for the worse? Before Vivi could ask, David barked at his father from inside the house.

"Let her in." David appeared beside his father. His flushed face warned of his mood. "Mom needs cheering up."

"I think I know what my wife needs, David," his father countered. "She's exhausted."

"Let's not pretend you're thinking of *her* needs right now." David reached past his father and yanked Vivi into the house. "I am, and she needs Vivi today."

Vivi watched the two men engage in a silent contest of will. Mr. St. James shocked her by backing down without another word and disappearing into his study. The door clicked shut behind him.

David glared at the closed door as if he could burn it down with his eyes. She reached for his arm, unaccustomed to seeing him so wound up. His chin dropped and his eyes closed tight. Were his lips quivering?

"What's wrong?" she asked. "Has your mom gotten much worse?"

He lifted his head, gazing at her through teary eyes. Instinct took over. She wrapped her arms around him, rubbing his back while pressing her head to his chest. His body trembled as he cried. Then quite suddenly, he straightened up and wiped his eyes.

"I'm sorry." He grabbed his keys from the entry table. "I've got to get out of here."

"Wait!" she called. "What's happened?"

She noticed his hands fist by his side before he said, "I can't say."

"You can tell me anything, David. Let me help you."

Except for the involuntary slow shake of his head, he stood perfectly still. His gaze remained unfocused until he looked directly at her.

"No, Vivi. Please don't pry." David closed the distance between them and gathered her to his chest. He laid his cheek against her head and spoke softly. "Thank you for caring. At least I know I've never misjudged *you*. You're the most generous, loving person I know. Don't ever change."

Without another word, he released her and strode out the door. Through the side transom window in the entry, she watched him jog to his car.

She hesitated, choosing between chasing him down and visiting his mother. The book in her hand helped her decide.

She glanced at the closed study door. No. She couldn't intrude on Mr. St. James to ask what had upset David. Something awful must have provoked David to fight with his much-adored father. Her stomach tumbled over at the thought. Perhaps she would find answers with Graciela.

She went upstairs toward the master suite. Family pictures hung on the wall of the now-familiar hallway of the St. James home. This would be Graciela's legacy—a beautiful, happy family. In many people's eyes, Graciela probably led a small life. But Vivi knew her love would leave an indelible imprint on everyone it touched. What mattered more than love?

She arrived at the threshold of the master bedroom, hesitating before tapping on the bedroom door.

"Come in." Graciela's voice sounded hoarse.

Vivi entered the dim room and crossed to the windows to part the drapes.

Used tissues were tossed on the nightstand. Graciela's eyes were red despite the smile she forced when she saw Vivi.

"*Mija*, come sit." She patted the bed.

Vivi loved being referred to with motherly affection. But as she slid onto the bed and sat crossed-legged, she grew concerned by Graciela's mood.

"Is everything okay?" she asked. "You look upset, and I've never seen David so shaken."

Graciela glanced out the window. Vivi noticed her lip quivering. Without meeting Vivi's eyes, Graciela clasped her hand.

"David will need time to wrestle with a demon. He'll need a lot of understanding, without demands." She turned her gaze on Vivi. "You be there for him when I can't, *Mija*. I know I can count on you. You love him and he loves you. When he confides in you, tell him family matters more than pride. Will you do that for me?"

"I'll do anything for you," Vivi said, puzzled by the request and message. "But you give me too much credit. David might not confide in me, and he certainly doesn't love me."

"I know my son." Graciela smiled and fingered a lock of Vivi's hair before cupping her cheek with a bony hand. "Now, enough of this. Where did we leave off with our little story?"

Vivi tamped down the thrill of hope coursing through her body. David loved her? Settling back against the headboard, she refrained from questioning Graciela further, and opened *The Help* to chapter sixteen.

Chapter Twenty-One

Present Day

Having spent most of August frustrated by her torn feelings for David and her inability to feel anything more than friendship for Franco despite his best efforts, Vivi welcomed the surge of optimism prompted by her first teacher in-service day. She loved the Catholic elementary school where she'd worked for the past four years. Soon the students' laughter and boundless wonder would fill her days.

For nine months of each year, Vivi soaked up their love and admiration like a dry sponge pitched into a lake. The accumulated hugs and approval always sustained her through the dry spell of summer.

Between grade-level team meetings, she'd stocked her art room with brushes, markers, crayons, paints, papers, clay, and glue. She'd revised and updated her curriculum for each grade, and decorated her classroom with a few personal touches. While she was checking her class rosters against the name tags she'd created, her phone rang.

"Hi, Cat," Vivi said.

"What are you doing right now?"

"Getting my classroom ready."

"Oh, well, don't forget about tonight. I've got birthday plans for you."

Vivi had seen Cat only once since Block Island, partly because Cat had been traveling frequently for work, and partly because Vivi had feared Cat discovering the secrets she'd been struggling to keep. Time apart had enabled her to sort out her feelings about everything that happened during that trip. Today she felt reasonably certain she could act indifferent if David or his dad came up in conversation.

"How could I forget?" she replied. "What have you planned?"

"Something fun and frivolous . . . so dress up."

"Will we be meeting up with Justin and his friends at some point?" Vivi's nose wrinkled at the thought. Cat had reunited with Justin soon after she'd returned from Block Island. Having learned more about Justin's private behavior had sickened Vivi. Then again, she'd never particularly liked him.

In fact, he reminded her of the typical asshole jock in every high school movie she'd ever seen. The arrogant, controlling jerk who dated the head cheerleader and laughed at her mean-girl antics. Vivi snickered at the analogy, considering he and Cat were sometimes only as mature as a high school couple.

Then again, Justin had never liked Vivi any better than she'd liked him. He'd so obviously considered her, with her average appearance and unglamorous job, far beneath him.

"No, I won't be seeing him tonight or any other night," Cat said.

Uh-oh. Trouble in paradise. Vivi should feel sad for her friend, but this news made her happy on too many levels.

"I'm sorry if you're unhappy." She tried to disguise the glee in her voice. "I guess we can talk about the gory details tonight."

"I'm sick of talking about Justin. I just want to have fun with my best friend on her birthday, okay?" Cat's overly bright voice was less than convincing, but Vivi didn't argue.

Besides, Vivi had earned a girls' night out on the town. Cat's plans would be fun. Of course, she didn't delude herself, either. The girls-only part would end abruptly after dinner.

Undoubtedly Cat would drag her all over Manhattan, where Vivi would end up playing the sidekick. Whenever Cat and Justin broke up, Cat needed to remind herself of the other fish in the sea by going out and being flirted with by every man within a mile of her presence.

Cat's insecurities boggled Vivi's mind, but she wouldn't deny her friend this indulgence. Everyone had their own way of handling loss. Who was she to refute Cat's right to party right through it?

"Sounds great, Cat. And I promise to do at least one thing to make you laugh, even though I know it will probably be at my own expense."

"That's why I love you!" Cat laughed. "Can you come by at seven?"

"See you then."

Vivi organized her name tags, cleared her desk, and put her phone in her purse before leaving the art room.

She strolled home, passing various cafés in her neighborhood and smiling at the patrons who sat at crowded café tables clustered on the sidewalks. Even the typical late-summer air—muggy, hot, and a little stinky—didn't faze her. Her hair, on the other hand, reacted with its usual flair, growing more unruly with each tenth-mile of her journey.

Vivi unlocked the front door of her apartment building. On the terrazzo tile floor of her small entry sat a bouquet of vibrantly colored Gerbera daisies and a small box. The cheerful flowers stood out against the vestibule's dull grays and browns.

She noticed her name scrawled across the small white envelope fastened in the plastic cardholder. David had sent the bracelet he'd bought her and two other floral arrangements during the past three weeks, so she guessed these and the gift were also from him.

She picked up the flowers and climbed the stairs to her apartment, thinking about the plans he'd wanted to make for her birthday. No doubt she would've enjoyed running around SoHo with him. These gifts made it hard to block him out, to not worry about how he was handling the upcoming wedding. But she'd needed to push him away in order to protect her heart, so she'd been refusing to speak with him ever since he left her apartment weeks ago.

Once inside, she set the vase on her table and sat down to read the card.

Happy birthday, Vivi. These remind me of the colorful, playful girl I miss. In lieu of my other birthday plans, I picked a gift for you. Let me know if you'd like to return it in favor of something else. P.S. Please forgive me.

Two months ago, she would've rocketed to the moon on unbridled happiness from this gesture. She would've danced around her apartment in victory, convincing herself he wanted more than friendship.

Today, the fuchsia and lemon-yellow blooms served merely as a reminder of her reckless behavior on Block Island. She'd fallen into bed with David the instant he touched her, without first demanding something in return.

No promise, no commitment—nothing.

And that's exactly what she got, too. No promise, no commitment. Nothing. In fact, she got less than nothing, because now they weren't even friends.

At first, she'd heaped all the blame on him. He'd wielded all the power, all the control. He'd taken advantage of her.

In hindsight, however, she could admit he'd warned her off, begged her to stop him before it went too far. She could also acknowledge the tremendous distress he'd been suffering, which clearly usurped his judgment that night. Unfortunately, her private admissions didn't mean she could easily resume the friendship they'd developed over the years.

She just didn't know how to face him in the wake of their lovemaking.

Not when the intense passion of their night together still affected her. When the imprint of his hands lingered on her skin. When the rapt look in his eyes haunted her every time she closed her own.

Thank God she'd agreed to keep their one-night stand a secret. David's discretion had spared her further humiliation. Now she needed time to put those memories and broken dreams behind her once and for all. Time to meet him on equal footing without wanting more from him than he did from her. That day seemed a long way off because, despite seeing David's flaws for the first time, she still loved him. Her irrational heart couldn't untangle itself from those bonds. She doubted he'd break down and attend his dad's wedding, but if he did, that still gave her a couple of weeks to prepare to see him again. Of course, each of David's attempts to soften her resolve distracted her for hours.

She fingered the firm, velvety petals of the daisies. Had David picked this arrangement himself, or had his secretary called in the order? She viewed the card again, confirming his handwriting. She doubted a Manhattan florist would deliver flowers to Astoria.

Had he come here hoping she'd answer the door? Her heart rate spiked. Tracing the neatly written words with her forefinger, she sighed and unwrapped the box to find a Lensbaby Pro Effects camera lens kit.

Oh my God. He'd easily dropped seven hundred dollars on this box of goodies. She wanted to be furious with him for thinking he could buy his way to forgiveness, but she knew that hadn't been his intention.

Naturally he'd remembered her drooling over these lenses in the past. She'd never been able to justify the purchase for herself. *Damn him.* She should send the gift back.

Times like this summoned her inner Scarlett O'Hara—she'd just worry about what to do with the gift tomorrow. Setting the card aside, she went to shower. Afterward, she stood at the far right side of her closet studying the extravagant clothing Cat had bought her over the years. Designer clothes she had worn once, or less often. Her generous friend's high-fashion outfits didn't quite fit with Vivi's low-maintenance lifestyle.

Knowing Cat's constant efforts to share her good fortune and love for couture were well intended, Vivi graciously accepted the gifts and hung them in her closet for a rainy day. Tonight would be a perfect occasion to break out something new. Perhaps she'd wear the jade bracelet, too. She was due for a little good luck. Wearing the bracelet had nothing to do with wanting David to be with her today. Nothing.

Since Cat was planning their evening, they'd probably eat at an exclusive restaurant, then end up at a hip, new nightclub surrounded by poseurs. Cat ran with the beautiful crowd even though, in truth, she had more substance than most of her superficial friends.

Although Vivi would be content to pop open a bottle of wine, eat spaghetti, and watch one of her all-time favorite movies, like *The Princess Bride*, a little adventure across the Queensboro Bridge might be just the change of pace she needed to cure her doldrums.

~

Cat's posh Upper East Side neighborhood, on 79th near Central Park, was another world compared to Vivi's artsy middle-class community. Stepping out of the cab, Vivi felt like an actress dressed in a costume. The high-heeled black leather boots with red soles she was wearing might as well have been stilts. Her green dress, with its thin black belt, revealed a hint of cleavage.

The humidity inspired her to style her hair into a diagonal French braid. For the final touch, she'd selected gold hoop earrings. She wasn't a model like her friend, but she looked pretty good.

"Whoa, look at you!" Cat eyed Vivi from head to toe when she opened her apartment door. "Nice boots!" Cat winked.

"These old things?" Vivi teased. "Someone tried to buy my affection with them."

"No. She knew she already had your affection." Cat smirked and crooked her finger, gesturing for Vivi to follow her into the living room.

Vivi's red soles tapped across the hardwood floors as she trailed behind Cat. Large windows with skyline views lined one side of the sleek apartment, which was appointed with a blend of glossy wood finishes and beige suede and silk upholstery.

Sleek and elegant lines, with a hint of femininity. Just like Cat.

Cat pushed a full glass of wine into Vivi's hands before sitting on the sofa. "I thought we'd have a drink here before we go out."

"Okay." Vivi wasn't a wine connoisseur. She merely guessed, from the rich color and bouquet of her drink, that Cat had broken out an expensive bottle. She swirled it around in her glass, inhaled its aroma, and then sampled it. "Ooh, this tastes good. Thanks."

"Brunellos are good for every occasion." Cat raised her glass in silent toast.

Vivi didn't know a Brunello from a Zinfandel, but she nodded just the same. Sometimes she preferred not to highlight the differences between her friend and her.

If viewed on paper, no one would believe the model living the good life in New York would be the soul sister of an eccentric art teacher from a dysfunctional home. Whatever. It worked for them.

Vivi often suspected she might be Cat's only true friend—someone who loved her for who she was rather than how she looked.

Before Vivi could ask about the plans for the night, Cat presented her with a gift-wrapped box. "Happy birthday."

"Oh, you really shouldn't have, Cat." Vivi untied the ribbons on the tiny box. Inside, she found a cool-looking silver John Hardy ring.

Before she could try it on, Cat blurted, "I know you don't love rings because you want 'unencumbered fingers' when you're working, but this is so flat and cute. And you're not working all the time."

"I actually love it. It's kind of funky, right?" Vivi smiled at Cat and slipped the ring on her finger. "It fits! Thank you." She hugged her friend.

"Jackson went in on that with me, so you can thank him later. He's decided to crash our little party later." The gift discussion was cut short when Cat's phone vibrated on top of the coffee table. She checked the screen, rolled her eyes, and placed the phone back on the table.

"Justin?" Vivi asked.

"No. David." Cat waved at the phone. "He's been calling a lot, but I promised Jackson I'd hold firm."

Vivi cocked her head. "Hold firm?"

"David is refusing to attend Dad's wedding. Jackson thinks we can force him to apologize to Dad if we just shut him out for a while." She straightened her shoulders and drank some of her wine. "If it works, we'll all be better off."

Vivi's stomach dropped. Despite her own issues with David, this treatment seemed cruel. Cat and Jackson would be ashamed of their behavior if they knew the truth about Mr. St. James and Janet.

"That sounds like bullying." Vivi eyed her wine, avoiding Cat's gaze. She uttered, "Don't go along."

"Gee, I'm *so* surprised you're taking David's side." Cat sat deeper into the sofa and curled her legs under her bottom.

Vivi ignored Cat's mockery. Poor David. Vivi now knew exactly how heavy a burden he'd been shouldering. If she could barely keep quiet, how the heck had he managed to do so while suffering their scorn?

"I'm not taking anyone's side." *Your dad is a lying jerk.* Oh, crap. Had she said those last words aloud? Relief washed over her when Cat didn't react. "All I'm saying is that no one knows what happened. It's possible your dad is at fault, you know."

"I doubt it." Cat tapped her fingernails against her glass. "If that were true, why wouldn't David just tell us whatever Dad did to piss him off?"

"Well, your dad's been just as tight-lipped." Vivi leaned forward and set her glass down. She was treading dangerous territory and totally unsure whether she could reach her goal without exposing the truth. "If I were you, I'd spend my energy trying to convince them to work it out rather than taking sides."

Contrition nipped at Vivi's conscience because of her failure to deliver her message about family and pride to David, especially because Graciela had given so much and asked so little.

Would hearing his mother's words help him finally begin to heal? The pull to run to him, to comfort him, tugged at her heart. *Soon.*

"Maybe you have a point. I'm uncomfortable with Jackson's plan anyway." Cat fingered her pendant necklace. "I feel awful about David, especially since he and Laney broke up. He works so much. I don't think he's reconnected with old friends yet."

Vivi felt a stab of disappointment. Perhaps he hadn't been sending her flowers and gifts because he missed *her.*

"Bullying won't make David attend the wedding." She gazed into her deep purple wine. "Let David and your dad work this out on their own."

Vivi wanted to give Mr. St. James a piece of her mind. Graciela had protected him in order to keep her family together. She would hate how her plan backfired by alienating David while Mr. St. James merrily built a new life for himself.

"Honestly, I'm not really looking forward to the wedding." Cat toyed with her long, silken hair.

"I remember when you first told me your dad had started dating, you seemed skeptical."

"I'd seen Janet around the club for years. I remember her first husband being sort of a pompous jerk. When she and Dad got together, it freaked me out to think she's almost twenty years younger than him."

"I met her only once, briefly. I didn't realize she is that much younger." Vivi leaned forward. "Do you like her better now that you've gotten to know her?"

"Mm, I don't dislike her. Dad's gaga over her. She kind of reminds me of Laney, actually." Cat grimaced and then laughed.

Like Laney? David's father had betrayed a vivacious, loving woman for a cool, distant one. Vivi shivered. David's words echoed in her mind. *God forbid we'd end up like them.* Maybe he'd been right.

After all, Vivi would probably embarrass him in front of his colleagues and Ivy League friends. She'd be out of place in his world. An unbidden image of her own parents crossed her mind. Maybe she didn't deserve a happy ending anyway, she thought.

Cat's phone vibrated again. This time her face blanched when she noted the caller.

"Oh, hell no."

"Who now?" Vivi finished her wine. "Jackson?"

"Justin." Cat's nervous laugh didn't fool Vivi. "He's becoming annoying."

"How so?" Vivi shed her boots and massaged her cramped toes. High fashion be damned, she preferred sensible footwear.

"We broke up on Wednesday—*don't* say it!" Cat stuck her hand out to silence Vivi. "Anyway, he keeps calling."

"Well, that's your pattern, isn't it? Break up to make up. Are you serious about ending it this time?"

"I think so. He's exhausting. I love his good points, but I can't take any more of his mood swings." Cat's expression reflected indecision mixed with regret. "Now he's convinced I'm already seeing someone else. He does this every time I go on location for work."

"Well, you *do* work with beautiful men." Vivi's brows went up. "I can see how that might be intimidating."

"Half of them are gay, Vivi. Damn shame, too." She blushed. "But I'm not a cheater. Either he trusts me, or not."

"True." Vivi's stomach growled, causing Cat to laugh. "Um, so where and when are we going to eat? Obviously I'm getting hungry!"

The resounding click of the front door's lock caught their attention before Cat answered. Stunned, they stared at each other and then at the entry, as if watching a movie. Seconds later, the front door swung open and Justin stepped inside.

"What the hell, Justin?" Cat leaped off the sofa and strode toward him, pointing her finger toward the door. "Get out!"

Justin scanned the living room, probably seeking evidence of the suspected boyfriend. Visible relief settled in his features when he saw Vivi sitting alone on the couch and only two glasses of wine on the coffee table.

Vivi studied him from her catbird seat. She might not like Justin, but he was a head turner. His ruggedly handsome face had a boyish quality, like Patriots quarterback Tom Brady.

"I can't believe you barged in here." Cat held out her palm. "Give me back my key. Obviously I can't trust you."

Vivi's brows shot up. If Cat hadn't already taken her key back, then she wasn't really done with Justin.

He slid the keychain into his front pocket, crossing his arms like a petulant child. "Not taking my calls now?"

"I'm not at your beck and call." Cat's eyes bulged. "We are over! Give me my key, then go. Vivi and I have plans tonight."

He studied Vivi's outfit, then looked Cat up and down, taking note of her sexy sandals and low-cut dress. "You ladies look fine." He fingered a skein of Cat's hair and whistled. "You're not dolled up to stay in and watch a movie. So, who are you meeting?"

Cat brushed his hand away and turned to reach for her phone. "Justin, get out or I'm calling security to come remove you."

"Put the phone down, Cat." His authoritative command startled both women.

Every muscle in Vivi's body went rigid and the hair follicles on the back of her neck tingled. Justin's face grew ruddy; his hands fisted by his side. Thinking back to Cat's reluctant confession on Block Island, it seemed quite possible they could all find themselves on tonight's eleven o'clock news.

Suddenly Justin changed tactics, softening his expression. "Just be honest with me. If you met someone else, then tell me." His shoulders slumped. He dipped his chin and lowered his voice. "Don't make me hear it from someone else, Cat. You owe me at least that much respect."

"Why bother? You never believe me." She stared at him for a minute. "There is no other man, not yet, anyway. *You're* the reason this never works. I can't take your accusations and crazy behavior anymore."

"I love you." He clasped her wrist. "How am I supposed to feel when I see the way every man leers at you? I know those photographers prey on women. Don't hate me because I care."

"I don't hate you, Justin. You suffocate me." She tried to pry his fingers off her wrist. "Please let go. Vivi and I are leaving for dinner."

He glanced back at Vivi. "Where are you going?"

"I don't know. It's a surprise." Vivi tried to appear sympathetic in order to defuse the situation. She didn't want to repeat old mistakes by doing something to make a bad situation worse. "I think you ought to work this out another time, after you calm down."

He ignored Vivi's request and turned back to Cat. "Are you meeting others tonight?"

"None of your business." Cat puffed out her chest.

Oh, frick! Vivi's stomach dropped. This wasn't the best time for her friend's defiant streak to join the party. Justin's and Cat's temperaments were too combustible. The air in the apartment felt positively explosive.

"I'll leave once you tell me the truth." Justin tightened his grip on Cat's arm. "Are you meeting others for dinner?"

"Let go." Cat's winced in pain. "You're hurting me."

Rather than release her, he rammed her against the dining chair. "Just answer my damn question, Cat. I'm not an idiot. Clearly you're dressed to impress, or maybe you plan to whore around with your friend and pick up strangers."

"Okay, Justin, this is getting out of control." Vivi stood, but her miniature frame was less than threatening. She took a step toward them. "Please let go of Cat."

"Quiet, Vivi. This is between her and me." He shoved Cat up against the wall, with his one hand firmly pressed on her breastbone and the other holding on to her hair.

The veins in his neck bulged, sending a tide of crimson rushing to his cheeks. "Are you planning to fuck someone tonight just to show me how much you don't care?"

Vivi recoiled at his ugly tone and language. Seized with panic, she couldn't think straight. On instinct, she bounded toward Justin and pounded on his back. He barely noticed, so she tugged at his arm, using her full body weight to try to pry him off Cat. Her heart kicked in her chest as she realized how little effect she had against his strength and size.

"Get off me, Vivi!" he spat. He turned and flung her away like a dishrag.

Her feet left the ground. In disbelief, she flew through the air, feeling as if she were moving in slow motion. A thunderous crack split the air, followed by a sharp burst of pain.

Then everything cut to black.

Chapter Twenty-Two

David tossed his cell phone onto his mahogany credenza and stared out the window. The late-summer evening light cast a peach glow across the city skyline. While both New York and Hong Kong were surrounded by water and boasted huge plots of densely clustered skyscrapers, he missed the dramatic mountain ranges surrounding Hong Kong.

He'd been in New York only a few months, yet his memories of Hong Kong already seemed ancient.

He glanced at his silent phone, willing it to ring. No such luck. Beside the lifeless phone sat a calendar with Vivi's birthday circled in red. Had she liked his gift? She hadn't called. She continued to ignore his e-mails, too.

She was locking him out of her life.

Nothing he'd done to date had softened her attitude. Seeking balance between pushing too hard and not hard enough, he'd chosen not to call her. Now he was beginning to feel desperate. Walking this tightrope required all his patience.

But he'd never quit.

He looked at the other date circled on the calendar—the one in black. Two weeks remained until his father's wedding. Cat and

Jackson had been refusing his calls in an obvious effort to strong-arm him into attending the affair.

He drummed his fingers on the arm of his chair, then swiveled his chair back to face his desk. To his right sat a silver-framed photograph of Vivi, his siblings, and him, taken at his law school graduation dinner. He lifted the picture, tracing all of their faces with his finger. Vivi's gap-toothed grin leaped off the photo.

"Ahem." Laney stood in the doorway of his office, holding a contract in her hands. Her finely tailored suit hugged her body, but David felt no lingering attraction for the woman who'd caught his eye and eased his pain not long ago. Of course, objectively she was beautiful. Her physical appearance and brains used to be enough. Now they left him cold.

He returned the photo to his desk and waved her in. Since returning from Block Island, they were engaged in a delicate dance of cordial behavior at work. Her noticing him staring at that photo might shred what little civility remained.

"Is that the indemnity agreement for the Ingram deal?" He smiled politely.

"Yes." She approached his desk and laid it on top of his desk blotter. "I think I've found a way to address the problems with the intellectual property protection. Let me know your thoughts once you review it." She turned to leave without so much as a smile or polite remark.

"Thanks, Laney." Without turning to face him, she raised her hand in the air to wave an acknowledgment. He called out, "Have a nice weekend."

Then she was gone. He glanced at the clock. Seven thirty. Friday night. Of course, he had no plans. Leaning back in his chair, he rubbed his face with his palms.

Three weeks ago he'd returned from Vivi's apartment feeling like the walking dead. Seeing himself through the lens of her eyes had sickened him.

Selfish. Cowardly. Hypocritical. Unforgiving.

All revolting traits. Traits that mirrored the sour pit in his stomach that kept growing larger each day.

When he'd arrived home after that confrontation, he'd found Laney sitting on the floor of his bedroom closet, poring through a midsize cardboard box she'd found stowed there. A box labeled "Vivi," which contained various photographs, works of art, and letters she'd sent him throughout the past decade.

Some of the letters appeared to have been read and tossed on the floor around Laney's slumped figure. Her hair had obscured her face while she sifted through the photographs, studying them intently. When David walked in on her, he'd been stunned by her invasion of his privacy. But the tears streaming down her cheeks had stopped him cold.

He'd been a jerk, not her. Vivi had been right about that much, at least. Laney had invested far more in their relationship than he. Even when she'd denied him being the reason she sought a transfer, he'd known she'd been hedging her bets with him. He'd been complicit in the deception, and then he'd failed her.

He'd touched her shoulder as he'd knelt down to pick up the papers from the floor.

"You love her." Laney's strained voice had only made him feel worse.

Of course he loved many things about Vivi. She'd been one of the most important women in his life, and possibly his truest friend. He nodded. "She's been my best friend for a long time."

"No. You *love* her." Laney had shoved the photos in his face. "Look at you. In almost every photo you're staring at *her*, not the camera. And there's so much joy in your face. You've never looked at me like that."

"Laney, let's not do this." He'd gently pried the photos from her hands and returned everything to the box. "Come on, let's talk in the living room."

He'd helped her up off the floor, made her some tea, and then listened to her cry. She'd railed against him for not coming back from Block Island sooner, for not ever saying he'd loved her, and for not making their relationship more important.

David hadn't wanted to cause her more pain. He'd bitten back any defense or justification that sprung to mind, accepting all the blame. Once she'd tired of complaining, she'd packed up the few things she'd kept at his home and walked out the door.

Now he glanced again at the photo on his desk. Laney had been right. He was always looking at Vivi. She made him feel light and cheerful in a way no one else ever could. These past weeks he'd come to privately acknowledge he did love her, and not merely as his friend. But what good was love that ended in heartache? And what good was love without forgiveness?

He desperately wanted her forgiveness. Yet as he remained unable to forgive his father, Vivi remained equally unyielding.

Of course, his father hadn't begged for David's forgiveness. After David had moved to Hong Kong, his father had sent a handful of rather impersonal updates by e-mail, but that was all.

His mother had always said forgiveness was a crucial element of love. It seemed the crux of David's problem turned on whether he loved his father enough to forgive him.

His mother had loved the man enough to forgive his betrayal—enough to beg David to do the same. So even if David didn't love his father enough, could his boundless love for his mother enable him to find room for forgiveness?

He blew out a breath and opened his eyes. The agreement Laney had left sat in front of him. He didn't feel up to reading it now. He stuck it in his briefcase, shut off his lamp, and went home.

~

He'd changed into shorts and a T-shirt and now stood alone in his kitchen. The weekend. Vivi hadn't called about the flowers and camera lenses he'd delivered earlier. She might have plans tonight, possibly with Franco, or some other man. Knowing so little about her love life bothered David.

She'd always kept it separate from him until Block Island exposed so much. Once again, he pictured Franco kissing her, like a recurring nightmare. His hand curled into a fist.

His phone vibrated against the thick concrete countertop, mercifully pulling him away from the imagery. His heart dropped to his stomach when he read his sister's incoming text message.

Need u ASAP. 911 @ home.

He called her, but she didn't answer. David pulled on his running shoes, grabbed his phone and wallet, and ran out the door. He sprinted the three blocks to Cat's apartment. Blue and red police lights lit up the front of her building. His muscles froze on his sharp inhale as his mind began racing. When he broke from his trance, he went straight to her apartment.

Her door was unlocked, so he let himself inside, where he was greeted by the jarring sound of walkie-talkies. Cat and Jackson stood on the far side of the living room talking to a police officer. David's muscles eased upon finding her unharmed.

She looked up and ran to him the instant their eyes met. Collapsing against his chest, she trembled and cried in his arms. He stroked her hair while looking over her head to throw Jackson a questioning glance. Jackson nodded but stayed by the cop, so David spoke softly into Cat's ear.

"What happened?" He kept the alarm from his voice.

"Justin." She sniffed. "He barged in and we fought. The police needed a statement. God, I was so scared." Her voice cracked behind another sob.

"Okay, calm down." He set her back and looked her over. "You're okay? He didn't hurt you?"

She touched her bruised bicep. "Not seriously." Then she glanced to her left and burst into tears again.

David followed her gaze to the living room coffee table and the bloodstain on the carpet underneath it.

"Oh, Jesus." His eyes darted back to Cat. "Did you hurt him? Do you need a lawyer, Cat?"

She shook her head, unable to speak through her sobs.

"Jackson," David called. "Whose blood is that?"

Jackson's grim face worried David, but didn't prepare him for the answer. "Vivi's."

David's knees buckled beneath him and he sank to the floor. Cat crouched down beside him.

"Is she . . . is she dead?" Unable to focus, he felt bile rising in his throat. He leaned forward and pressed his fingertips against the hardwood floor.

"No. She was unconscious when the EMTs took her. Her head was gashed open."

"What the hell happened?" He rose to his feet as adrenaline began pumping through him, causing his muscles to twitch. As Jackson approached, David barked, "Where's Justin? I'll kill him!"

"Shut it, David." Jackson grabbed David's arm and backed him into the corner of the room. "The cops are here. You know better than to make threats."

The room spun again, so David gripped Jackson's arm while refocusing.

"Justin took off when Vivi hit the table." Jackson scowled as his eyes drifted to the bloodstain. "Fucking coward."

"Did you see her?" David couldn't control his shaky voice. "Did you see Vivi?"

"No." Jackson put his hand over David's. "She'd been moved before I arrived."

Tears clouded David's vision. He had to go to her.

"Take Cat to your place when the cops leave. I'm going to the hospital." Without waiting for Jackson's reply, he kissed his sister's head and hurried out the door.

David sprinted without stopping. The eight blocks to Lenox Hill Hospital whizzed past in a blur. When he arrived, the emergency room coordinator advised him to take a seat and be patient.

Vivi had been taken for CT scans, MRIs, and EEG tests. No one would provide him any information about the severity of her injuries. Frustration mounted as he met with one dead end after another.

Stuck in the waiting room, he spent the next two hours researching skull fractures and traumatic brain injuries on his phone. Each page he read made him sicker and more concerned: hematomas, swelling, neurological damage, and worse. When he noticed how hard his knees were bouncing, he stood to stretch and move around.

Hospitals reminded David of the months he'd spent with his mother during her chemo and radiation therapy. Images of holding her hair back when she got sick from the chemo, wiping her forehead with cool cloths, and holding her hand while she rested all replayed in his head.

He hated hospitals, and prayed this visit ended with better results than his mother's had. Losing Vivi would be crippling. He loved her. He'd taken her, and her love, for granted for too long. If she made it through this incident, he swore he'd not waste another moment. One way or another, he'd win her back.

To distract himself, he called Jackson to check on his sister. He breathed a sigh of relief upon learning the police had issued a warrant for Justin's arrest on charges of third-degree assault. Once they found him, he'd be in jail for at least a day until he was arraigned. Cat would be safe with Jackson until Justin was in custody.

By eleven o'clock he'd eaten his third bag of chips. Dinner. A mixture of salt, grease, and worry settled like a hard lump in his stomach. Exhaustion overwhelmed his senses. He slouched into the uncomfortable vinyl chair while nodding off.

When the nurse finally called his name, it startled him. He bounded from his chair, leaving the crumpled bag of chips discarded.

"How is she?" He studied the nurse's stone-faced expression for clues, only to come up empty-handed.

"She's resting and conscious." She pushed open the doors leading to the emergency room beds. "You can see her now."

"Does she need surgery?" He held his breath.

"The scans looked clean. She needed twelve stitches on her scalp, but nothing more serious. She's got a significant concussion, so she'll be on restricted activity for a while. We'll release her tonight. Someone should be with her for the next day or two to wake her periodically and watch for warning symptoms such as vomiting or changes in vision, just to be safe. We'll give her a packet of information on how to handle her recovery."

David nodded at the nurse, although he'd barely heard the details. He'd stopped listening once he'd learned she'd come through this intact. Tears filled his eyes. His body quaked from fatigue.

The nurse drew back the curtain surrounding Vivi's inclined bed. When Vivi saw David, her eyes grew wide and teary.

"Oh, God. What's wrong?" She looked terrified, then held a hand up to her head and winced. "What happened to Cat?"

"Nothing. Cat's fine." He walked to the bed, resisting the urge to take her into his arms. "She's fine. Jackson took her to his home. The police have issued a warrant for Justin's arrest, so they're looking for him now."

"Cat must be so upset." Vivi sighed before closing her eyes. Then her eyelids flew open. "If Justin didn't hurt her, then why are you here looking like a wreck?"

His chin drew back in surprise.

"Because I've been sitting here for hours imagining the worst-possible scenarios about *your* injuries." Her bed squeaked under his weight when he sat on its edge. He gave in to his emotions, laid his head in her lap, and wrapped his arms around her thighs. "My God, Vivi. I'm so happy you're all right."

"Oh." She didn't touch him. The surprise in her voice floated above him. "I'll be fine as long as I don't overexert myself for a while."

"I know." He sat up and wiped his eyes. He yearned to touch her, to comfort and be comforted. "I've tried calling your dad all evening, but he's not answering the phone or returning my messages. Is there anyone else I should call?"

"I'm sure you're shocked my dad's a no-show." She glanced down at her hands, wearing an indescribable expression in her eyes.

David was pissed at her father, yet selfishly celebrated the fact that he wasn't available, because it gave him the opportunity to spend time alone with her. He ignored the remark, though, so as not to upset her.

"So, no one else to call?"

Vivi tilted her head. "Like who?"

"I don't know, maybe Franco?" he asked cautiously, praying she'd say no.

Her puzzled expression turned uncomfortable. "No."

He suppressed the grin he felt turning up the corners of his mouth. No Franco. No Franco was very good news. It meant he had a chance.

He blew out the air he'd been holding in his lungs, then took charge of the situation.

"We'll get out of here soon." He flashed an encouraging smile. "My house is close by, so you can get settled and rest within the hour."

"Your house?" She shook her head, then winced and touched the bandages covering her stiches. "I'm going home, to my place."

"No." He stared at her without blinking. "You have to be observed for at least twenty-four hours. I live near the hospital. If anything happens, we can rush right back." He pulled his phone from his pocket and texted his sister an update on Vivi's condition. "Please don't argue. I can't take any more stress tonight, and neither can you. Cat's with Jackson, so you can't go there. You can call them when we leave."

"I'll go home to my dad's, David. I won't be alone, but I can't stay with you."

She sat in the bed, blinking at him. Her tiny form looked fragile. He didn't want to fight. He wanted to curl up beside her, hold her, and make everything better. She, however, clearly wanted nothing to do with him. He rubbed his hand over his face, sighing.

"It's too late to go all the way to Connecticut tonight. And your dad isn't even home." Her dejected expression burned him. "Vivi, do you hate me so much? Please, let me help you. You can go back to ignoring me once we know you're out of the woods."

She bit her lip. With a defeated sigh, she finally said, "Fine."

"Thank you." David lifted off the bed and sat in the chair with a sense of despair. She hadn't answered his question. Perhaps she did hate him.

The nurse returned and handed Vivi a small box with her personal effects. David noticed the jade bracelet among the items Vivi had been wearing. He looked at her, wondering if she could feel the hope in his heart. He fingered the bracelet. "It didn't work."

"What?"

"Jade is supposed to bring luck and protection. If you were wearing this tonight, it didn't work." He frowned, envisioning her being tossed by that brute.

"Or it did. My injuries could've been worse," she said, shrugging. Then, speaking to no one in particular, "My dress is bloody."

"Hold on," David said as he grabbed the curtain. "I'll be right back."

He returned promptly with a set of medical scrubs. "Wear these and we'll see if the dry cleaner can get those stains out of your dress tomorrow."

"Thank you," she said, clutching the blue scrubs. "But I doubt I'll ever wear that dress again."

David squeezed her ankle and then stepped away. "I'll step out while you change. Then close your eyes and rest until they bring the discharge papers."

They didn't get to his home until after one o'clock in the morning. Jackson had called to inform David the cops had taken Justin into custody. When David updated Vivi, he expected her to express relief.

Instead, she rubbed her eyes and stared at the floor. David decided not to press her about what had happened, or how she felt. Reliving the evening's events now would be unwise. She needed to relax.

Vivi quietly followed David into his building, up the elevator, and into his condo. He noticed her eyes taking in her surroundings as they walked back toward his bedroom, but she said nothing. Did she like his home? Could she be happy here? he wondered as he turned on the bedroom light.

She looked uncomfortable in her high-heeled boots and the too-large scrubs. She kept scratching at the stiff cotton smock.

"Let me get you something softer to sleep in, then you can crawl under the covers." He went to the dresser to find a large T-shirt. "Those boots look uncomfortable as hell. Are they one of Cat's bright ideas?" He preferred Vivi in her own clothes, or his.

"This is your room." Her hands toyed with the belt of the dress in her arms. "I'll stay in the guest room."

"No, stay here." He pulled out an old Georgetown T-shirt. "You'll want a private bathroom in case you don't feel well."

Her eyes darted to his bed and back to him. He noticed her head shaking ever so slightly.

"Don't worry. I'm not planning on staying here with you." He placed the shirt on top of the comforter, then stacked and fluffed the pillows so she could rest at an incline. "Go ahead and change. I'll come back in to check on you before I go to sleep."

He left the room without looking back. After getting a glass of water from the kitchen, he paced the hallway for a minute before knocking on the door.

"Come in."

She sat on the bed with the blanket pulled over her legs, looking afraid and vulnerable. How had they gotten to this place? Gone were the loving, trusting eyes that had always adored him. She was as skittish as a colt around him now, and it sucked. Somehow he had to fix things between them. The edge of the mattress flattened under his weight as he sat beside her.

"I have to wake you up every few hours." He placed the glass of water on the bedside table. "Doctor's orders."

"I know."

He stood to go, then stopped. "Vivi." He fell silent while she simply blinked at him. All of his words caught in his throat. He shook his head, feeling foolish. "I wanted to see you on your birthday, but not like this. I'm sorry about everything that's happened, tonight and before." He inhaled deeply and sighed. "I'll be right next door if you need anything."

He walked out of the room, shutting the door behind him. In the guest room he stretched across the bed and stared at the ceiling.

This was his last shot. Twenty-four hours to win her forgiveness. But forgiveness wasn't all he wanted.

He rolled onto his side and pictured her in his room. Despite the distance between them, she looked so right sitting in his bed. She belonged there—belonged here with him.

His head and his heart had stood on opposites sides of the fence these past several weeks. Now he was at the precipice with respect to their relationship. All or nothing. Those were her terms when they'd last spoken. He loved her and hoped he was capable of giving her everything.

When he offered, would she take it from him?

Chapter Twenty-Three

City lights streamed through the sides of the bedroom window blinds, spilling onto a framed drawing on David's nightstand. Vivi recognized it as the one she'd sent David after his mother died. She reached out and brought the small portrait close to her face for a closer inspection.

Graciela's smiling face stared back at Vivi. *I know my son.* Vivi's hands trembled. She'd held on to the promise of those words for too long. Maybe David did love her, just never enough. She clutched the frame to her chest, seeking comfort.

But the charcoal image couldn't wrap Vivi in the warm embrace she remembered. It didn't smell like the spicy perfume Graciela had worn, or whisper motherly endearments in her ear. It was only a drawing, and a poor one at that, Vivi thought with some regret. She'd never been very good with portraits.

When she set the frame back on the bedside table, she glanced at the clock. Five in the morning. David must be sound asleep. She sunk her head back into his pillow and inhaled. She could smell him. Unable to stop herself, she rolled onto her side and inhaled again, indulging the sensation of lying in his bed.

Without thinking, she ran her hands over the T-shirt she wore, as if she was somehow touching him, or he was touching her. Vivi stretched her hands across the mattress, wondering which side he usually slept on. Nearer to the bathroom, or the window? Then she shook away the thoughts before sorrow and regret could strike.

The space behind her eyes ached. Her fingers touched the bandage covering the itchy stitches. An ugly reminder of Justin's brutality.

How long had she been unconscious? She recalled nothing between the time Justin had flung her off his back and when she'd woken up in the ambulance. Luckily, neither she nor Cat sustained permanent injuries. Then again, she didn't feel very lucky right now.

Although thinking about last evening's events made her head pound, her growling stomach demanded attention. No surprise there. Her last meal had been yesterday's lunch, which meant she was a meal and several snacks shy of her usual intake.

Swinging her legs out of the bed and onto the floor, she stood slowly. Once she felt steady, she began searching for the kitchen to find something to eat.

Along the way she noticed a large collage of photographs covering one entire section of the hallway wall. Even in the shadows, she recognized many of the pictures.

Each photograph transported her back to a specific moment in time—some vague, others vivid. Cat and Vivi smiling in their high school graduation caps and gowns. Cat's sweet-sixteen party. The Christmas cookie debacle, when Vivi and the St. Jameses had all ended up covered in colored icing. Her varied, and sometimes frightening, hairstyles captured and depicted here for all eternity.

And Cat looked so young and unworldly. Her pre–modeling days. Cat lost that doe-eyed look years ago. The past twenty-four hours probably wiped out whatever innocence remained, Vivi thought glumly.

She proceeded down the hall, then turned on a small lamp in the living room. Earlier she'd noticed the handsome details of David's home, but had been too tired and uncomfortable to comment. Now she could take her time and inspect his things.

The modern kitchen had concrete countertops and stainless steel appliances. The living room and dining room areas were separated by a see-through bookshelf. The entire condo smelled like him, just like his sheets.

When he'd first returned from Hong Kong, she'd waited for an invitation to visit. Standing here now felt surreal, and sad, especially under the circumstances. Once more, her thoughts slid to Cat and Justin. Thank God things hadn't turned out worse for everyone. She couldn't afford to lose more family.

She poured herself a glass of milk, grabbed a handful of grapes, and snagged her prescription bottle of painkillers from the counter. *Please, God, let the food and pills dull this headache.*

She ate in the dark. Other than an occasional rumbling truck engine and screeching set of brakes, she heard very little external sound, which was unusual in the city.

After finishing her snack, she meandered through the main living space, touching David's collection of books and knickknacks. All the rooms were accented with interesting lamps and thick Tibetan carpets.

She loved his home, and that made her sadder. She didn't want to love it, or him, any longer. With her glass in her hand, she strolled into the study and sank listlessly into his leather desk chair. On one corner of his gorgeous, burled-wood desk sat a framed picture of her blowing a kiss to the camera.

She studied the photograph, unable to recall the occasion. Her mop of hair was cropped at her jaw at that time, so it was probably six or seven years ago. Mindlessly, she tugged at a section of her long hair and wrapped it around her hand.

"Vivi? Are you feeling all right?"

She turned, feeling self-conscious sitting at his desk, looking frightful as ever. David stood in the archway wearing an old T-shirt and shorts. He still stole her breath away, especially when he looked deliciously sleepy, rumpled, and concerned.

"I was hungry. I'm sorry for waking you."

"You didn't wake me." He rubbed his hand over his face and then stretched both arms over his head. "I set my alarm to check on you. You weren't in bed." He noticed the pill bottle. "Does your head hurt?"

"Yes."

"Do you feel sick to your stomach?" His reached toward her and then withdrew his hand when she flinched. "Is your vision okay?"

"Just hungry." She quirked a small smile before lightly touching her fingers to the bandages again.

David's eyes darkened, but he said nothing as he came to lean against the edge of the desk. Then he noticed the photograph she'd been studying.

"Do you remember that day?" He smiled.

"No." She shook her head. "But obviously it was another of my many bad hair days."

He chuckled and leaned closer. "That's the day you left for your freshman year of college. You were so excited."

"Was I?" She looked back at the picture. She'd never liked school. Perhaps she'd just been happy about gaining some freedom and distance from her father, his constant depression, and her regrets. "Did you take this before I left for the train station?"

He nodded, then rested his hands on his thighs. For weeks she'd avoided him in order to give herself time to gain emotional distance. But the intimacy of the wee hours and memories made it impossible not to feel pulled toward him, as always.

"Why do you keep this here?" she asked, wishing she hadn't.

He hesitated before answering. "Because seeing your face makes me happy."

Vivi gulped and then held her breath. His calm reply contradicted the intensity of his gaze. "I don't remember seeing all of these pictures displayed in your old apartment."

"They weren't. Until recently, I'd kept them in a box." He crossed his arms. "After Laney left, I put up my favorites. You've all shut me out now, so this is all I have left."

"Stop it, David," she started. "Emotional blackmail's not your style."

"It never was, but desperate times . . ." He let the old saying die without finishing.

"Do you miss Laney?" Vivi asked, then cast her eyes downward.

"No. I don't miss her at all. I miss you." Lifting himself off the desk, he kneeled down before her. "I miss you so much. More than I could've imagined."

Vivi's mouth opened involuntarily. When she failed to respond, he continued.

"Tonight, when I saw the bloodstains and Cat told me you'd been taken away unconscious, I panicked. I was terrified you might wake up a different person because of brain trauma, or maybe not wake up at all. I knew then I wouldn't want to face a future without you in it." His eyes suddenly darkened to coal black. "I could kill Justin for what he's done, but I'll settle for burying him in lawsuits."

"The criminal charges will be punishment enough," Vivi said.

"Hardly." David scowled while gripping the arms of the desk chair until his knuckles turned white. "He'll plead out and be slapped on the hand with community service and a small fine at best. We'll hit him where it hurts . . . his wallet. Off the top of my head, I can think of several torts, like trespass, assault, battery, intentional infliction of emotional distress—"

"I'm not interested in revenge or greed, I just want to heal and move on." Vivi sensed David's disbelief. "Legal battles will only prolong his contact with Cat. Don't force her, or me, through that, David. Time to forgive and forget."

"Are you serious?" He rocked backward slightly. "You're going to let *him* off the hook?"

"He's hardly off the hook. Fines, a criminal record, and most importantly, he's lost Cat, and maybe some of his self-respect, too." Her eyes fluttered closed as she actually empathized with Justin about those last two blows. She knew exactly how much pain he would feel because she'd been in his shoes twenty years ago . . . and every day since then. That special kind of hell was worse than anything David could throw at Justin. "Let it go. I won't cooperate."

"I know I'm not as compassionate as you are, but in this case your big heart is steering you wrong. The way you forgive your dad year after year amazes me, but this is different. Justin's got to face the consequences of what he's done—"

"Stop it! Please." The stress of the night's trauma converged with her memories, causing a sudden breakdown. Hot tears spilled onto Vivi's cheeks. The truth about her relationship with her dad pressed up against her ribs, begging for release. Shame and fear and regret mingled together, tightening her throat. "You don't know what you're talking about, especially when it comes to my dad. Sometimes people make mistakes they can't take back. It doesn't mean they aren't sorry. It doesn't mean they don't think about it all the time. Trust me, people can punish themselves enough without needing anyone else to pile on."

David looked confused by her wellspring of emotion. "Vivi, I don't want to upset you, but honestly, how would you know? You've never hurt a soul in your life."

Vivi started shaking her head with her eyes squeezed closed. "That's not true."

"When? I can't think of a single time when you've hurt another person."

"I have!" Vivi replied before looking in David's disbelieving eyes. "I have and I've paid the price every day."

"Every day?" When he reached for her hand, she withdrew. She didn't deserve his comfort. "Does this have something to do with your father?"

"It's about me." Her voice caught in her throat. "You've blamed my dad all these years for the way he treated me. But the truth is . . . the truth is . . ." The words lodged in her throat so tight, she had to force them out. "I'm responsible for the accident that killed my mom and brother."

David's eyes widened and his jaw came unhinged. The room felt close and hot as silence stretched between them. Her mind raced, unsure of whether the fuzzy feeling arising from her confession was a sense of relief or stupefaction.

"How is that possible?" David asked, his voice distant. "You were only six, so you weren't driving."

The unpleasant images came quickly. As always, it saddened her that her only sharp, clear recollection of her mother's voice revisited her with this particular memory.

"We were driving through a snowstorm, down a winding road. My mom was begging me to settle down so she could concentrate. But I kept teasing my brother in the backseat. He screamed when I pinched his leg." Vivi felt her face crumpling as she recalled those final moments in the car as if she were watching a horror film. Her heartbeat sped up. Her head throbbed. "His screech made her take her eyes off the road for just an instant, and then we slammed into the tree. If I'd have listened"—her raw voice barely croaked out the words—"if I'd have behaved, they'd be alive. They'd be alive, and my dad wouldn't be brokenhearted. He wouldn't have turned into a drunk. So, you see, it's not about *me* forgiving *him*. I deserve to suffer for what I did."

David wrapped his arms around her and rubbed her back while she sobbed. "My God, Vivi, you were a kid. It was an accident that most likely had nothing to do with you and everything to do with the ice." He kissed her head and tried to reassure her. "It's not your fault. You have to know it isn't your fault."

She couldn't tell him his words fell on deaf ears. The truth couldn't be wiped away by wishful thinking about ice and snowstorms. She eased away from his embrace. "The point is no one else can punish me more than I do myself. That's what happens when you hurt someone you love."

Her comment appeared to shift something within David. His eyes softened with some weird mix of yearning and understanding. He squeezed her hands and, when he finally spoke, his voice cracked. "I do understand that much. Listen to me. I want to talk more about your guilty conscience when you're ready, but right now I need you to forgive me for being an ass last month. I'll keep asking until you do. I want you back in my life."

His hands brushed the tops of her thighs. When he looked up at her, his eyes darkened with desire. She heard his breathing fall shallow. Once again, extreme circumstances were affecting his judgment. She couldn't go through another round of frustrated expectations with him, especially here and now, when she'd been completely depleted by her confession. "Don't, David. Please stop."

He straightened up, looking strung out. "I'm sorry. I know I've made many mistakes with you, especially recently. But I have to ask, can you please give me some sign that you . . . won't lock me out of your life forever?"

She glanced at the photograph he kept on his desk. The room pulsed with crazy, confused emotions. "Even if I wanted to completely shut you out, I doubt I'd succeed. It won't be forever, but some things take a long while to heal, as you know."

"You're referring to *my* dad now." His voice sounded hollow as he leaned against the desk.

She nodded in response.

"It kills me to think I've hurt you as much as he hurt me. I'll never forgive myself for that." His grim expression emphasized his words. "You believe me, don't you?"

"I do."

His gaze grew fuzzy and distant, as if his mind were wandering someplace else. She watched, waiting for a clue about where he'd gone. When he looked at her, she held her breath.

"I assume you're going to his wedding," he said, his voice tight.

"Yes. It won't be easy to sit there in silence with Cat and Jackson, pretending to be happy, now that I know the truth. Of course, I won't tell. I wouldn't do that to you, or your mom." Vivi realized she'd stumbled upon the perfect opportunity to keep her promise to Graciela. "Actually, I remembered something recently. Something your mom told me shortly before she died. A message for you. At the time, I had no idea what she was talking about. Now I realize it was about your dad."

David looked nearly panicked in his anticipation as he slid to his knees. "You have a message from my mom?"

Vivi nodded. "She assumed one day you would confide something troubling and, when you did, I should remind you that family is more important than pride."

His eyes widened. "That sounds like her."

"Yes, it does." Vivi watched David's face reflect the love he felt for his mom. She barely stopped herself from reaching out to touch him. "And I think she's right. Don't let your pride, or your dad's, destroy your relationship with your entire family. I know it's hard to accept what's happened, but you're the only one suffering from holding on to hate. It's ruining your life, David. You need to let go."

"I agree. But how? How can I face him? How can I stomach this marriage?"

"Take one step at a time." Just like she had done for so many years with her own dad. "Go to the wedding without thinking about what comes next."

David closed his eyes, his face pinched as if he were sucking on a lemon. A slight tremor quaked his shoulders, then he opened his eyes and searched hers. "Will you go with me? Please."

She hadn't expected that plea.

"I'll get a car service to take us back and forth from Wilton, and you can talk me off the ledge on the drive up. Honestly, I don't think I can do it alone, Vivi. Please say yes."

David remained kneeling before her, begging for help. How could she deny him when he'd been there time and again when she'd needed support? At some point she would need to take one step toward some kind of friendship with him, so it may as well be now. "Okay. I'll help you through that day . . . for you and your family. And because I loved your mom."

David wrapped his arms around her calves and briefly rested his head in her lap. "Thank you."

"You're welcome, but don't read more into my decision than what it is. You need me at the wedding because I'm the only one with whom you can be truthful about Janet, so I will be there for you this one time. It doesn't mean things between us are fixed. I'm not falling back into old patterns with you."

"Understood." He sat upright, looking slightly less sick to his stomach than he had minutes earlier. "You look exhausted. You should rest."

He stood and then followed her back to his room. After she crawled beneath the sheet, he drew the comforter up to her chest. His gaze locked on hers, full of warmth, as he ran a hand over her hair. "Sleep, *Muñequita*."

~

In the morning, Vivi woke up alone, wondering if her concussion caused her to hallucinate the discussion with David in his study. She licked her lips as she replayed the scene in which she'd agreed to go to the wedding with him.

He walked into the bedroom carrying two cups of coffee just as she sat up.

"Here, sorry it's decaf. Doctor's orders." He handed her a mug and sat beside her on the bed. A strand of her hair fell in front of her eyes, so he tucked it behind her ear. "How do you feel today? Groggy, nauseated? Is your vision normal?"

"I'm tired. My head hurts."

He set his coffee on the table. "Are you hungry?"

"Surprisingly, not yet." She frowned, thinking it odd since she usually woke up starving. Then again, she wasn't usually waking up in David's bed with a massive concussion. The reminder of Justin's rage stopped her short. "Have you spoken with Cat today? Is she okay?"

"Yes. Funny how she's taking my calls now." His tone conveyed irritation and hurt. "She's fine, other than being worried about you."

"You do realize she and Jackson are trying to force you to make up with your dad by avoiding you? She hates doing it, just so you know." Vivi peered at him. "Now that you're going to the wedding, things will improve."

"Thank you again for agreeing to go with me. I could never go otherwise. " He glanced out his window. "I guess I should talk to my dad first. I know I've got to find a way to forgive him."

"Yes, you do." Vivi sipped her coffee, her heart thawing with each minute she spent near David.

"He hasn't asked for my forgiveness, which may be part of the problem. It won't be easy to take the first step." He glanced at her and grinned. "Why are you smiling?"

She looked at him and bit her lip. "It's nice to be the one being leaned on for a change."

He cocked his head before shaking it in apparent disbelief. "Why have you always believed you needed me more than I needed you? That's never been true. I've always relied on you, on your love and friendship, on your ability to make me lighten up a bit."

"I already agreed to go to the wedding, David, so you don't need to pour it on so thick." She patted his hand, smirking.

He grabbed her hand and kissed it. "I mean every word."

Chapter Twenty-Four

David finished cleaning the lunch dishes and went to his study while Vivi slept. He sat at his desk, staring at the phone. He'd been avoiding his father since returning from Hong Kong. He couldn't procrastinate any longer. If he didn't call now and accept the invitation to the wedding, he might chicken out. Blowing out a breath, he dialed the phone.

"Hello, David."

"Dad." His posture stiffened; his heart thudded inside his chest. Neither spoke for several seconds.

"I take it you're settled in at work and a new apartment." His father's typically authoritative voice faltered.

"Yes." David paused, uncertain of how to begin. Five seconds later, the words tumbled from his mouth. "I'm calling about the wedding. I thought we should try to clear the air so I can attend."

Another brief silence unfolded between them.

"I'd hoped after all this time you'd finally let go of that, David."

"Trust me, I wish I could. I'm trying, but I'm still pissed. And your attitude hasn't helped matters. You've shown no remorse. You've also allowed Cat and Jackson to blame me for this friction. Instead of shouldering any blame, you've protected yourself and let me twist in the wind."

David heard his father sigh before he replied.

"Your mother begged us *both* to keep my affair a secret. I've simply been respecting her wishes. Honoring them was the least I could do to make amends." David was mulling over the unexpected response when his father continued. "As for the rest, I didn't thank you because I knew you weren't staying silent for my benefit. You were doing it for her.

"I am sorry for the backlash you've suffered from Cat and Jackson. But, David, I won't apologize for anything else. What happened in my marriage, and with Janet, is not your business. That was between your mother and me, and Janet."

"That's not true. It affected everything and everyone."

"Only because you found out. The problems in my marriage were my business, not yours."

"How lucky for you Mom's death freed you to be with Janet without having to publicly own up to the affair or your decision to break up our family."

"You're out of line, David. I mourned your mother's death. Despite what happened, I loved her, and I cherished the family she gave me."

"How can you say you loved her when you betrayed her, not to mention how you betrayed *me*? Christ, I spent my life admiring you, seeking your approval. No one could've made me doubt your integrity. You say you cherish your family. But when Mom was dying and we all needed you more than ever, you let Janet become more important than the rest of us.

"Your selfishness turned my whole world upside down. It's caused me to question everything I ever believed about you, our family, and love. So don't lie to yourself and pretend what you did wasn't any of my business."

A short silence ensued while David tried to calm his heaving chest.

"I'm not proud of how I handled things in the past." His father's tone sounded tired, if not defeated. "I'm sorry I disappointed you, but I can't undo it. What would you have me do now?"

Unable to muster another reply, David's stomach burned.

"David? Are you still there?"

"Yes." His mind raced. "I don't know what else to say right now. I can't talk about this anymore. I'll just see you at the wedding."

"Okay. I'm glad you're coming. I'm sorry things between us are still uncomfortable, and I hope we can eventually fix it."

"I'll speak with you later, Dad." David ended the call. A tremor whipped through his body. He didn't feel better or worse for having had that long-dreaded discussion—only numb.

He slouched in the chair while replaying the conversation. The dissatisfied part of him already wanted to cancel his plans to attend the wedding, but he wouldn't give up a chance to spend the day with Vivi.

Right now he needed a distraction. He turned his computer speakers on low so he wouldn't disturb her by listening to music while he worked. He was editing the first ten pages of the agreement Laney had given him yesterday when the doorman called to announce visitors. Moments later, he opened the door to greet his brother and sister.

"Where's Vivi?" Cat pushed past him, scanning the empty living room.

"Shhh," David said. "She's resting."

Jackson crossed between them and went straight to the refrigerator to get a beer. Once he popped the cap, he looked at David, who merely shook his head before continuing his discussion with Cat.

"The doctor told her to refrain from most activity. No TV, computer, books, or music. No physical exertion for a few days, either."

"But you said she's okay." Cat's accusatory tone carried a layer of concern.

"No one expects her to suffer any permanent damage," David began, "but concussions are tricky. She needs to protect her brain while it recovers."

Cat bit her lip and tapped her foot several times, lost in thought.

"Well, when she wakes up, I'll take her home with me." Cat hopped onto a kitchen stool. "I'm sure it'll be more comfortable for everyone that way."

"No, it won't. Taking her back to the scene of the crime so soon is a terrible idea." David sat beside her and let his eyes drift between her and Jackson. His brother looked worn down. Obviously, they'd all had an exhausting night. David returned his gaze to Cat. If he wanted a future with Vivi, he'd need to face the music with his sister and Jackson. He hoped they'd prove him wrong by reacting well to his news. "Besides, I want her here. I also want you both to know that I'm in love with her."

"What?" Jackson's shocked expression bordered on disgust. He set the bottle down and stepped closer. "David, she's like our sister. What in the hell are you saying?"

"She's *not* our sister. She's not related to us at all." He looked directly at Jackson, who was looking at him as if he were a stranger. "I love her, Jackson. The whole time I sat in the emergency room praying for her recovery, I promised God, if given the chance, I'd be honest about my feelings. I don't know what I would've done if she hadn't come through so well."

"I don't get you at all." Jackson waved his hand in the air, unable or unwilling to comprehend David's sincerity. "First Dad, now this. Did you lose your mind in Hong Kong?"

"You're being an insulting ass. You both know she's always been important to me. We had our own relationship apart from her friendship with you two." He scratched at the back of his neck. "I'm sorry if it makes you uncomfortable. For the time being, please put her recovery above your own feelings. I haven't said anything to her because"—he paused, unwilling to confess everything that had happened on Block Island—"the nurse said it's imperative she doesn't become overexcited for a while. Once she's out of the woods, I'm going to tell her how I feel, and then we'll see where things lead." He looked at his sister's strained expression. "I'd appreciate your support. Failing that, at least allow us to decide what we want without interfering."

"I'm not particularly comfortable, but I guess I'm not shocked, either." Cat's fingers tapped against the granite, her mouth set in a firm line. "I sensed something happening on Block Island. Guess Laney had a right to be pissed."

"Let's leave Laney out of this, please." He stood and shoved his hands in his pockets. "And I'm not asking for your consent. Ultimately, this is between Vivi and me."

"It affects us, too, David. If you two break up, do we lose our friend? And what if I don't want her telling you things about my life, but she feels obligated because she's your girlfriend? Or worst of all, you break her heart. Hasn't she been through enough in her life, without having you give her hope only to disappoint her?" Cat rolled her eyes and dropped her chin into her palm. "Don't pretend this doesn't have the potential to change everything for all of us."

"Isn't it possible that everything will change for the better? Besides, Vivi's never revealed secrets between all of us before, so there's no reason to suspect that would change. And I *won't* break her heart." David sighed, aware that he actually had broken her heart recently. Time to change the subject.

He looked at Jackson, who'd grown quiet while finishing his beer. "About Dad. I'll be coming to his wedding, but not because of anything you two have said or done."

Jackson's sideways glance annoyed David. "Why the change of heart, then?"

"I have my reasons. Last night's scare was a wake-up call about how short life is, and it's important to Vivi that I mend things with Dad."

"Oh, well if it's important to Vivi, then by all means, do it." Jackson's sarcasm revealed his own hurt feelings, so David let it pass without defending himself. "Are you ever going to tell us the real reason why you've been acting like a jackass toward Dad?"

"No. And before you jump all over me, consider that perhaps I'm doing it for your own good. There are some things you don't need or really want to know." David lowered his head briefly. "I will tell you I'm offended by how you both dump all the blame on me. When have I ever given either of you reason to doubt me?"

Jackson opened his mouth to respond, but then his eyes darted sideways and his expression swiftly changed from somber to welcoming. "Hey, V. How are you feeling?"

Cat slid off her stool and hugged Vivi.

"I'm so sorry, Vivi." Cat's voice broke over her tears. "You warned me about Justin. I should've listened. I'm so sorry he hurt you."

"It's not your fault, Cat." Vivi patted Cat's back. "I'm just glad you're not hurt."

"It should've been me, not you," Cat cried. "I'm the fool who kept taking him back. I'm so stupid, Vivi. I'm so sorry!"

"You're not responsible, Cat." Vivi looked Cat in the eye. "Just promise me it's really over now, no matter how much he apologizes or begs. I—"

"Oh, it's over. Trust me. If he comes anywhere near either of you, *he's* over, too," Jackson interjected. "And you're both going to testify if that bastard doesn't plead guilty."

When he hugged both women, his big hand grazed Vivi's bandage, causing her to yelp and break up their huddle.

"Sorry, V." Jackson grimaced. "I'm an idiot."

"My favorite idiot, anyway." She grinned and punched his arm.

"I'm serious about Justin, though." Jackson's expression turned grim. "He's gonna pay, right, David?"

David looked at Vivi, who seemed to be holding her breath. Before he responded to Jackson, Vivi turned to Cat. "Is that what you want, Cat? Do you want to get involved in a bunch of lawsuits and drag everything out?"

"No. I just want to make sure he can't come near us again." She looked at David. "I just want out."

David shot Jackson a defeated glance. He couldn't disagree with both women more, but he wouldn't push this topic in light of his and Vivi's discussion last night.

"We'll get a restraining order in place right away," he promised his sister. "No one needs to make any decisions about civil suits right now. We have time to file, if that's what either of you decides to do once the dust settles."

"I don't need time." Vivi's voice sounded agitated. "I already told you, I'm not going to be part of any civil suits."

"Relax, Vivi. David can't force either of us to do anything." Cat grasped Vivi's hand and shot her brothers a death stare. "This all can wait until another time. You're supposed to stay calm. Let's stop talking about Justin."

"Cat's right. You need to stay calm and relaxed. No stress." David handed Vivi a glass of water and a painkiller. In his peripheral vision, he caught sight of Jackson, who now appeared lost in thought, almost haunted.

Cat pushed some of Vivi's hair behind her ear. "Hey, let's lighten the mood. I have some cute scarves you can use to hide those bandages. Want me to go get them?"

"My God, Cat." Vivi swallowed her pills with a large gulp of water. "Scarves . . . seriously?"

"Well, I always feel better when I look pretty." Cat shrugged and offered a weak smile.

"I'll be fine with these bandages." She touched her head, wincing. "Thanks for checking on me, but standing here is making me a little light-headed. I think I need to sit."

David immediately stepped closer, hovering his hand just below her elbow in case she started to faint.

"We shouldn't tax you with a long visit, anyway." Cat's eyes drifted away from David and Vivi as she fidgeted with her purse strap. "We'll leave you to rest. I'll check in later."

Jackson gave Vivi another quick hug and followed Cat out the door. Vivi seemed oblivious to Cat and Jackson's abrupt departure. She was obviously preoccupied with her own memories and feelings. The legal conversation must've once again stirred her awful memories of the car accident.

David was thankful she'd stopped pushing him away, although she didn't seem to realize the subtle shift in her attitude. At least he'd made a little progress with her during the past twelve hours. His relief was tainted by a feeling of impotence with respect to the irrational guilt she'd been carrying around. Had she really suffered in silence all these years, believing she'd killed her mother? It explained a lot about her, but it didn't excuse her father from not getting her the help she needed to put that accident in proper perspective.

Now wasn't the time for that discussion, so he let it drop. "I think you should go lie down. I'll wake you for dinner."

"Okay," she began. "After dinner, I'd like to go home."

Her words depressed him. Winning her back would be an uphill battle. But it wasn't about him or his needs. It was about her. She'd waited for him for years; the least he could do was be willing to return the favor.

He wouldn't push her now, despite his heavy heart. He'd take his time, regain her trust, and then beg for a second chance. "Whatever you want."

~

Nearly two weeks later, Vivi pulled the tray of lasagna out of her father's oven and set it on the stove. While letting it cool slightly, she poured herself a soda and then stared out the window. The lawn was in dire need of cutting.

Mindlessly, her fingers slid along her scar, where the stitches had recently been removed. When she'd last visited her dad, three weeks ago, she never could've predicted the ways in which her life would keep changing. But every day since Block Island had built toward the confrontation she'd planned for tonight.

She could do it. After all, she'd drawn a line with David. Only after weeks of his begging, and her near miss with tragedy, did she consider letting him back in her life. For the first time since they'd met, she saw herself as his equal. An incredible reversal for her, and one that gave her courage today.

Courage needed to draw similar boundaries with her father.

Unloading two decades' worth of guilt had been terrifying yet freeing. David had worked hard to make her accept the possibility that the icy roads were at least as much to blame. At this point in time, blame really didn't matter.

Accidents happen. Mistakes were made. The only way to move forward was through forgiveness and acceptance—of others and one's self. Vivi could do that for herself, and tonight she would ask her father to do it for her, finally.

She placed two large squares of lasagna on plates and set them on the kitchen table. "Dad?"

When he didn't answer, she wandered into the living room. He sat, asleep in his recliner, one hand clutching a near-empty glass of whiskey. Vivi walked over and gently removed the glass. "Dad, dinner's ready."

Startled, he opened his eyes and blinked, confused. "Vivi."

She nodded. "You fell asleep. Dinner's ready."

He hefted himself out of the chair and slowly followed her into the kitchen. He went to pour a fresh glass of booze, but she reached for the bottle. "Before you drink more, I want to talk."

"About what?" he asked, taking a seat without thanking her for the meal she'd prepared.

"About you and me." She unfolded a napkin across her lap while he forked a bite of his dinner. "I told you Mr. St. James is getting remarried tomorrow at his country club. That's why I'm staying here tonight."

"So?" He glanced at the half-empty bottle of Jack Daniel's on the counter. "What's that got to do with you and me?"

"Well, the unexpected events of the summer and his wedding have made me realize something. A lot, actually, but one thing about you in particular."

He set his fork down and crossed his arms in front of his chest. "Oh yeah? And what's that?"

"All these years I put up with your drinking—your neglect—because I knew how devastated you were by Mom's accident." Her throat tightened a little. "I lived with shame and regret because I survived and Mom and Tommy didn't. I knew seeing me only reminded you of them, and I convinced myself your grief justified your behavior, no matter how destructive."

"Destructive?" He snatched his fork again, waving it dismissively before using it to stab his lasagna. "I'm not destructive."

"Yes, you are. You're self-destructive and you've hurt me, too. I thought I'd been handling it well all these years. Now I know I was wrong." She leaned forward, reaching across the table in vain. "*You* were wrong."

"What the hell are you talking about?" He scowled before taking another bite of his meal.

Everything about his posture and expression warned her to stop. Nothing would change. But she had to finish. She had to draw her line.

"People lose spouses and children every day, some in tragic accidents, others to illness, the way Mr. St. James lost his wife. But unlike you, they move on. Mom and Tommy died in that crash, not you. *You* still had a life. A daughter. A reason to get up and be the best man and father you could. You had the possibility of finding love again, eventually. We could've had a happier life here, together." She found the courage to look him in the eyes. "Instead of choosing to live—instead of choosing to invest in me—you curled into a ball. You left me alone and neglected and feeling unloved for most of my life. And I took it. I kept coming back, making excuses, feeling guilty. That's over now. I can't keep going down this road with you. You need to make changes, or you won't be seeing me nearly as often in the future."

"What the hell do you know about losing a wife or a son? You can't know how I feel or tell me the way I handled my feelings is wrong." He shoved his plate aside and leaned forward. "Neglect you? Didn't I keep a roof over your head, food in your belly, clothes on your back? Yes, I damn well did, Vivi. I never neglected you."

"I didn't say you abandoned me. I said you didn't take care with my feelings. You never helped me grieve, and, believe it or not, I, too, lost a family that day." It wouldn't help to allow her own emotions to spiral out of control, so she took a deep breath to settle herself. "You've never taken an interest in my art, my friends, my job. Our whole relationship has been about me giving to you, me caring for you, me visiting you. Jeez, Dad, you didn't even come see me after I got injured the other week. You were content to let David and Cat take care of me."

"Seems to me you always preferred those St. Jameses anyhow, so you should be grateful." He stood up and walked toward the counter. After dropping his plate into the sink, he moved toward the bottle.

"Don't drink that now. We're talking." She put her fork down, holding her breath.

"I'm done talking." He swiped it off the counter and started strolling out of the kitchen. He paused at the doorway, glancing over his shoulder. "You do what you need to do, but don't tell me how to live my life. And don't ever tell me I didn't love you. That's a bald-faced lie, Vivi."

She sat in her chair, blinking back tears. What had she hoped for? A sudden change of heart? A tearful apology and warm hug?

His reaction was exactly what she should've expected. Cold. Removed. Unapologetic. Just as always.

Maybe he had done the best he could do, which wasn't saying much. Perhaps some part of his heart died and got buried with her mom and brother, and what was left only had so much love to give her. She'd probably never know anything other than the fact that he preferred the comfort of his beloved booze to her company.

But she'd said what needed to be said, and now she would not go out of her way to make sure to visit twice a month. She would no longer worry about whether or not he was eating right. She'd treat him with the same detached sentiment with which he'd always treated her.

Although the dinner was not a rousing success, she had stood up to him for the first time. Pride stole through her—something she'd almost never felt sitting in this kitchen. That, at least, marked a change for the better. A new era.

And she would heed her own advice, too. She had choices to make in her life. Risks to take. Happiness to grab. Love to give.

Chapter Twenty-Five

The next afternoon, David took a car service to Wilton to pick up Vivi before going to his father's wedding. Given his dark mood, he suspected he should've rented a hearse.

He shook away the thought, vowing to use this occasion to move forward with his life, and with Vivi. He walked up to her door, remembering the times throughout the years he'd picked her up or dropped her off here. It looked exactly as he remembered it, but everything else about this moment felt different. Charged. He rang the doorbell, and she appeared a minute later.

Unlike her typically loud clothing, today she wore a conservative nude-colored dress with a scalloped hemline. Its feminine lace overlay had the barest hint of metallic sheen. Her arms extended from the cap sleeves, and the fabric gathered at the waist before dropping to her midthigh. The back had a peekaboo opening, making him ache to touch her bare skin. She wore platinum sandals and pinned her hair up into a simple French twist, which hid her fresh scar.

He'd never seen her look more elegant. "You're gorgeous."

She broke into a wide smile, revealing the gap between her front teeth he loved so well. "You look pretty good yourself." She straightened the knot in his tie, then squeezed his forearm. "All set?"

"As much as I'll ever be."

"That's all anyone can ask."

It had been twenty months since he'd laid eyes on his father. He hadn't seen Janet since the day he caught them together outside of Starbucks. A wave of nausea curled in his stomach, just like every time he pictured that woman. He could never have attended this wedding without Vivi at his side.

"You know, I've been a little nervous about seeing your dad and Janet, too." Vivi fiddled with her earring as they walked toward the car. "I've tried hard to find the silver lining in all of this, and may have one for you."

"There's a silver lining?" His skepticism couldn't be masked. "This ought to be good."

"If you think about it, isn't it better that your dad is *marrying* Janet? At least you know he truly loved her when he cheated on your mom. That's better than if it had been a careless, cheap fling."

He halted, processing her remark, before joining her at the car.

"I guess there's something to that twisted bit of logic." He frowned while helping her into the backseat.

"It's not twisted," she said, batting his arm. "I know you don't think he's been punished enough, but your mom forgave him."

"Not punished enough?" David scowled. "Try not at all!"

"You already know how I feel about this topic. Just because he didn't beg for forgiveness, or confess his sins, doesn't mean he hasn't suffered. He knows he hurt her and you. He knows he lost the respect of both of you as a result of his behavior." She clutched her little purse in her lap. "Maybe if you think about it that way, you won't feel so agitated today. And for all you know, maybe your mom even encouraged him to find someone once she knew she wasn't going to live long. She loved him, David. She would've wanted him to be happy after she died. Maybe she knew he wouldn't do well on his own."

"If that were true, she would've told me so at the time I discovered the affair." He closed his eyes. "Let's stop speculating. It's not making me feel any better. Are you saying all this because you're worried I'm going to create a scene?"

"No." She shook her head. "I just want to help you mend fences with your dad, and with Cat and Jackson."

"Well, you're more forgiving of sins of the father than I." As soon as he spoke, he wished he could retract his insensitive remark. Vivi had offered gentle support and he repaid her by throwing her own shitty situation in her face. "I'm sorry. That was rude."

"It's okay." She stared straight ahead. "I know you're not yourself today."

"Don't make excuses for me." He turned to her. "It was uncalled for and cruel, especially after everything you shared with me recently. You're the absolute last person in the world I ever want to hurt."

"Fine. You big, mean jerk!" She stuck her tongue out at him, then smiled. "Better?"

He cocked a brow and grinned. "Yes."

They pulled under the expansive portico of the Rolling Hills Country Club and walked across the Belgian block driveway to the entry. The wedding ceremony was being held on the covered side patio. A center aisle had been created by rows of gold-and-white chairs.

Despite a gentle fall breeze, David felt perspiration gathering all over his body and immediately regretted his decision. He froze, considering turning around, then Vivi's voice anchored him again.

"Ooh, you look handsome, Jacks!" Vivi fingered his brother's bow tie and ran her hand along the lapel of his tuxedo jacket.

Apparently Jackson was his father's best man. It made sense, under the circumstances, but it also highlighted the vast gulf between David and his father.

"Where's Dad?" he finally asked.

"Checking on last-minute details." After an awkward pause, Jackson asked, "Shall I escort you to your seats? Cat's already here."

David noticed his sister in the front row on the right.

"Lead the way."

Jackson stuck his arm out for Vivi, and David followed behind them.

"You look pretty, Cat!" Vivi said. "Is that new?"

"No." Cat's forced smile didn't fool David. He wished her attitude were due to the wedding rather than her discomfort with the idea of him and Vivi. If he failed to win back Vivi's affection, Cat would probably rejoice. "You look good, Vivi. I'm so glad you're recovering well."

"I'm fine." Vivi touched the place on her head where the stitches had just been removed. "However, I doubt I can do much dancing later."

"This doesn't look like much of a dancing crowd," Cat whispered, then she leaned forward to look at David. With an even tone, she said, "I wasn't sure you'd actually show up, let alone stay very long. Have you seen Dad?"

"No. I spoke with him on the phone. I'll see him after the vows." *Vows.* His own words stunned him. God Almighty, the next thirty minutes would be torture.

The string quartet began playing Pachelbel's Canon in D, putting an end to the uncomfortable conversation. David sighed, bracing for the long afternoon. He surveyed the fifty or so attendees—a collection of close family, business colleagues, and friends.

He felt like a fraud sitting among them, celebrating something for which he felt no joy. When David first saw his father standing at the makeshift altar, his stomach clenched. The man hadn't changed much, excepting a few extra silver hairs and a new general air of fitness.

They looked at each other, which caused David to recall the many times their roles were reversed. For years his father had been the one standing on the sidelines watching David play lacrosse or pose for prom photos or accept an academic award. The man had never been demonstrative, but he'd been proud. Always proud. And now, despite David's anger, he acknowledged a tender surge of emotion, a desire to resolve things and be close again. That goodwill vanished as soon as Janet began her march down the aisle.

Janet. His soon-to-be stepmother.

His stomach burned as if he'd devoured a bowl of hot peppers. His intense dislike didn't stem solely from what she'd done to his mother, although that alone justified his position.

For years he'd watched her and her former husband interact with everyone at their country club. Good-looking social climbers. A plastic pair that air-kissed everyone, smiled too often, and tried too hard. Insincerity incarnate. Now she would be part of his family.

Part of his life.

He reached for Vivi's hand. If she minded his sudden, tight grip, she didn't react. He supposed she was taking pity on him, which was fine with him as long as she didn't pull away. Occasionally she wiggled her fingers to encourage him to loosen his grip, but she never let go. He took that as another hopeful sign. The only truly good part of his day.

"I can't stay here," he whispered.

She looked him in the eye and whispered back, "Leaving won't change anything or make it better. In fact, you'll end up feeling worse. We can make it through this day."

"I hate her," he said, not as quietly as he should have.

"I know." She squeezed his hand. "I'm sorry."

Beside her, Cat shifted uncomfortably and shot him a disapproving look. He straightened his shoulders and inhaled a long, deep breath. He would stay. He would say hello to his father, let Vivi eat something, and then convince her to slip away with him, unnoticed.

Instead of watching the rest of the ceremony, he wondered how someone like Janet had been tempting when his father had already had an amazing wife. Then David thought of Laney, and how he'd been ready to settle for a lesser relationship when Vivi had been right in front of him all along.

A shudder ran through him. Reflexively, he tugged her hand up to his chest. *I* will *make you mine*. She shot him a bewildered look.

After the ceremony, David and Vivi followed Cat into the reception area in the main ballroom. Afternoon sunlight spilled through its French doors, transforming it and its bouquet-filled tables into a beautiful garden.

David picked glasses of champagne off a passing tray. He considered getting drunk, but thought better of the idea. Some of his father's colleagues were clients of David's firm. He sipped his champagne and twisted his neck to and fro, running his finger along the inside of his collar.

"Is it hot in here?" he asked Vivi.

"No." Her empathetic smile suddenly changed and her eyes widened.

"David. You look good, son." His father's voice startled him. "Thank you for coming."

Vivi elbowed David, who'd turned to stone and not spoken. He snapped himself from his daze and extended his hand.

"Congratulations." The words tasted bitter, as though he'd stuck his tongue on the tip of a battery. He swallowed the lump in his throat and barely acknowledged Janet with a shallow nod of his head.

"Mr. St. James, congratulations," Vivi thankfully interrupted. "Hi, Janet, I'm Vivienne. We met briefly last year, but you might not remember. I love your dress."

"Thank you," Janet said in her chirpy voice.

A tense moment passed before Vivi spoke again. "So, Janet, Cat and I would love to hear about your honeymoon plans, wouldn't we?" She began stepping away from David, but he tugged at her hand, panicked. She went up on her toes and kissed his cheek. The casual gesture was something he'd have taken for granted weeks ago. No longer. Now he savored it. "I'll be back in a minute." Then she looked at Mr. St. James and said sotto voce, "I suspect you might like a minute with your son."

The three ladies moved several feet away, leaving David alone with his father. With downcast eyes, he cleared his throat and waited for his father to speak. He finally looked up to notice his father staring at Vivi with an odd expression.

"Are you dating Vivi?" The undisguised surprise in his voice irritated David.

"Not yet, but I intend to if she'll have me." David's eyes warned his father to tread lightly.

"I'll be damned," his father said, smiling. "Graciela was right about you."

Everything in David's body tingled with awareness. Hearing his father speak his mother's name, today, and in reference to Vivi, stunned him.

"What are you talking about?" He narrowed his gaze.

"Whenever I'd comment about Vivi always being underfoot, your mother would tell me to get used to it, because one day you'd realize you loved her." He smiled at a private memory. "Of course, I didn't believe her. You kids were so young, and so different. I suppose she always did understand you better than I did."

His mother's premonition burrowed into David's heart, injecting it with warmth so unexpected at this occasion. She'd loved Vivi, not just for herself, but for him, too. She might have been the only person in his family who'd be truly supportive of them exploring a romantic relationship.

He could almost hear his mother's accented voice making the bold prediction. Tears mounted in David's eyes, so he shook his head to clear them.

"I guess she did know me best."

Suddenly a missing piece fell into place, thawing more of the ice surrounding his heart. David's mother was dead. No one would or could replace her in his memories or heart. Now, if he could get out of his own way and risk everything, he could have someone wonderful in his life. Someone with whom he could build his own happiness—love that his mother had foreseen and sanctioned.

His father's choices were his own, and he'd live with the consequences—good, bad, or indifferent. David hadn't wanted to be defined by his poor behavior during the past year, so perhaps he should stop defining his father solely by his faults. It had taken him too long, and too many mistakes, to figure out the person granting forgiveness gets the greater reward: freedom from prolonged grief.

It was time to focus on his future.

"I am glad you showed up today, son."

Vivi had been right about taking this one step, even if David still couldn't envision a civil conversation with Janet.

"Well, I may never like Janet." David looked his father in the eye. "But I'll be respectfully polite, for everyone's sake."

His father's response was halted due to Vivi and Janet's arrival.

"David, let's grab our seats. I'm starving!"

~

Sixty minutes later, David convinced Vivi to leave the party early. He sat beside her in the car, anxious for reasons having nothing to do with his father or Janet.

"I'm proud of you, David. How do you feel?"

"Glad it's over."

"I'm sure." She chuckled.

"I couldn't have done it without you. Thank you."

"You're welcome. I hope things get easier for you with time." Her eyes looked misty just before she turned and looked out the window.

"Vivi." He hesitated, desperately hoping she'd agree to one more favor. "Do you mind taking a detour with me?"

"Where to?" She cocked her head.

"I want to go home."

Her brows furrowed before she realized what he meant. "To your dad's?"

"Yes, while I know neither he nor Janet are there."

Vivi pressed her lips together as if she were struggling to make the right decision. "Okay. I haven't been there since . . ." Her voice trailed off. He squeezed her hand, knowing she meant she'd not returned since his mother died. Neither had he.

The car turned into the driveway, causing David's heart to skip a beat. The formerly butter-yellow colonial had been repainted white. His mother's vibrant flowerbeds had been replaced by an assortment of smart-looking shrubs and small boulders. Had these changes been made at Janet's request, or was this his father's handiwork?

David drew a deep breath before exiting the car.

"Are you sure about this, David?" Vivi asked, her eyes appearing to catalog all the changes. "I'm having second thoughts. I don't think you're going to feel better after this visit."

"I need to accept what's happened, including all the changes. Otherwise, I can't move forward." He withdrew the keychain from his jacket pocket and tried the front lock. It still worked, he thought as the tumblers clicked. After stealing a quick glance at Vivi, whose wary expression matched his own, he swung the door open and stepped inside.

The house smelled completely different than he remembered. Throughout his youth, it had always smelled like a mix of fresh herbs and his mother's spicy perfume. Now it smelled citrusy, like a spa.

More shocking than the new scent was the change in decor. Gone were the golds, greens, and reds of his childhood. Floral patterns and heavy drapes had been replaced with neutral shades of pale blue, gray, and cream.

He was trying to process all the changes when he heard Vivi cluck her tongue. Her eyes were wide with disbelief. "I hate it," she said without thinking, then slapped her hand over her mouth. "Sorry!"

Her gesture made him chuckle. "I hate it, too." He truly did, yet he was mesmerized at the same time. "Dare we check out the kitchen?"

Vivi nodded and followed him to the back of the house.

"Oh my God!" Vivi's eyes popped open wider when they entered the remodeled space.

Gone were the cherry cabinets and copper pots. The "new and improved" kitchen contained white cabinets and whiter quartzite countertops, neither of which looked like they got much use.

A sniffle dragged his attention away from the new flooring. Vivi was wiping a tear from her cheek. "There's no trace of her."

David nodded in silence. Apparently Janet had made sure there was nothing of his mother, or of their family life together, in this house.

He would've expected these sweeping changes to make him scream or cry or break something. Perhaps shock and disbelief had chased away those emotions, leaving behind a numbed sense of calm. Perhaps seeing his dad look happy at the wedding had tempered his hatred. Or perhaps he'd just grown tired of carrying around ten tons of anger.

He looked at the new kitchen table—cold glass, of course. The cushioned chairs looked more comfortable than the wooden ones from his youth, but again, he doubted his father and Janet ate many meals at this table.

He sat in one and tried to envision his family in this space. Impossible. Those images existed only in his memories—very happy memories. He couldn't re-create them, but he could take steps to build new ones of his own. And those would all start and end with Vivi.

"Sit." He pointed at the chair across from him. Without a word, Vivi took a seat, her gaze scrutinizing every inch of the kitchen.

So adorable.

"I couldn't have made it through the day, or that dinner, without you. My family owes you so much. I owe you." He leaned forward, elbows on the table. "Do you remember this is where we met? Right here, at a table very *unlike* this one." At least he hadn't lost all sense of humor.

"I remember." She smiled, and he could tell she was reliving that evening, when she'd drawn his portrait and eaten a ton of Oreos.

"I'd never met anyone like you before that day. You were this tiny, direct, eager little wisp of a girl with bright pink stripes in your hair. I could see you absorbing every detail about my family. You piqued my curiosity in a big way." He grinned at his own memory of seeing her for the first time. And then his thoughts swiftly ran through everything from that day until this one. "My father told me something surprising tonight."

"What was that?" She sat upright, her round eyes fixed on his.

"He said my mother always suspected I loved you." He reached across the table and laced his fingers with hers. "Apparently she knew how I felt before I did."

Her breath caught. "What does that mean?"

"I always knew how much I liked you, but it's more, Vivi. So much more. I love you. I don't know why I didn't see it sooner. Maybe I've buried and denied my feelings for all the reasons I explained in your apartment weeks ago. Maybe I'd needed to go away for a while in order to see you as a woman instead of a girl. I don't know exactly how or what changed. All I know now is how much I love you."

"You do?" she asked, her voice barely above a whisper.

"I'm in love with you." He stood and walked around the table to sit beside her. "I've thought about our night together so many times this month. I want the right to touch you, kiss you, and make love with you again." He raised her hand to press a kiss into her palm. "I want it all back. Maybe I don't deserve it, but please give me another chance. If you do, I'll give you everything you said you wanted."

He kept hold of her hand, his heart in his throat as he waited for her response.

"Why now?" she asked. "None of the circumstances you feared have changed."

"*I've* changed, Vivi. I know I haven't given you much reason to believe me lately. I swear I'm still the person you were always able to trust in the past. Trust me again and I'll make it worthwhile."

His heart thumped inside his chest. When she threaded her fingers through his hair, he groaned, shuddering with relief and pleasure. He touched her face before his lips claimed hers. He kissed her gingerly, as if she might disappear, but then she pulled back.

"Are you really sure about this? You won't change your mind tomorrow, or at the first sign of trouble? You'll take the heat from Cat and Jackson?"

"I'm sure." He kissed the tip of her nose and let his fingertips trace her upper lip before kissing her again. "This is the happiest I've felt in years. And if I can say that here, standing in the childhood home I no longer recognize, after fleeing the wedding from hell, that ought to tell you something."

She dabbed at her misty eyes and revealed the gap-toothed smile he loved. "It doesn't feel quite real."

"It is real." He kissed her again, and this time she didn't retreat. Electricity zipped through his veins as he pulled her onto his lap. When her body nuzzled against his, he felt himself grow hard. "Vivi."

"David," she murmured in his ear as his hands cupped her breasts. His elbow hit against the glass table, reminding him of where they were.

"Wait, not in here." He looked around, wishing he had thought this through better. He couldn't be with her here in his dad's and Janet's house, but he couldn't wait another hour or longer to get back to the city, either. Hell. "The pool house."

Her eyes crinkled as she blushed.

"No good?" he asked.

"Oh, it's good. Growing up, I had a lot of fantasies about you whisking me off to the pool house." She looked up at him from beneath her lashes. "Dirty fantasies."

"You naughty girl. Come show me." He pulled her out of the chair and practically ran out of the kitchen door.

As soon as they closed the door to the pool house, David yanked her onto the sofa. "I wish we were anywhere else. Are you sure this is okay?"

"It's perfect. Now stop talking and make one of my old day-dreams come true." She unbuckled his belt and unzipped his pants as he fumbled with her zipper. Within minutes, they were skin to skin.

Despite his desire, he moved slowly, wanting to remember every second of this sweet surrender. Memories of making love on Block Island rushed back, adding to his anticipation. But unlike then, now he felt no doubt, no worry.

He peppered her body with kisses, running his hands and mouth from her neck to her knees. Drawing himself up against her body, he let his finger trace the line of her jaw and then dip down to the vulnerable notch below her throat before kissing her there.

"It's hard to believe I'd lost all hope of ever feeling like myself again. Now I've never been happier." His eyes locked on hers.

"Me too."

He peered down at her with a lopsided, doubtful grin. "I hope so, because you may be stuck with me, and me alone. I'm afraid the more time we spend together, the quicker I'll be falling off the pedestal you've always put me on."

"No more pedestals. No more girlish dreams." She entwined her fingers with his and raised them to her lips. "We'll take it one day at a time."

Everything about the moment felt sacred to him, so he held her gaze when he finally entered her. She moaned his name, and he tightened his grip on her.

"I love you," he said.

"I love you more," she replied, and kissed his neck just behind the ear.

"No, Vivi. I love you most."

Epilogue

Three Months Later

Vivi rode up the elevator to David's home, fidgeting as she wondered why he'd insisted she run over here tonight despite the fact she'd been busy writing out report cards. He'd sounded weird on the phone. If they hadn't enjoyed the most amazing fall together, she might be worried. But the only snag they'd encountered had been Cat's initial discomfort with their relationship.

The lock tumbled when she turned the key, so she pushed the door open to step inside. The lights were off. Candles were lit throughout the apartment. Red paper arrows lay on the floor, which was also sprinkled with rose petals. Her hands went to her cheeks.

She followed the arrows back toward the bedroom and noticed every fourth one had a word written across it.

You. Own. My. Heart.

Her body began trembling and she plastered one shaky hand to her heart before opening the bedroom door.

David was sitting cross-legged in the center of the bed holding something in front of him.

"What's all this?" she asked.

He reached out his hand to beckon her to the bed. She didn't want to get her hopes up, but she couldn't help it. This setting was exactly the kind of schmaltzy romantic scene she'd wistfully described to David recently, after her friend had received a less-than-romantic proposal from her boyfriend.

She crawled onto the bed and looked at the little package in front of him, but it wasn't a ring box. Tamping down her disappointment, she picked up the scroll of paper tied with a red ribbon and held it up. The well-worn paper felt as soft as fabric and was marred by deep creases.

"What's this?"

David stretched his legs out to encircle her. "Open it and see."

Vivi untied the ribbon and gently unrolled the delicate paper to see her own childlike handwriting staring back at her. Her cheeks heated as she recalled writing this love letter. Her heart had beat as hard when she'd hidden it in his computer case as it was beating now.

Had he kept this letter all these years? She could barely read the note through the tears collecting in her eyes. When she came to the final lines of the letter, she read them aloud.

"I know I'm too young now, but when I'm grown up, I'll find a way to own your heart just the way you'll always own mine."

She looked up at David, who was holding an emerald-cut diamond ring in his hand. A tiny sob escaped her throat. He reached for her left hand and slid the sparkler on her ring finger.

"You made me a promise all those years ago, and I intend to hold you to it." His shy smile always melted her heart. "You do own my heart, Vivi. Be my wife, so I'll always have you with me."

She lunged at him, knocking him down on the bed before smothering him with kisses. "You'll always have me, no matter what, David. I love you. I love you with all my heart."

"Is that a yes?"

"Yes! Yes, I'll marry you."

He rolled her onto her back and traced his fingers along her brows and nose and lips. "I love you so much it scares me." Then he kissed her. Her last lucid thought during the ensuing hours was envisioning her soon-to-be new name in purple ink, just the way she'd scribbled it thousands of times on dozens of sheets of notebook paper since she'd first met David.

Vivienne St. James.

ACKNOWLEDGMENTS

I would like to thank my husband, children, parents, brother, and friends for their continued love, encouragement, and support.

I am grateful to my agent, Jill Marsal, as well as Helen Cattaneo and the entire Montlake family, for believing in me, and for working so hard on this story.

I owe so much to my earliest readers—Christie Tinio, Siri Kloud, Katherine Ong, Suzanne Harrison, Tami Carstensen, and Shelley Eccleston—for their input on various drafts of this manuscript.

I am also indebted to the wonderful members of my CTRWA chapter for their support, feedback, and guidance through the years.

Finally, I want to thank my readers for making my work worthwhile. With so many available options, I'm honored by your choice to spend your time with me.

ABOUT THE AUTHOR

Jamie Beck is a former attorney with a passion for inventing stories about love and redemption. In addition to writing novels, she also pens articles on behalf of a local nonprofit organization dedicated to empowering youth and strengthening families. Fortunately, when she isn't tapping away at the keyboard, she is a grateful wife and mother to a very patient, supportive family.